AMERICAN OUTRAGE

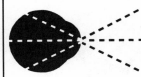

This Large Print Book carries the
Seal of Approval of N.A.V.H.

AMERICAN OUTRAGE

TIM GREEN

THORNDIKE PRESS

An imprint of Thomson Gale, a part of The Thomson Corporation

Detroit • New York • San Francisco • New Haven, Conn. • Waterville, Maine • London

LIBRARY OF CONGRESS CATALOGING-IN-PUBLICATION DATA

Green, Tim, 1963–
　　American outrage / by Tim Green.
　　　p. cm.
　　ISBN-13: 978-0-7862-9712-2 (hardcover : alk. paper)
　　ISBN-10: 0-7862-9712-3 (hardcover : alk. paper)
　　　1. Television journalists — Fiction. 2. Birthmothers — Identification —
Fiction. 3. Human trafficking — Fiction. 4. Large type books. I. Title.
PS3557.R37562A44 2007b
813'.54—dc22   2007016821

Published in 2007 by arrangement with Grand Central Publishing,
a subsidiary of Hachette Book Group USA.

Printed in the United States of America on permanent paper
10 9 8 7 6 5 4 3 2 1

For Illyssa, because meeting you was the best thing that ever happened to me.

ACKNOWLEDGMENTS

With each book I write, there are many people who help with essential steps along the way, and I would like to thank them.

Esther Newberg, the world's greatest agent and my dear friend, for her wisdom. Ace Atkins, my dependable, brilliant, and talented friend, for his careful reading and fantastic ideas. Jamie Raab, my publisher, and Jaime Levine, my editor, who polished this story with unmatched insight and creativity. As well as all my friends at Hachette Book Group, beginning with our leader, David Young, Maureen Egen, Chris Barba and the best sales team in the world, Emi Battaglia, Karen Torres, Jennifer Romanello, Flamur Tonuzi, Martha Otis, Jim Spivey, and Mari Okuda.

My parents, Dick and Judy Green, who taught me to read and to love books and who spent many hours scouring this manuscript so that it shines.

7

A special thanks to former FBI agent John Gamel, who helped me navigate the inner workings of the FBI and kindly took my calls at all hours of the day. Deputy Chief Michael Kerwin, the good cop who's been with me from the beginning. Kevin Harrigan and Marc Harrold for their insights into international adoption. Onondaga County District Attorney William Fitzpatrick for his friendship and guidance. Jim Costello, who appears in the book as himself, for his insight into mortuary science. And Christine Hagan, my friend from *A Current Affair,* who also appears as herself and is the most brilliant First Amendment attorney I know.

I'd also like to thank Peter Brennan and the entire staff at *A Current Affair,* who welcomed me into the world of tabloid TV with a warmth that I learned is the exception rather than the rule.

1

Sam's head was back against the wall, his eyes painfully closed, wearing the look of a refugee. Crusted blood caked the edges of his nostrils and sloppy crimson smears marked the trail that must have run down either side of his mouth and off the chin. His white Yankees T-shirt, oversized to hide a stomach that spilled over his belt, was stained and rumpled.

Jake's jaw tightened and he drew deep breaths of air through his nose. He flung open the door and Sam looked at him, blinking back fresh, seventh-grade tears. The principal, Ms. Dean, burst out of her office, shooting her glare at Jake, then at Sam, then back to Jake. Ms. Dean wore a frumpy blue dress. She had a small, grandmother's face, with curly white hair and petite round glasses, what you might expect on a can of baked beans. She tapped the backs of her fingers against the open door of a conference room and said, "In here, please."

Jake put a hand on Sam's husky shoulder, giving it a squeeze before he followed the principal's orders. She snapped her fingers at Sam. Jake cleared his throat, felt his cheeks go warm, and sat down at the far end of the table after folding his raincoat and laying it over the back of the chair to drip. Ms. Dean pointed to a chair and Sam sat down at the opposite end of the table. The principal put a piece of paper in front of Jake, handing him a pen.

"An order of suspension," she said. "This is three. The next one and he'll be expelled, Mr. Carlson. We can't have this fighting."

"Ms. Dean," Jake said, offering her the same smile that he used to open the hearts of total strangers.

"No, Mr. Carlson," she said, showing him her trembling palm. "I know it's been hard for Sam, losing a parent. But this school is supposed to be a safe zone for my students."

"Are you sure about what happened?"

Ms. Dean frowned, the little crescent wrinkles at the corners of her mouth rippling outward and down toward the tuft of fuzz on her chin.

"He *bit* them," she said.

Jake flashed a look at Sam, who only hung

his head.

"I saw the teeth marks," she said. "And there's blood on his braces."

Sam tightened his lips and winced.

Jake scrawled his signature below the principal's.

"Come on, Sam," Jake said. He got up and grabbed his coat, walking past his son and letting himself out into the office.

"I think he should see Dr. Stoddard," the principal said, raising her voice. "Obviously, whatever you're doing privately isn't working."

Sam followed close behind, filling the entryway with his large presence. Jake wasn't a big man, but at just thirteen, Sam was nearly as tall and weighed about the same. It wasn't unusual for people to overestimate his age by three or four years.

Outside, Jake held the umbrella for Sam, giving him all the protection it could offer against the teeming late spring rain. He saw Sam into the passenger side, slamming the door before collapsing the umbrella and tossing it into the trunk. He climbed into the seat of his BMW coupe and wiped away the courses of water running down his face.

"You *bit* them? Are you kidding me?"

Sam slumped further into the seat and deepened his scowl. He folded his thick arms across his chest and angled his head away so that Jake could see nothing of his features except the ends of those long dark lashes and the tip of his pug nose. Jake slapped the steering wheel, whipping droplets of rain from the stringy ends of his hair across the burl-wood dashboard. He cursed, slammed the car into gear, and raced off into the downpour toward home. The wipers pounded out their beat, fighting off the hissing buckets of rain as they crossed the bridge to Atlantic Beach.

"My father would have kicked my *ass*," Jake said. "Is that what you want? Is that what this is about? I'm too easy on you? I'm your buddy and you want some goddamn assurances that I'm in charge?"

Jake pulled up short at a light, stomping on the brake so that Sam bumped his head against the dash.

"Where's your goddamned seat belt?" Jake said. "Can you follow at least one rule?"

Jake just stared at Sam until he popped open the door and ran out into the rain.

All Jake could do was watch as he ran across the parking lot, a husky, hunched-over shape in tennis shoes, whose bear-gait sent him into the misty gray rain coming in off the ocean until it swallowed him completely.

"I don't belong," Sam said, his face contorting as if someone had pinched his skin, then let go.

"I'm sorry, Sam," Jake said. He knelt down and touched Sam's shoulder.

Jake hadn't bothered with the umbrella when he went after him. His suit clung tight to his body and dark blue dye stained the backs of his hands. Sam sat balled up underneath the boardwalk with his head in his knees, trembling. Heavy drops from the boardwalk above plunked into the lake of water surrounding them and the rain hissed as it struck the dunes beyond.

"They say you're not my dad," Sam said, his head back in his knees, his shoulders shuddering. "Everyone sees you on TV and they say you're not my dad. I tell them to shut up, but I don't *look* like you, and if someone hits you, you always said to hit them back."

"Sure," Jake said, moving his hand from Sam's shoulder to his dripping head, "but you don't bite people, Son. You just don't."

Sam's head jerked up and his big dark eyes had that red cast.

"There was three of them. Mike Petroccelli was choking me from behind and I put my head down. I didn't bite him. He was pulling my head off and my braces cut his arm. There was three of them. I didn't bite. I swear to God."

"Is that what all these fights are about?" Jake asked. "You being adopted?"

Sam nodded his head and dropped it between his knees. When he spoke, his words were muffled. "I want you to find my mom."

Jake lost the feeling in his arms and legs and his head felt light.

"Your mom's gone, Sam," Jake heard himself say.

"No," Sam said, his voice barely audible above the shattering rain on the boardwalk above, "not Mom, my *real* mom. I want you to find her."

Jake felt his lunch pushing up into his throat and he swallowed it back down.

"The records are gone. That was part of how we got you. We wanted you so badly, your mom and I. You have to know how bad we wanted you, Sam."

"Someone knows."

"What do you mean?"

"I mean, someone out there knows. There are things on the Internet about everyone."

Jake shook his head. "You're talking about

14

finding a person. You don't just go Yahoo! it."

He studied Sam for a moment then looked at his watch. "I know you don't want to hear this, but I've got to get you home and get to the city. I got the nanny Angelina Jolie just fired."

Sam rolled his eyes.

"I know," Jake said. "Who gives a shit, right? But we get to live in a house on the beach and eat Häagen-Dazs by the gallon."

"You find everyone else," Sam said, looking up at him, his eyes looking into Jake's. "That's what you do. You find people. They talk to you. That's your job. I want you to do that for me. I want to find her."

Before the crap he was doing now, Jake had spent time in the streets of Kabul and Baghdad. He'd seen the mobs, the fighting, smelled the gunpowder, the burnt and rotting flesh. That didn't scare him the way this did because this wasn't someone else's problem that Jake was there to give an account of. This was *his* problem, and he knew it was a problem. His instincts, the same ones that had launched his career as a journalist, had told him back then when they got Sam that something was wrong. It wasn't anything on the surface, all the documents were there. The lawyers had signed off. There were assurances.

But Karen had gone through the first of many operations back then, and she was desperate for a baby, desperate because she knew that no matter how it turned out she could no longer have children of her own. And back then, when they were praying that maybe she'd been cured, Jake wanted to give her that baby more than he'd ever wanted anything. To make her a mother. To make her life complete. And as hungry as Jake was for his own success, it paled next to the yearning he felt for Karen to have what she wanted and for her to be happy.

So, he had pushed it.

Jake realized Sam was still looking into his eyes and it made him start. Sam was a boy whose eyes usually shifted, his head tilting down, and his face disappearing beneath that dark thatch of unruly hair. This time, though, Sam held his gaze. And maybe it was because Jake had seen that same desperate look in the faces of so many strangers that, despite the fact he was scared, he said yes.

"Okay, Sam," he said. "I'll find her. I'll try."

2

Jake cinched up his tie and went to sit down in the barber chair nearest the door.

"Oh, I'm sorry, Jake," the makeup girl said, covering her mouth. "That's Nancy's new chair. Can you use this one over here?"

Jake looked from the girl to the other chair. Nancy Riordin was the host of *American Outrage.* Jake had been hired as the show's number two.

"Nancy's not here, is she?" he asked.

The girl shook her head, but patted the other chair and smiled at him through the mirror that ran along the entire wall, round bulbs above and below.

"Please."

Jake started to say that he'd seen Sara Pratt, another reporter, in Nancy's chair the previous Tuesday, but bit his lip instead and sat down.

While he had the makeup applied and his hair sprayed down, Jake ran his eyes over his script and wondered if he really was the top correspondent anymore. He'd been hired as that, promised that, but things had subtly changed during the past year and a half since Karen had taken a turn for the worse. The candy dish he kept on his desk didn't get mysteriously filled anymore, and when he left his shoes on the floor of his dressing room, they were no longer guaranteed to be shined by the next day. Twice in the last month he'd had to pick up his own dry cleaning.

The stage manager poked his head into the room and said, "Two minutes. We've got the nanny on the set with her mother."

"Her mother?" Jake said, squinting at the stage manager in the mirror.

The stage manager shrugged and disappeared. Jake took out his cell phone and dialed his friend Meghan Lisson, a reporter from NPR who had met the nanny over in Africa.

"Jake, Jake, Jake," she said when she answered the call, "flowers are fine. Roses. No candy. Happy to help, but how the hell does a guy like you go from pirates in the Gulf of Oman to Angelina's nanny?"

"What's up with the mother?" Jake asked, flexing back his lips and checking the perfect white teeth in the mirror for food.

"You know she's booked tomorrow on *GMA, The View,* and *Larry King Live*?" Meghan asked. "Did you know *American Outrage* is the only evening magazine with an interview?"

"Why is the mother here?" Jake asked. "Who is she?"

"I speak French, so it didn't even cross my mind," Meghan said with a laugh, "but the girl doesn't speak English. Her mother is probably there to interpret."

"Is she interpreting on *GMA*?" Jake asked.

"You don't think Diane Sawyer speaks French?"

"The audience doesn't. Christ."

"Settle down, it's been done before. Everyone else will be doing it too. Maybe subtitles. Gotta go. Do pink roses, will you? The red ones smell."

Jake hung up. The makeup girl brushed out his eyebrows and whipped off the cape.

"You want me to run a quick iron over that suit?" the makeup girl asked.

"It's a three-thousand-dollar suit," Jake said, looking down and brushing the sleeve.

"It's pretty wrinkled."

"Yeah, I'm okay. The stripes will hide it, but thanks."

He got up and the show's lawyer, Christine Hagan, appeared waving a copy of the script.

"You can't say 'when Angelina hit you,' " she said, her face turning colors. "We'll get sued and lose. We don't know if she hit this girl. She could be some crackpot milking this thing. You have to say 'allegedly.' Every time you talk about her being hit, you have to say that."

"Got it," Jake said.

"You got it, but it was in the script. You say she hit her and I'll bury the whole piece. I'm not letting us get sued by Angelina Jolie."

Christine kept after him all the way down the hall and Jake just smiled and nodded.

He walked into the studio with an audio man fixing the microphone to his lapel and clipping the transmitter to the back of his belt. He stepped up onto the set and gave the girl his best smile.

"Antoinette," he said, holding out both hands. "No, don't get up."

He bent down and kissed her good cheek, scanning the other side of her face for the red finger marks where she'd allegedly been slapped by the movie star for her impertinence, wherein lay the tragedy. He then looked at the mother, who quickly spoke to the girl in French. The girl blushed and looked down, saying something.

"What'd she say?" Jake asked the mother. She was an attractive woman, well built like her daughter but with blond hair that had faded and wrinkles around her eyes from too much sun.

"She says she thought Brad Pitt was the most handsome man in America, but maybe not now."

"Thank you," Jake said. He looked at the girl and gave half a bow. *Merci.*

"Oh?" The girl perked up. *Monsieur, parlez-vous français?*

"No," Jake said, looking from mother to daughter, "I don't. No French."

"Mr. Carlson," the mother said in a low tone, leaning forward in her chair, "I know you pay my daughter's fee, but you misunderstood that I also have a fee."

Jake took half a step back and placed his hand on his chest and asked, "Did you get Antoinette's check?"

"Yes," the mother said, taking it out of her purse and holding it up.

"Fifty thousand dollars," Jake said, tilting his head toward the check.

"Yes," the mother said. "But fifty thousand *each.*"

Jake's mouth fell, and before he could respond Joe Katz, the show's executive producer, burst into the studio waving his hands. Jake signaled him to calm down and Katz checked himself. He took a deep breath and cleared his throat before calmly explaining to the mother that they weren't even getting a twenty-four-hour exclusive and that they just couldn't pay more than fifty.

The lawyer for the girl's family slipped into the mix with his back up and began to argue with Katz. The volume of their voices steadily grew. Somehow, Jake ended up with the check in his hands and the girl ran off the set crying. The lawyer and the mother stormed out after her, yelling that they'd sue for breach of contract.

"Great," Katz said, frowning at Jake. "I thought you had this nailed down."

"Yesterday you said I was the only reporter in America good enough to outdo the networks," Jake said, tugging the corners of his mouth into a false smile. "Now they pull a bait-and-switch and that's on me?"

"Don't be so goddamn smug, will you?" Katz said. "We ran promos all day promising the nanny."

"You think our audience will forgive us?" Jake said. "I mean, now they'll never know if Billy Bob Thornton's influence is still lingering, if that's what pushed Angelina to slap this girl, or if someone just forgot to change a diaper."

"Funny," Katz said, turning to go, "but when the suits out in LA ask, this one's on you."

Jake waited until he was alone, then kicked a chair and went back to the makeup room. He threw himself down in Nancy's chair and snatched a handful of baby wipes to remove his makeup. The makeup girl peeked in, but saw the expression on his face in the mirror and quickly disappeared. Jake scowled at himself, the tightness in his chiseled jawline and the dark brooding in his glass-blue eyes, and ran a hand through his dirty-blond hair to break up the spray. He went to his dressing room and tore off his suit, replacing it with jeans and a T-shirt that clung to his muscular frame, before he too stormed out of the building.

On the drive out to Atlantic Beach, Jake dialed up his agent in LA and related the story. She knew about it already because another client of hers was the executive producer of *Entertainment Tonight* and they'd snapped up the girl and the mother before Jake had his makeup off.

"Do you know I was actually thinking today that no one fills my candy dish?" Jake said. "How sad is that?"

"I'm sure you're sick over it," she said.

"You know what I'm sick over?" he asked.

"Mary Hart's smart-ass grin?"

"No," Jake said, holding the phone away from his face, looking at it. "I'm sick of me."

3

The next morning, Jake huffed and wiped the sweat from his face, churning up through the beach grass. He was just forty, but fit enough to have run a marathon two summers ago even though he still had the thick muscular frame from wrestling in college. The sun wasn't up yet and the fog was thick, but his white contemporary home rose up like some futuristic temple, a cluster of giant rectangular boxes standing on end, rigid and riddled with glass cubes, nearly glowing in the thin dawn light while its neighboring shake-shingled beach houses still hid in the gloom. A single orange rectangular glow came from the window in the master bathroom and that's where Jake headed.

He climbed the split-level stairs and stopped outside Sam's room, the bed unmade, and wondered if some of his own decisions as a parent had precipitated Sam's slide.

No one except Juliet, their housekeeper, knew that Sam slept with Jake on the far side of his king bed, with Louie at their feet. Jake told Sam that if he ever told his therapist that the party would be over. All the books said not to do it, but it had started when Karen went to the hospital for the last time. Sam would come into Jake's bed in the middle of the night, sobbing and trembling. A week or so after the funeral, Sam just made it his own space. Louie came later, which Jake didn't like, but tolerated, so that when he traveled, Sam wouldn't be alone. And after a while he got used to the big warm presence at his feet.

He climbed the next set of stairs and walked into the master bedroom with its sixteen-foot-high slanted ceiling and sliding glass doors that opened onto a wide balcony. The radio on the alarm clock was playing Beethoven's Ninth, but not loud enough to drown out the sound of the surf that came in through the open doors. Sam was still out cold with his mouth hanging open and a wet spot on the pillow. Louie raised his head, blinked, and thumped his tail three times on the bed.

"Come on, Sam," Jake said, tugging on a

thick big toe. "Alarm went off fifteen minutes ago."

Sam sat up, his straight dark hair going in every direction, his bulk lost in a triple-X Jets T-shirt. He yawned and looked blankly at Jake.

"Come on, goddamn it," Jake said.

"You swear a lot," Sam said, rubbing his eyes.

"Every morning I tell you, if you're going to listen to the radio during the day, turn up the volume for the alarm at night," Jake said.

"You think I was listening to *that?*"

"Well, get dressed," Jake said, peeling off his sweaty shirt and stepping into the bathroom. "We've got Dr. Stoddard."

"Dr. Stoddard's an asshole," Sam said from the bed.

Jake stuck his head back out into the bedroom. "Hey, don't get suspended for fighting and you won't have to see the school shrink. Turn that off and get ready."

When Jake got out of the shower, Sam was nowhere to be seen. He went to the doorway and shouted down the stairs. "Hey, you making eggs?"

Sam shouted back that he would if Jake wanted them.

"Scrambled, okay?" Jake yelled.

He walked over to the dresser, where his cell phone rested amid Karen's hand cream bottles and the stack of books she'd been planning to read. Their covers seemed faded under the blanket of dust. The professional advice Jake got was to put them away, that it was time, but Jake couldn't do that. He was afraid even to touch them and he'd instructed Juliet that the top of the dresser was off-limits. The cell phone's red light blinked at him. Messages. Three of them.

Jake wrapped the towel around his waist and put the phone to his ear. The first message was from one of the show's field producers, Conrad Muldoon. Frantic. The wife of a murdered FBI agent was finally going to talk. The agent had been investigating a senator's connection to an Indonesian child pornography ring. Jake, Muldoon, and several of the show's other producers had been orbiting the woman for months, sending notes, flowers, e-mails, angling for an interview.

The FBI was telling the woman to keep quiet, even though their investigation had stalled. That same agency had yet to track down a mysterious black Mustang seen by several witnesses racing away from the scene. That bizarre inconsistency had finally hit home with the wife. Muldoon had a crew set to shoot at nine a.m. at the woman's home in Brooklyn.

The second message was from an elated Joe Katz, telling Jake congratulations, he had heard the news, and that an interview like this was just the kind of thing he needed to call off the wolves. The third message was from Muldoon asking where the hell he was.

Jake called the producer while he dressed, explaining that he'd be a little late, but would do his best.

"You're kidding," Muldoon said.

"Relax," Jake said, "these people are mine. They'll wait."

"I'm the one that got the call from the mother," Muldoon said.

"Conrad, first of all, Katz assigned this story to me," Jake said. "Second, the only reason the mother talked to us in the first place was because she used to hear me on NPR. I'll get there when I get there."

4

The school psychologist had a full, salty beard and long greasy hair that he wore tied into a ponytail with a red rubber band. The elbows of his corduroy blazer were patched with worn leather and it was missing the same leather button that had been missing since the first time Jake met the man two years ago.

"Sam and I need to be alone," he said.

Jake shifted in the wooden chair outside Stoddard's office. It was library quiet. The hallway of the administration building smelled like old carpet and floor wax. Every so often, someone would walk past and mount the creaky stairs to the second floor. Once a door across the hall opened and a heavy woman with pink cheeks and curly hair peeked out before closing it. Jake looked at his watch and the cell phone rang again.

"I'm doing my best to keep her," Muldoon said. "What's it look like, buddy?"

"Not long," Jake said. "Thanks, Conrad."

"No promises," Muldoon said pleasantly, "but I'm doing everything I can."

Fifteen minutes later, the knob on Stoddard's office door rattled and turned. Sam came out hanging his head.

"Well," Stoddard said, clasping his hands, "we've had a good beginning. Why don't you step back inside for a second, Mr. Carlson?"

Jake looked at his watch and forced a smile. The psychologist offered up a small nod. Jake went in and shut the door, draping an arm over Sam's shoulder. Stoddard slipped behind his desk and sat down, but Jake stayed on his feet.

"One of the things I think Sam now understands, Mr. Carlson," Stoddard said, "is that who we are is nothing more than a series of choices. Sam told me he wants to find what he calls his *real* mother and that you've agreed to help him."

Jake just stared.

Stoddard shook his head and said, "A disaster. Sam has to understand that he was born, and given away. His real mother is *not* a life-detail because she never impacted a choice. Now, this imagined figure may be one of the excuses Sam likes to attribute to

31

his own poor choices, but we cannot allow this. Not if he's going to get well."

Jake bit the inside of his lip and nodded. It was enough for Stoddard, who then said he'd see Sam every morning of his week-long suspension at eight-thirty, and once a week after that.

"I think I can help," he said solemnly.

Jake kept his arm around Sam all the way across the wet parking lot. The sun was a yellow splotch now, burning away at the mist. When they were in the car, Sam turned to him with wet eyes and a protruding lower lip.

"Dad, you promised you'd —"

Jake held up his hand as he started the car and backed out.

"I don't care what that guy says," Jake said.

"Really?"

"I told you I'd try to find her."

Sam sat back in his seat and let out a big breath, shaking his head.

"But the school says you have to go and I don't want you to blow it with Dr. Stoddard," Jake said, taking a corner fast enough for the wheels to screech. "Deal?"

"He's such an asshole."

"Hey, come on," Jake said.

■ ■ ■ ■

When Sam asked where they were going, Jake told him he had to get straight to an interview. When they arrived at the woman's Brooklyn address, Jake dashed up the steps and into the open doorway, adjusting his tie. He found the crew nearly finished taking down the lights. The equipment stood waiting in a cluster of black cases, the kind that always reminded Jake of his days in the high school band. Neither the woman nor Conrad Muldoon were anywhere in sight.

Skip Lehman ran the crew, and when he saw Jake he suddenly became fascinated with collapsing a tripod. The crew began filing past him, carrying the boxes out to their van. Sam slipped through the doorway and stood with his hands jammed into his pants pockets.

"What the hell happened?" Jake asked the crew leader.

"Hi, Jake," Skip said. He shrugged and shook his head and held his palms up. "I really don't know. Muldoon said to shoot it. You know it's not my decision."

"Muldoon did the interview himself?" Jake asked.

"No," Skip said, "Sara was here."

"Sara Pratt? When did she get here?"

"I guess about nine, maybe a little before."

"That fucking asshole."

Skip Lehman tilted his head to one side, stroking his ginger beard and glancing at Sam before he went back to work.

"Where's the woman?"

"Upstairs," Skip said without looking. "She said we could finish and close up. She got kind of teary."

"She cried?" Jake said.

Skip nodded.

"She cried in *my* interview, which I didn't do," Jake said. "You people are beautiful."

"Hey, Jake. We just shoot what they tell us."

"Yeah, what they tell you. Great."

Jake walked out with Sam in tow. They got into the car and headed for home so he could drop off Sam.

Juliet, their housekeeper, was used to keeping an eye on Sam and she did a good job of it. Sam didn't steal or light fires or commit vandalism. He didn't smoke or drink or do drugs. His trouble wasn't at home, it was in school. It was teachers and principals and other kids. It was forgetting his sneakers for gym class. It was not sitting still. It was outsmarting his teachers, laughing at the wrong time, fooling around, and getting grades that didn't come close to his IQ.

Karen had had him tested years ago. He wasn't ADD, but he had some of the characteristics. He wasn't depressed or schizophrenic or bipolar or anything they could put a label on except trouble, too smart for his own good. At home, though, he was just Sam. He liked to read books. He'd take their golden retriever, Louie, for long walks on the beach and come back at dark with smooth pieces of glass and shells that he kept in a big jar on his desk. It wasn't that Sam wasn't friendly, but he didn't have any friends. Karen used to say he was waiting for the right person, someone he could trust, someone who saw the world the same way he did. Jake used to tell her that apparently he wasn't in any hurry.

They pulled into the driveway.

"You going to find her now?" Sam asked.

"It's not like calling 411," Jake said. "If I can find her, it's going to take time. It won't be easy. Right now I've got another disaster to attend to."

"You will," Sam said.

Jake told him to behave and that he'd try to make it home for dinner.

5

The *American Outrage* offices were set up like a newsroom, with the executives along the walls behind closed doors and the production staff working at desks in a big open space. Three hours remained until the show went to air and every day it was the same, the place abuzz with people darting between desks and production bays and shouting into telephones. Joe Katz had the corner office looking out over the East River. He held the phone to his ear, but motioned for Jake to sit down while he wrapped up his call.

Jake took a spot on the leather couch, crossed his legs, and grabbed hold of his shin, trying not to listen. Katz had dark curly hair that had receded halfway up his narrow skull. His glasses were stylishly rectangular, like his black, open-collared Hugo Boss shirt. When he hung up, he smiled at Jake and rested his hands flat on the desk in front of him.

"I know," he said. "You're mad, but we needed the story and the wife didn't want to wait. We got the exclusive with her, Jake. It'll be huge."

"He didn't try," Jake said. "He was planning to do this to me. Sara didn't just happen to be in the neighborhood, Joe. Shit, the little bimbo lives in Jersey City."

"He knew you might not make it," Katz said, examining his pen. Then he looked up. "Hey, she made a play for you. Get over it. Most guys would be flattered."

"See this?" Jake said, holding up his hand with the wedding ring. "A play for a guy with one of these is a bimbo."

"Jake, can I be honest with you?"

His tone jolted Jake. Katz was quintessential Hollywood. Everything was great, even when it wasn't. Jake nodded.

"First of all, Sara did a good job," Katz said with a sniff. "She's probably going to be the next weekend anchor."

"How nice for her."

"Jake, you're making a lot of money and ad sales are down. It's not just this show, it's everywhere, but they're down."

"I saved you fifty thousand on the nanny interview."

"Funny. Another thing I caught shit for."

"You came to me for this show, Joe. I was pretty happy where I was."

"Except that NPR pays like you're an English teacher."

"They don't have producers who'd steal your story."

"It's not your story, Jake. It's the show's story. We've been through this. You know how TV works. Remember *Nightly News*? Before your career move? Look, it doesn't matter. The problem here is your salary and what you've produced."

"Joe, my wife was sick."

"You know I'm sorry. I am."

"My son is having problems."

"Nancy's son just went into rehab, Jake," Katz said. "But she's still hosting the show. You didn't see her miss a single day."

"See any connection there?" Jake said, uncrossing his legs and leaning forward.

Katz wrinkled his brow and frowned in puzzlement.

"Look," Katz said, "you need a big story."

"Like the one that bimbo is tracking right now?" he said, raising his voice and stabbing his finger toward the edit bays. "Like that?"

"You need a *couple* big stories. It's beyond me now. The lawyers in LA are asking me to justify re-upping your contract next month and I'm having a hard time."

"Now the lawyers are making decisions? Jesus. Why don't you just fire me?"

Katz put his pen down. "I like you, Jake. You can write. I've seen you get great interviews. You got balls. Maybe too much. Who takes on the U.S. Army?"

Jake blinked and nodded his head.

"So, I want to help," Katz said. "Remember the guy up in Syracuse who was holding those women prisoner in that bunker?"

"I remember hearing about it."

"Well, the pretty one, Catherine Anastacia, the blonde, is going to talk," Katz said. "No one ever got her and she's good TV. The guy goes on trial next week and I think it could give the story new life, especially with her talking. I want you to go up there and get him, too. Word is the lawyer can be bought. Get the DA if you can and a couple other victims. You see how I'm helping you here? We could do a five-part series for sweeps and it'll go a long way out in LA."

"My son is —"

"You used to work up there, didn't you?"

"At the CBS affiliate," Jake said. "That's where I met Karen. That's where we got Sam."

"So, you'll go."

Jake ran the edge of his thumbnail up and

down the space between his front teeth for a minute, then said, "Yeah. I'll go."

6

The kitchen in Jake's beach house also looked out over the Atlantic Ocean. The table sat in an alcove of glass, separated from the rest of the room by a white marble bar. Since Karen died, Jake and Sam ate at the bar with their backs to the view, even though Juliet scolded them for not sitting down like a normal family. They enraged her even more when they had a forty-inch plasma screen put up over the refrigerator so they could watch *SportsCenter* while they ate.

And, while Juliet was a good cook, she made mostly Caribbean-style rice dishes and salads. So the bulk of Jake's and Sam's diet was what they cooked themselves on the grill. Sam was more finicky than Jake, so if it was something like steaks or lobster tails, he cooked. When it was burgers and dogs, Jake got to man the fire. Juliet's food they lavished with praise, but mostly just pushed around on their plates.

After steaks, plantains, and a cabbage-and-pepper salad, Sam went to walk Louie while Jake helped Juliet clean up. He talked with her about staying for a few days to watch Sam, then went upstairs to pack enough things for a week upstate.

Jake's office was on the same level as Sam's bedroom. His desk was a thick sheet of glass resting on a black lacquered base with drawers. The chrome-and-leather chair sat facing a big square window that also looked out over the dunes and the ocean beyond. Once his briefcase was ready for the trip, Jake sat down and stared out at the sky, thick clouds brewing over a white-capped ocean.

He drew a deep breath and let it out through his nose, then turned on the computer and began the first stages of his search for Sam's biological mother. He didn't know how long he'd been there before he realized that Sam was back from his walk.

"I got an idea," Sam said.

"Uh-huh," Jake said, clicking on the Web site of an international adoption agency only to find that it specialized in babies from China.

"This guy Stoddard's a joke," Sam said.

"Mmm," Jake said, adding the word *Alba-*

nia to his search requirements.

"Matt Parker once," Sam said, "he went to the Grand Canyon on a family trip. He was gone for a week."

"I'd like to see that sometime, too," Jake said, clicking on a new site. "We'll do it one of these days."

"I mean, you're gone all the time," Sam said. "I'm sick of being alone."

"Juliet's here," Jake said.

"She goes to bed at like, eight-thirty and I can't stand that gospel music."

"You like her."

"I know, but I don't even *have* school this week."

Jake let his hands fall to his lap and swung around. "You want me to go do this thing, or not?"

"I do. With me."

"Oh, that Grand Canyon? No. You got Stoddard, jerk or not."

"Definitely jerk."

"You want to find where you came from, this trip couldn't come at a better time."

"I'm not saying I mind you going for this," Sam said. "I'm just saying in general you go too much."

"You gotta take the bad with the good," Jake said, without turning his head.

Instead of going to his room, Sam hovered

over Jake's shoulder. Jake tried to ignore it and keep working, but Sam's heavy nasal breathing cut right through his concentration.

"Sammy, I love you, man," Jake said. "But you're huffing and puffing on me."

Sam grinned at him and nodded. "This is my world."

"Yeah?" Jake said. "It's called the International Children's Adoption Agency of Central New York. I can barely say it, let alone find it."

"You're using the wrong search engine," Sam said, pulling up another chair, nudging Jake over a bit, and letting his fingers scamper across the keyboard.

"Google," Sam said.

Jake watched Sam riffle through a series of screens. Finally Sam stopped and shook his head.

"The only thing I get for agencies in Syracuse is Catholic Charities and the World Adoption Agency that's like some franchise. You sure about the name?"

"I'm the one that got you."

"It's not there. Not in any phone books, no directories. No Web connection for sure. You sure you're sure?"

"Hang on," Jake said.

He left Sam in his study and went upstairs.

On the floor of the bedroom closet, Karen had a fireproof lockbox. Jake opened it with a key from his sock drawer and found the papers from Sam's adoption along with the house deed, Jake's will, and a copy of his TV contract, which he couldn't help checking for the date of expiration because it didn't seem that three years would have really passed by the end of next month.

Sam's papers included a declaration of abandonment from an Albanian state-run orphanage and an order of adoption from a court in Tirana and their English translations. At the back of the envelope was a letter that Karen had saved. It was from Ron Cakebread, the man who ran the upstart adoption agency they'd heard about through a woman Karen had met during her treatments. Back then, they didn't know if they'd have the three to five years to wait for a domestic adoption to go through, and Karen's friend told them about Ron Cakebread.

The letter had come only two weeks after their first meeting and it announced that the agency had found a perfect baby boy for them to adopt. Jake held the letter up to the light and wondered if the small round spot on the lower corner had been a tear of Karen's or just something Ron Cakebread spilled on his desk. Jake remembered Cakebread as a scarecrow of a man in a camelhair blazer with a pale purple tie whose knot was the size of Jake's wallet.

Jake went back downstairs and handed the letter to Sam.

"The agency name was right," Jake said, "but how about this?"

On the letter's heading, Cakebread was listed as Ronald O. Cakebread.

"That's a good name," Sam said, typing it in. "I'll find him. You guys have AutoTRAK, right? Can you give me the account?"

Jake raised an eyebrow. "How'd you know about that?"

Sam huffed and said, "*Dog The Bounty Hunter?*"

"The bleached blond guy with the pony-tail?"

"It's a cool show. He uses it."

Jake nodded, gave Sam the account information, and watched him search. After half an hour, Sam slapped his hand on the desktop and looked over at him.

"What did I miss?" Sam asked.

"I think you did everything I could think of and more," Jake said. "That's how it goes sometimes. The Yankees are playing. Let's watch the last couple innings. You make some popcorn and I'll get the drinks."

"But we're not giving up?"

"Hey, we just started."

Jake looped his arm around Sam's neck and pulled him tight.

In the morning, Jake ran on the beach while it was still dark and kissed Sam on the forehead in his sleep before slipping out. He had a late-morning flight out of La-Guardia and just enough time to stop at the Albanian Embassy on the Upper East Side. It was a long shot, but it was on his list of possible leads and it was right there, fifteen minutes from the airport. Jake pulled to the curb when he saw the red flag with the black double-headed eagle. The street sign read DIPLOMATS ONLY but there was still space for another car, so Jake got out and went up the steps. Through the glass and steel bars, Jake saw a squat bald man sitting at a security desk.

After Jake rang the bell, the man got up and looked him over before opening the door to ask in a thick accent what he wanted. Jake showed his press credential and asked to speak with someone who might be able to help him find the mother of an adopted Albanian child. The guard scowled, but let him in and told him to have a seat before he picked up the phone in one hand with the credential in the other and said something Jake didn't understand. After setting down the phone and the credential, the guard returned to his original position, with his bare head settled back into the thick rolls of his neck, staring blankly ahead like a toad.

Jake looked at his watch and waited. After fifteen minutes, he got up and peeked outside to make sure his car wasn't being towed, then walked to the desk, politely asking if someone was going to be able to help him. The guard blinked at him and picked up the phone once more, talking in his thick Slavic-sounding dialect back and forth in quick staccato bursts with someone on the other end.

When he hung up the phone, he said, "Twenty minutes, maybe thirty."

Jake sat back down and took out his BlackBerry, sending out a flurry of e-mails to help get things organized for the shoot up in Syracuse. When two men and a young woman, all wearing dark suits, came in through the front door, Jake stood up. But after glancing at him, they spoke to the guard and passed through the inner door.

Jake stayed on his feet. After thirty minutes had passed, he stepped toward the desk once more. Before he got there, the inner door opened and a young man with fashionable frameless glasses and a buttoned-up navy suit stepped out, picked up Jake's press credential off the desk, and began to study it. Jake had seen the type. Embassy brats who grew up to be diplomats themselves. They were like lab rats, colorless and practiced at running the maze. This one surprised Jake when he looked up, extended his hand, and apologized for the delay.

"I'm sorry about just dropping in," Jake said, "but I'm on my way to shoot a story upstate for the show."

The young man introduced himself as Peter something, the embassy's assistant press secretary. He said he'd seen Jake's show. He led Jake into a small office down a narrow hall. Jake sat and explained his situation. The young man's eyes stayed on his except when they drooped sympathetically in a way that filled Jake with hope. Jake handed the papers across the desk and the man studied them for a minute before handing them back.

"I'm sorry, Mr. Carlson," he said. "But without a birth certificate, finding your son's mother is impossible. The certificate of abandonment means that he was a foundling."

"What about someone at the orphanage?"

Jake asked.

Peter shook his head and again said he was sorry.

"Would you have any way of helping me find this organization?" Jake asked, handing the letter from Ron Cakebread across the desk. Peter looked at it and said no.

"But they were bringing Albanian babies over here," Jake said. "Lots of them. Not just Sam. These are government papers. Someone has to know, right?"

"Mr. Carlson," Peter said, "that was a difficult time. The government fell apart. Soldiers were in the streets. Our country is still working its way out of everything bad that happened. It's a new government now."

"You know who Arnold Schwarzenegger is?" Jake asked.

"Austria's practically a neighboring country to Albania," the young man said.

"Exactly," Jake said, standing up. "So, I'm doing a sit-down with Arnold this one time and I ask him if he remembers the name of the guy who took second in his first body-building contest, you know, to do a kind of comparison to how close that other guy was to all Arnold has done.

"So, Arnold says he doesn't know and there's no way of him really finding out and I said, 'Just take my card. Something might come to you.' The Governator rolls his eyes, but he takes it."

The young man raised his eyebrows.

"Two weeks later," Jake said, "Arnold calls me. Said it just came to him in the shower. It was a great piece. The guy's a motorcycle mechanic in Munster and a huge Arnold fan."

Jake pushed one of his cards across the desk.

"So . . . you know," Jake said, and saw himself out.

7

Jake got a hotel in Armory Square, the renovated part of downtown Syracuse, and set up shop. Catherine Anastacia, the blonde Katz had talked about, was being handled by the show's booker in New York. That interview was set for tomorrow. The rest of the interviews that would round out the story were up to Jake and the producer for the series, one of the show's best, Barbara Simon. Jake would work in tandem with her and after his blowout with Muldoon, he wanted to send a message that he was still very much a team player.

He called the DA's office to get the ball rolling there, and began leaving messages for the list of women, besides Catherine Anastacia, who had also been victims in the concrete bunker. The lawyer for the monster who had kept them there — one for nearly three years — was an easy play. He wanted money and *American Outrage* was willing to pay ten grand for a jailhouse interview with a two-week exclusive. The lawyer was even going to smooth the way to get their cameras inside the jail and suggested he might be able to get them in the same room so they didn't have to shoot through the visitation glass.

With some work done, he dialed Sam and asked how it had gone with Dr. Stoddard.

"Did you find her?" Sam asked.

"Sam," he said, "you gotta stop doing this. If I can find her — and it will be really tough, Sam — but *if* I can, it's going to take time. These things sometime take years. I've got an idea I'm going to check out later on. I'm working here, too, don't forget. Now what about Stoddard?"

The school psychologist was still an ass-hole, but Louie was good and Juliet was making pasta with vodka sauce so Sam was okay.

"Good," Jake said. "Okay, I gotta go."

"What can I do?" Sam asked.

"Take care of Louie and Juliet and don't give Stoddard a hard time. That's help enough."

"Give me a job. Something on the computer. I'm good at it."

Jake agreed that if he had something, he'd call. He told Sam he loved him, hung up, and checked his e-mails. One was from Katz apologizing, because Barbara Simon, the producer he'd promised to Jake, had had a breakthrough with Russell Crowe, nailing down the first interview with him since he kicked a dog he caught pissing on his Bentley. Barbara had to go straight to LA, so Katz was sending Muldoon.

Jake snapped his phone shut.

"Jesus Christ," he said, shaking his head. "Russell fucking Crowe." He put on his suit jacket, scooped up his briefcase, and walked out into the afternoon sun. The trees along the street were fat with budding leaves and as he walked along, Jake believed that he could smell the first hints of warm mud and baking grass, the promise of an early summer.

The building where the agency had been was only a few blocks away. Inside, a sleepy-looking security guard straightened up in his chair and eyed Jake while he waited for the elevator.

"Hey," the guard said, "aren't you that guy?"

Jake let his face go slack and he gave the man a blank look.

"On TV?" the guard said. "I seen you, right?"

The guard started snapping his fingers, trying to connect a name with a face. Jake shrugged and shook his head like the guy was nuts.

"Sorry," he said.

"Aw, you look just like that guy," the guard said.

Jake shrugged again and got onto the elevator, taking it to the third floor. Jake thought he remembered the tan paint on the frame of the door. Missing chips exposed the dark metal below. The nameplate read AA EUROPEAN TRAVEL, INC.

Jake walked in and stopped cold. He straightened his back and tightened his stomach and stared. The girl behind the gray metal desk had her head angled down at some paperwork and the flourish of her pen. Beside her, a small CD player buzzed with David Gray. On either side of a comfortable-looking couch was a potted tree. A coffee table rested on a worn Oriental rug and the air was thick with the spicy smell of incense, reminding Jake of a college dorm room.

The girl's long straight hair was glossy and black. Her eyes were large and dark and their lashes swept up toward her olive-skinned brow and down toward high cheeks and a long narrow nose. It wasn't until she raised her head that he saw the bone-white scar that ran nearly the full length of the far side of her face. Where it curved across the corner of her mouth the full lips were dimpled, giving her a permanent half-frown.

"Can I help you?" she asked with the hint of an accent.

"I'm Jake Carlson," he said, his face warming. He crossed the open space and extended his hand.

"Zamira," she said, taking it. She wore a short-sleeved taupe sweater that revealed the subtle curves of her chest and shoulders.

"Uh, there was an adoption agency that used to be here."

"We do travel," she said, turning the music down. "For groups."

"And you don't know anything about the people before, I'm sure," he said, forcing his eyes from the scar. "But do you know who owns this building?"

She gave him a vacant stare and shook her head.

"Do you know who would know?" he asked, looking at the closed door that led into the offices beyond. "Is the manager around?"

"He's out for the rest of the day," she said.

"Can I get his cell phone number?"

"I'm sorry," she said. "I can't. But I can

try him. Hang on."

She dialed and waited, then shook her head and hung up.

"Will he call in or anything?" Jake asked.

"Usually."

"Maybe I could check back with you?" Jake said. "Would you mind asking him who owns the building? I'll be here for a few days. I'm working on a story for a television show."

She stared.

"*American Outrage*?" he said, taking the press credential out of his wallet.

"Oh."

"We're doing a piece on that guy who kept those women in a concrete bunker."

She blinked.

"The trial starts next week," Jake said. "So, can I check back later, after you talk to your manager?"

"Wait. I can try the leasing agent down-stairs," she said, picking up the phone. "He'd know."

She held it for a minute or so, then rolled her eyes and said, "Surprise. Half the time I have to slide the rent check under the door. Here, I'll write his number down. You can leave a message and maybe he'll call you back. Ask for Joe."

Jake took the paper and peeked at her left

hand. He saw no ring. His heart skittered and he said, "I appreciate the help. Maybe I could buy you a cup of coffee when you get done? At that Starbucks? Around the corner?"

Her cheeks flushed and she adjusted the curtain of hair on the scarred side of her face.

"Only if you come with the name, though," Jake said, repressing a smile.

She looked up at him, studying his face.

"Kidding. How about five o'clock? Meet you there?"

"All right," she said, allowing the hint of a smile. "Sure."

On his way out, the security guard snapped his fingers and hailed him as the guy from *American Outrage.*

"I knew it, man," the guard said.

Jake gave him a goofy grin and kept going. Out on the street, he slung the briefcase over his shoulder and twisted the wedding ring around on his finger. He felt naked when it slipped off, but instead of putting it back on, he clutched it in his fist.

Steve Cambareri came out right away, wearing a light gray suit and a thin mustache. He slapped Jake on the shoulder, telling him that he watched his show all the time, before leading Jake back into his office. The two of them used to go drinking when Jake was a young reporter and Cambareri was working traffic court.

"You ever marry that girl who worked for the judge?" Jake asked.

Cambareri grinned and spun the picture frame on his desk to show off his kids.

"Remember Grimaldi's?" Jake asked. "We'd order a plate of spaghetti and old Freddy would send out steaks and lobsters? You still getting the treatment?"

Cambareri laughed at the memory. "No, the old man passed on. You help somebody with a loading zone today and they ask why it's only thirty minutes instead of sixty."

"That loading zone was the only way you and me were getting a taste of lobster."

"Back then," Cambareri said. "You must be eating five-star now. Jake Carlson, TV star."

"Nah."

They talked for a while longer before Jake said, "I know it's a long shot, but I wondered if you ever heard of a guy named Ron Cakebread?"

Cambareri shrugged and asked what that had to do with the trial.

"Nothing," Jake said. "It's personal. He ran an adoption agency."

"Name rings a bell. If he ran an agency, maybe one of the family court judges would know," Cambareri said. He picked up the phone and after a minute got a judge on the line, asking the same question Jake had asked him.

"You sure it's the same guy?" Cambareri said to the judge, leaning forward with his elbows on the desk and raising his eyebrows at Jake. "Yeah, I remember, I just didn't remember that he ran an adoption agency. Okay. Thanks."

Cambareri hung up and began absently cracking his finger joints one at a time.

"I knew I heard that name. We never found out who did it," he said, gazing out the window.

"Did what?" Jake asked.

"Your guy?" Cambareri said. "This Ron Cakebread? If it's the same guy — and they're telling me it is — they found him about seven years ago. His car was parked in back of some grocery store. Fatal gunshot wound to the head. They ruled it a suicide, but I think it was a little sketchy."

8

"Anybody asks, I'm not chasing this stuff down for you. You got it yourself, right?"

Jake nodded. While Cambareri searched for the file, Jake went down the hall and locked down his interview with the DA for the next day before returning to his old friend's office.

As he walked in, the phone rang. Cambareri answered it, handing Jake the thick file off his desk and pointing to the little conference room across the hall.

Jake peeled back the cover and saw the name Ron Cakebread. A black-and-white photo showed Cakebread's profile, one vacant eye and the dark exit wound in the back of his skull. Jake sat down in the conference room and dug in. There were several newspaper articles as well as the police report. No arrests were ever made. The coroner's report said suicide. There was ample powder residue on the fingers, but it was noted that there were also faint bruises and abrasions around the upper arms that were consistent with restraint and that Cakebread's blood alcohol level was .23.

The list of interviews was unimpressive. Cakebread's mother, who lived in Tupper Lake and swore her son didn't have an enemy in the world. Cakebread's landlord, who said the guy kept to himself. He had a grown daughter he never spoke with. The only thing of interest was the ex-wife. The report said she refused to cooperate and asked immediately for a lawyer. After that, there was nothing. Jake jotted down her address as well as the name of the investigating officer, Sergeant Fred Blane.

The report mentioned the adoption agency, but only as Cakebread's self-owned business. A cashier found the car next to a Dumpster in the back of a shopping center called Westvale Plaza. Jake jotted down the location on his yellow pad, closed the investigation file, and returned it to his friend's desk. Cambareri was still on the phone and he signaled Jake that he would give him a call later.

It was nearly five when Jake stepped out onto the sidewalk and wove his way through the crowd of workers spilling from the office buildings. Zamira sat at a small table in the Starbucks by herself, staring out the window. She wore a trim brown leather jacket over her sweater and its matching skirt. The long scar faced him, but he still felt the urge to touch the long silky hair.

"What do you like?" he asked, stepping up to the table.

She stood up, shaking her head, and said, "I have to go, but I brought you the number. My boss wanted me to ask why you wanted it."

She handed him a scrap of paper. He took it, looked at the name, and said, "Come on. You've got to let me live up to my part of the bargain. Too late for coffee? You want a drink?"

"What happened to your wedding ring?" she said, glancing at his hand.

His face warmed and he took a breath.

"My wife passed away," he said, looking into her eyes. "About a year ago. I usually wear it anyway."

She held his gaze, studying him before she said, "I think it's nice that you wear it."

"But not that I took it off," he said. "Stupid. Anyway . . ."

"Anyway," she said, sitting back down. "I'll have a cappuccino."

Jake got the coffee and sat down across from her. He kept his eyes fixed on hers and felt his heart pick up. The white scar only made him think about how perfect her face must have been.

"This show I do? I interview all these Hollywood assholes who leave their wives for every other costar," he said, taking a sip. "I try to be different."

"Wearing the ring is different," she said. "A year is a long time."

"First time I took it off," he said. "Something about you, I guess. A feeling."

Her brow furrowed.

"Funny thing was, she tried to make me promise I'd move on," Jake said. "How many women would do that?"

"I think I would," she said. "If you care about someone, you want them to be happy."

Jake looked at his coffee and took a drink, then he looked out the window.

"So," she said after a few moments, "why do you want to know about the owner of the building?"

"Did you know about the guy who ran the agency that used to be in your office?" Jake asked, turning his attention back to her. "Did you hear about him? What happened?"

"Is it something to do with the women in your story? The women in that bunker?"

"No," he said, "this is a separate thing. He was killed. They're not sure if he did it himself, or someone else."

"Are you doing a story about him?" she asked, sipping her drink and looking at him over the rim of her cup.

"Not a story," Jake said. "Not yet anyway. Maybe. I wasn't planning on it, but in the work I'm in I guess you're always looking for a story. Everyone has one. You too, right?"

"I guess," she said.

Jake's cell phone rang. The caller ID read it was Muldoon. Jake held up a finger and answered it. He didn't say anything to Muldoon about what had happened in Brooklyn, but he spoke with a cool detachment as he shared the interview times he'd already set up for the DA and the bunker man. Muldoon had just landed and he asked Jake to meet him for dinner so they could go over the schedule. Jake told him he already had plans, but that he could meet him later at the hotel bar.

When he got off, Jake said, "So, how about your story? Where are you from?"

"Albania," she said. "Fifteen years ago I came over. Things were bad."

"Albania?" Jake said. "Your English is excellent."

"Thank you," she said. "I went to school at night, and I like to watch old movies."

"Like, black-and-white old?"

"Katharine Hepburn. Cary Grant. Orson Welles. All of them."

"Ever see *Touch of Evil?*"

"Charlton Heston."

"They did a director's cut," he said. "Cut it the way Orson Welles supposedly wanted it. It's amazing."

"I didn't see that," she said.

Jake sat back in his chair, studying her.

"Ever been married?" he asked.

She lowered her eyes. "No."

"Fought them all off," he said.

Her fingers strayed to her face.

"I do need to go," she said, swinging her legs around to get up.

"Wait. I'm sorry. My wife and I adopted our son through the agency that used to be in your office," he said, touching her arm. "He's going through a hard time and I want to find his mother for him. His biological mother. If there's a story to it, well, okay, like I said, but that's not what it's about. It's about my son."

"I'm sorry."

"He's from Albania, my son," Jake said. "The agency had a pipeline over there for children. I just don't think it's total coincidence that you're from there, too."

Her eyes widened and she opened her mouth for a moment before snapping it shut.

"What?" he said.

"Many people came to this country from Albania. I'm sorry. I wouldn't know anything about your son. Thank you for the coffee."

She stood and Jake got up with her, shouldering his case and walking her to the door.

"My pleasure. Hey, do you want to maybe have dinner one of these nights?" he asked. "Tonight, even. What did I say? Just dinner."

"I have to go," she said. "Thank you."

She turned and hurried down the sidewalk, back in the direction of her office.

"Can I call you?" Jake said. He was sure she heard him, even though she made no sign.

He watched until she disappeared around the corner.

9

Jake found a rib place called Dinosaur Bar-B-Que a few blocks away. While he waited for his food, he dialed the real estate company that owned Zamira's building. There was no one in, so he left a message, saying he was interested in some space in the same building as AA European Travel. Then he called information and got the address of the real estate company, jotting it down underneath Zamira's writing on the same scrap of paper. The food came quickly.

Jake knocked down two pints of Blue Moon Ale and ate a rack of ribs so good he scraped the bones clean with his teeth. The sun had dropped by the time he walked out, but the warm air left him feeling unhurried. Three motorcycles rumbled past with girls clinging to the backs of their riders. Jake touched his wedding ring before taking a toothpick out of his front pocket and going to work on the shreds of meat stuck in his teeth as he walked back to his hotel.

The lobby smelled newly renovated. Up by the ceiling, a strip of masking tape still clung to the molding bearing the colors of the sea-foam-green wall. Brass floor lamps and hanging fixtures gleamed and sparkled. The corners of tables, chairs, and sideboards cut perfect angles, unmarred by the usual chips and dents. The faux-marble floor leading into the bar bore one lone black scuff mark. Muldoon hadn't arrived at the bar and that was just as well. Jake went upstairs to use the bathroom and call Sam from his room.

"How'd it go?" Sam asked as soon as he picked up the phone.

"No 'I miss you, Dad'?" Jake said. "No 'This place just isn't the same without you, Dad'?"

"What'd you find?"

"Not much," he said. "I went back to the agency where we got you and it's not there anymore."

"What happened?"

"I don't know."

"Did you check the phone book?"

"Of course."

"A lot of cities have a business directory. Did you go to the other agencies? They might have just changed the name."

"I looked. There's nothing."

"What about the people who worked there?"

"I only knew the director," Jake said, thinking about the bloody cavern in the back of Cakebread's head. "He's . . . not around either."

"How about your friend in the FBI? They've got stuff people don't even know about."

"Tell you what," Jake said. "I'll give him a call. That's one thing I didn't do."

" 'Cause like you said, this isn't going to be easy."

"You're right, but with the Dynamic Duo on it, she doesn't stand a chance."

The phone was silent for a minute. Jake thought he heard Sam breathing.

"That's like, Batman," Sam said.

"I was kidding," Jake said.

"You think she's alive, right?" Sam said in a flat voice.

"There's no reason to think she's not. I'm sure she's a young woman."

"Mom died," Sam said.

"Most don't," Jake said, his throat tightening.

"I know," Sam said. "They say stress causes cancer lots of the time."

"Lots of things do," Jake said.

70

"I wasn't always a bad kid, right? I mean when I was little?"

"You're not a bad kid now. What are you talking about?"

"Just all the trouble," Sam said.

Jake heard him cover the phone for a moment.

"You know what you were to her?" Jake said. "You were what she dreamed about. You gave her ten years they said she didn't even have."

Tears ran down Jake's face, but he kept his voice even and strong.

"You think?"

"I do," Jake said. "Now get to bed. I love you."

"I love you, too."

Jake hung up and wiped his face, then blew his nose in the bathroom and looked at himself in the mirror. The blue in his eyes seemed duller. No question the blond in his hair had faded, closer to gray than the wheat it had once been. Wrinkles radiated from the corners of his eyes. For TV, his agent did her best to sell looks like these as rugged or distinguished. A woman with chinks like his would get labeled as old.

Jake looked at his watch and hurried downstairs so that he could get around a few more drinks before he had to see Muldoon. Two women in business suits gawked at him. He walked to the far end of the empty bar for a stool, ignoring the blonde with the bright red lipstick when she winked at him. From that spot, he could watch the entrance without looking at the women and still keep Muldoon from sneaking up on him. Jake sniffed at the smell of new carpet and ran his hand over the glassy surface of the oak bar. The bartender had a stutter, but turned out to be a friendly college kid who poured a heavy-handed vodka tonic.

The corners of the ice cubes in his first drink had melted off when his cell phone rang. Cambareri gave Jake a cell phone number for Sergeant Blane.

"I asked around," Cambareri said. "They ruled it suicide because it fit and there weren't any suspects. The wife's alibi was rock-solid, some engineer's conference in Miami. No real connection between her and Cakebread since their divorce three years earlier anyway. They wrote the lawyer thing off to paranoia."

Jake thanked his old friend and dialed Blane. The sergeant reinforced Cambareri's recollection of the wife acting strange, but gave him nothing he didn't already have, so he ordered a fresh drink and called information. There was a D. Cakebread in Otisco. Jake took the notepad from his briefcase. The address matched the one he'd written down from the police report.

Muldoon barged in halfway through Jake's third drink, gut first, wearing snakeskin cowboy boots and stonewashed jeans with a matching jacket. The buttons on his white oxford pulled hard enough on their holes that Jake could see little flecks of pink skin. Muldoon's collar-length hair was ghost-white and swept straight back off his florid face.

He crossed the room calling Jake's name as if he'd discovered gold and the other handful of people in the bar stopped their conversations to look. In Muldoon's hand was a yellow notepad and a pen and he slapped them down onto the bar, ordering a Scotch and soda before clasping Jake's hand and saying it was damn good to see him.

"Right," Jake said, his teeth slightly numb.

"I am," Muldoon said, sipping his drink with one pinky extended and winking. "This is huge. *American Outrage* locks down the bunker-man story for sweeps. It'll be big news in the trades. I'm thinking Emmy for you on this one."

"I was thinking Emmy for the FBI agent's wife in Brooklyn."

"Come on, Jake," Muldoon said, soft-punching his shoulder. "You're a newsman. We both are."

"The DA is set for ten at his office on the third floor of the public safety building," Jake said, knocking down his drink and ordering another. "I'm sure you saw the e-mail from New York. The bunker man is lined up for tomorrow at two. The jail's out in Jamesville. What time's the crew call?"

"Jake."

"You're right, Conrad," Jake said. "We're pros. I'll do my job, you do yours. Otherwise, you can go fuck yourself."

Muldoon stiffened and his smile went blank.

"I booked one of the victims, Bethany Cross, for eight in the morning at her house out in Liverpool," Muldoon said. "Crew call's at five. I'll have a PA pick you up in front here at six-thirty. Try to make it this time."

Muldoon started to walk away, then spun around and stuck his finger in Jake's face.

"Let me tell you something, asshole, that woman was *my* interview and I wasn't going to wait around for you to get your personal life in order."

Jake squinted at him and shook his head. "You're pathetic."

"She didn't even *like* you, Jake," Muldoon said. "I know that's hard for you. I know women are supposed to swoon when they see you walk in the room, but that lady wasn't impressed. You had the mom, I give you that, but the wife was *mine*."

Jake muted a chuckle.

"Go ahead, laugh," Muldoon said. "But believe it or not, some women like the fat kid who got picked last because they know that guys like you are selfish assholes they can't trust."

Muldoon started to walk, then spun around again. "And another thing. That shit you did over in Iraq? You think you're some kind of hero? Think again."

"No hero," he said. "Just my job. Where were you? Looking up Pamela Anderson's skirt?"

"Yeah, you were real clever," Muldoon said, "you tricked a man who was fighting to protect us on a live feed. You stood up for a couple towelheads who got caught in a cross fire, then you come back all proud, like you're better than the rest, some moral paragon because you win the Murrow Award. Well, just so you know, there was about two hundred million people in this country who were damn glad when you got shitcanned."

Muldoon turned and this time sauntered all the way out with his duck-footed walk. Jake turned back to the bar.

"S-s-s-s-son of a bitch didn't pay for his d-drink."

"I got it," Jake said, pushing his money stack toward the edge of the bar. "He's a really good friend."

"Oh," the bartender said, his face turning red. He took the money and changed it out.

Jake knocked down two more drinks and ordered another, even though the lights had been turned down and the last couple of patrons were wandering out.

Jake hunched down over his drink, rolling the glass around on its base so that the ice swished softly, until he heard the clicking sound of a woman's heels on the wood floor. He widened one eye and cast it back over his shoulder.

She wore the same short leather jacket from earlier in the day, but now she had on snug, low-riding jeans with a belt buckle that matched her turquoise T-shirt. The shirt was cut low enough to reveal the swell of her breasts and short enough that he could see a honey-colored swatch of her hips and stomach.

Zamira slid up onto the bar stool next to him, exposing the good side of her face. She arched her back and wiggled out of the leather jacket, then she turned just a bit, smiled, and asked if she could have a drink.

10

Jake returned her gaze, then signaled the bartender.

"Red wine," she said. "Pinot noir, if you have it."

The bartender stared at her for a moment before reaching for a wineglass.

"Small world," Jake said.

"I had dinner with some friends at a place around the corner and thought I'd stop by," she said.

"How'd you know I was here?" he asked.

"You mentioned it."

"Did I?"

"That or you hypnotized me."

She smiled and nodded, taking the glass of wine from the bartender. She raised it, and when he lifted his drink she touched the lip of her glass to it with a small clink.

"What are we drinking to?" Jake asked.

"New friends?"

"And a whole new attitude, right?" he

said, hoisting the glass again and taking a slug.

She sipped hers and said, "A couple of my girlfriends have seen you on TV. They said I was crazy to walk away like I did. We had a few drinks, and, well."

"A few drinks is always good," Jake said, sliding around in his seat and putting one foot up on the footrest of her stool.

Zamira took another drink, nearly finishing the glass, and turned so that one leg fell across his at the calf.

"They thought that at least I should find out more," she said. "Like you said, everyone has a story."

"I like the beach," Jake said.

"Right," she said, "and surfing and blondes."

"I'm more about the inside, but if it's a quiz, brunettes."

"But you're a blond," she said.

"Opposites attract."

"What about accents?"

"Love them. Especially Albanian."

His left hand was up on the bar and she squeezed it, then let go with a gust of laughter.

"So," she said, "how much of what you said today is true and how much of it is part of the TV act?"

"TV is bullshit."

"So, you really have a son who was adopted?"

"Yeah," Jake said, smiling. "Sam."

"And that doesn't have anything to do with your TV show?" she said, grinning and taking another drink.

"No," he said.

"I thought you said you were always looking for a story."

"Well, sometimes the best stories have a way of finding you," he said. "I could use a good one."

"Why?"

Jake glanced at the bartender, who was drying a glass while he watched an NBA game on the screen in the corner.

"Great expectations," he said.

She wrinkled her brow.

"In TV, you're only as good as your last show."

"And what was your last show?" she asked.

"Someone took another shot at Snoop Dogg."

"Sounds more exciting than a thirteen-year-old adoption story."

"You saying there's a story?"

She ran her finger around the rim of her glass and looked away from him.

"You gotta have more than an empty office and a guy who killed himself. That happens fifty times a day. Got anything more?"

"I've been thinking. There was a lawyer," Jake said, hesitating. "Polish-sounding name. Kalaski or something. I can't remember. I only saw him in court once. Everything went through the director, Cakebread."

"You must have a name somewhere," she said. "The lawyer's. Have you checked your records? The Albanian community is large but perhaps I could help."

"Trust me," Jake said. "This is what I do. If I had it, I'd know. So, if I break something, you want me to interview you? Be on TV?"

"No. It's just interesting."

"You're interesting," Jake said, lowering his voice. He reached over and let the backs of his fingers trace the length of her silky hair. The scar seemed faded. He saw only the high, proud cheeks and the big liquid eyes.

"American women say if you want something that you should take it," she said, letting her left hand come to rest on his thigh.

He could feel the sharp edges of her red nails through his pants.

"And the friends you had dinner with are Americans?" he asked, swallowing.

"Very," she said, tracing a figure eight with one nail. "Me, too. I'm trying, anyway. I'm a citizen."

"You pledge allegiance to the flag?"

"Of course," she said.

Jake touched the side of her face and leaned close. Their lips barely touched. He closed his eyes and felt the warmth of her breath. He smelled perfume and a hint of shampoo. When he opened his eyes, she was looking at him. He grinned.

"Upstairs?" he asked.

She stared, and nodded her head ever so slightly.

11

The shrill sound of the phone cut the darkness and Jake bolted upright. His head throbbed and he worked his mouth open and closed to moisten it. Sun shone through the curtains. A glaze of sweat beaded his forehead. The clock read nine-twelve.

Jake snatched up the phone, expecting Muldoon.

"You go now," the voice said. It was a man with a thick eastern European accent. "This TV story is not good for you. Very dangerous."

The phone went dead.

Jake blinked and swung his feet to the floor, grasping his head in both hands. He staggered to the bathroom and tore through his shaving kit for the Advil. He swallowed four of them and refilled the plastic cup, drinking down three more refills before letting the cup clatter into the sink. He braced a forearm against the wall above the toilet and relieved himself.

The phone was ringing again. He crossed the room and snatched it up.

"Who the hell is this?" he asked.

"Me," Muldoon said. "I did the interview myself. I figured we could do a standup with you later for a bridge. Not bad for an off-air guy. Look, I don't know what the fuck you're doing, but if you no-show with the DA, I'm calling Katz."

"Was that you that just called?" Jake asked. "Who was that?"

"I got no idea what you're talking about, man," Muldoon said. "All I know is I'm on my way to the DA's office and you better be there or we're going to have serious problems."

"Where's the goddamned PA?"

"He knocked on your door three times and figured you took a cab."

"He didn't knock goddamn hard enough."

"You blaming a kid now? Nice."

"Fuck you."

Jake hung up. He turned on the shower and looked at himself in the mirror. There was a bottle of Visine in his kit and he let the cold drops fill his eyes, blinked for a minute, then held them tight before wiping them on his arm and checking the mirror again. Steam curled up out of the shower and he stepped in, scrubbing and trying to reconstruct what happened.

He remembered the bar and the kiss. He was certain that had happened. He remembered the feel of her lips and her nail on his thigh. Then they were in his room. He had a fuzzy notion of a black lace bra and matching panties, then nothing. He strained his thoughts and even tried to invent a naked scene that would jar his memory. As he dried off and dressed in a suit and tie, he decided to try another tack. He'd stop trying to remember and just let it come back to him, the way he did when he forgot a name.

He took the elevator downstairs and stopped at the front desk. The young woman behind the counter wore a cheap cranberry business suit. Her nameplate read MAGGIE.

"Maggie," he said, "I just got two calls. I'm in 311. Do you guys have a caller ID? Can you tell me the numbers that came in from the calls I just got?"

"We do," she said, walking to another part of the desk and punching some buttons on the phone system. She gave him the number, then said, "The one before that was . . . restricted."

"Can you give me the exact time? My clock said nine-twelve for that first call. Is that what the system says?"

"Uh, nine-eleven."

"Any other calls come in at that time?"

"Just the two for you, then nothing for about ten minutes," she said.

"Great, thanks," Jake said. "Can you get me a cab?"

"Right out front," she said.

He took one of the cards with the hotel's number out of the cardholder on the desk and wrote NINE-ELEVEN a.m. on the back of it before he slipped it into his pocket.

He got to the DA's office with enough time to check in with Cambareri and ask him to get the number of the restricted call made to his hotel. While incoming calls could block themselves on a caller ID, the phone company had them and someone like Cambareri could get them with a phone call. Jake told his friend what happened while Cambareri slid the card between his teeth, cleaning out a piece of his breakfast before angling it to the light.

"Sounds like you messed with the wrong girl," Cambareri said. "She married?"

"She said she wasn't," Jake said. "I don't think it was that."

"Ask her."

"I will, when I finish with these interviews."

Jake looked at his watch and went for the door.

"I'll get the number and give you a call," Cambareri said.

The DA wore a dark blue pin-striped suit and a red tie. His shirt collar was high, and before they began the interview he hooked his finger inside it and tried to tug it loose. Muldoon was there, wearing a white shirt with blousy sleeves and an open leather vest, pestering Skip Lehman about the lighting. He made a point of ignoring Jake. Jake ignored him right back. When Jake started the interview, Muldoon positioned himself over Jake's shoulder, which Muldoon knew Jake hated.

Jake didn't take the bait. He focused on the DA, conducted the interview, and even paused patiently when Muldoon cut in. When they were finished, Jake made small talk with the DA until he excused himself for a court appearance. Muldoon was in the corner, reviewing the tape and making notes to himself. Jake gave Skip Lehman a look and the crew manager emptied the room.

"I'm sorry about last night," Jake said, pulling up a chair. He slapped his hands on his knees, then extended a hand to Muldoon, who glanced up at it before going back to his notes.

"I was a little drunk," Jake said. "And I'm going through some personal things. I don't want to spend the next week going at it with you, Conrad. We can make each other's lives miserable or we can bury the hatchet."

Muldoon looked up at him and said, "I'm not the one who's on thin ice. This series turns out shitty, it ain't gonna make or break me. Paycheck's the same."

"You've got more pride than that," Jake said. "You know it."

"Do you?"

"Of course."

"Enough to get out of bed?"

"Something happened," Jake said, leaning forward and lowering his voice. "I could be on to something, Conrad. A story. Something big. I think I might have been drugged last night."

Jake told him about Zamira and the adoption agency, then the strange phone call. Muldoon nodded his head, listening with apparent interest.

When Jake was finished, he said, "You know who the last person was who told me to fuck myself?"

"No."

88

"Tim Simmons."

"Who?"

"Exactly," Muldoon said, leaning forward himself and lowering his voice. "See, assholes like you come and go."

"Did you even listen?"

"Focus," Muldoon said. "That's your problem. We're here to do the bunker man and you're getting shitfaced and chasing pussy."

Muldoon went back to his notebook.

Jake returned to Cambareri's office, but the ADA had gone to a meeting. Jake left a message with the secretary, asking that Cambareri call him if he got any information from the phone company, and then walked outside. The travel agency was only a few blocks away. When he got there, he hurried past the security guard with an offhand wave. On the third floor he went to the door where he'd been the previous day. It had the same chipped tan paint on the frame, the same brushed-silver knob, but the door had no nameplate. When Jake tried the handle, it refused to budge. He knocked, then put his ear to the door before he stepped back to look. He walked up and down the hall, examining the other doors, but certain that he had had the right one in the first place.

Only one, at the other end of the hall, had a nameplate: ROBERT ANTONACCI & AS-SOC., LLP, CPA.

Jake turned the handle and walked in. A secretary looked up from her computer and removed her headset.

"Can I help you?"

"The travel agency down at the other end of the hall?" he said. "Do you know what happened to it?"

She gave him a puzzled look.

"This is the third floor, right?"

"It's the third floor," she said. "There might be a travel agency, but not that I ever saw."

12

"It used to be an adoption agency," Jake said. "There's a woman there. Pretty. Long dark hair with a scar on this side of her face?"

"I'm sorry," she said. "Maybe you have the wrong building. That happens sometimes."

Jake went back down the elevator and approached the security guard, who sat on a stool behind his lectern.

The guard looked up from his newspaper and said, "The TV man."

"Hi," Jake said.

"Hey, you found your personality?"

"I was wondering if you've seen the woman from the travel agency on three?" Jake asked.

The guard shrugged and yawned.

"Look, I get pretty focused," Jake said. "I'm sorry if you thought I was rude yesterday. Can you help me out?"

"What do you need?"

"What can you tell me about the travel agency and the girl that works there?"

"I got no idea what you're talking about."

"The travel agency," Jake said, raising three fingers along with his voice, "on the *third* floor."

The guard made a show of examining the front of his little lectern.

"Do you see something that says information desk?" he asked. "I don't think so."

Jake clamped his mouth shut and blew out through his nose. He took the scrap of paper from his pocket that Zamira had given to him and showed it to the guard.

"Is this the company that owns this building?"

The guard took the paper and gazed at it for a minute, then handed it back.

"Tell you what. You give me a phone number. I'll think about it and get back to you. That's what they say in TV land, right? 'I'll get back to you.' "

He rattled his newspaper and brought it back up in front of his face.

"Asshole," Jake said under his breath.

Outside, he stared up at the building. Painted brick. Tall old windows. Five stories. Not unlike the rest of the buildings up and down the block. He remembered the words of the secretary in the law office and jogged down the sidewalk, into the lobbies of the buildings on either side. One was 200, the other 240. They were similar, but not the same, and neither had the security guard. When he went back into 220, he stared at the guard until he looked up from his paper.

"Do you ever sit in the other buildings?" Jake asked.

The guard just snorted and shook his head.

"That too tough a question for you?" Jake asked.

"Hey, asshole."

"Do you sit in the other buildings or not? Just answer the fucking question or I can call your boss and tell him I'm doing a story on belligerent rent-a-cops who mistake themselves for the real thing."

The guard puckered his mouth and shook his head. "No. This is where I sit."

"And this is the company who owns this building?" Jake asked, producing the paper.

"Yeah," the guard said, then raised his paper so Jake couldn't see his face.

Jake had an hour before he had to be at the jail, so he took a cab to the real estate company.

On the way, he called Muldoon and told him to have the PA drop a car off at his hotel. He'd drive himself out to the jail. He tried Cambareri again, but with no luck. When he arrived at the real estate company, the receptionist thought the best person to answer his question would be Peter Finn, the owner. Jake showed his press credential and asked her to please tell Peter that *American Outrage* would like to quote him for a story. Two minutes later, a secretary appeared and led him into the owner's office.

"I've got to admit that I don't watch your show," Finn said, rising from his desk to shake Jake's hand, "but my wife does and she'd kill me if I sent you packing. Sit down. How can I help?"

Jake took a chair and told him about the travel agency and asked him to check all three buildings.

"There isn't a travel agency on the third floor of any of them," Finn said after several minutes on his computer.

"Who's on the third floor of 220?"

"Two companies," Finn said. "The tax lawyer and some Tarum Jakul International."

"What's that? Is that Albanian?"

"No idea," Finn said.

Finn picked up the phone and asked his secretary to have someone bring him the leasing file on 220 Warren Street for Tarum

Jakul International. While they waited, Finn asked if it would be too much for Jake to get a photo of Nancy Riordin, the show's host, signed for his wife. Jake took one of Finn's cards and said he'd be happy to do it.

The file came in a thick standing binder.

"Whoever they are," Finn said, examining the papers, "they've been there for the past fourteen years and they pay their rent every month."

"It said AA European Travel on the door," Jake said.

"I don't know. This is the only other tenant on three besides the lawyer. This is their third five-year lease they're in now," Finn said, flipping through the pages.

"Who signed the lease?" Jake asked.

"It just says *President of Tarum Jakul International* under the signature and I can't read it," Finn said, holding the paper up to the light, then showing it to Jake.

"I have no idea," Jake said, squinting. "The first name looks like it starts with an *M*, but that's about all I can tell. Do you have any more information on whoever this is, or the company?"

"Uh, Ivan Lindgren did that lease," Finn said. "He's not with us anymore. Went to Arizona, I think."

"Forward address for him?"

Finn shook his head. "It wasn't a happy breakup."

Jake wrote down the company name anyway. He looked at his watch and thanked Finn for the help, assured him that he wouldn't forget to send Nancy's picture for the wife, and stepped out.

Jake got to the bunker-man interview at 1:58, three minutes from being late. He ran his fingers through his hair, straightened his tie, and slid into the chair. The room was crowded with cameras, lights, and cables. The audio man clipped a microphone to his lapel and the bunker man, dressed in a blaze orange jumpsuit, blinked at Jake from behind the glass with flaps of skin drooping from the tendons in his neck, thinning gray hair, and sad saggy eyes. He looked like a harmless old man, not someone who could have abducted, raped, tortured, and in some cases killed more than a dozen women in the past twenty years.

"Couldn't do anything about the glass. Sorry," the lawyer said, stepping up to shake Jake's hand. He wore an olive-green suit and his hair was slicked back. His next sentence was to ask when he'd get the check for the interview.

"I've got it right here," Muldoon said, patting the envelope that poked up out of his front shirt pocket. "Soon as we're done, it's all yours."

The lawyer smiled and flicked his eyes from Muldoon to Jake. The interview turned out to be mostly a rehearsal for the bunker man's defense at trial, his story about how the women in his underground vault were there consensually. The responses were canned, with the lawyer giving embarrassing verbal cues to the old man. The questions Jake asked didn't matter. The old man would look right at him and regurgitate his trumped-up story.

Around and around they went, with Jake pressing, the old man sidestepping him, and Muldoon signaling Jake to keep going. Muldoon finally stopped the tape. The guards led the bunker man away and Muldoon handed the envelope to the lawyer without looking at him.

In a voice the whole room could hear, he said to Jake, "I want to do some stand-ups by the bunker and a walk-through of his house tomorrow at nine. We've got the blonde at eleven. I'll e-mail you an itinerary. They also lined up the husband of one of the dead women when he gets out of work. The guy's got tattoos all over his neck and he's ballistic. It'll help to spice up the counterpoint to the crap we just got."

The lawyer gave Muldoon an offended look and walked out of the room examining the check. Jake told Muldoon to e-mail him the itinerary with the addresses and directions, that he'd keep the PA's car and drive himself.

"Where you headed now?" Muldoon asked.

Jake unclipped the microphone from his lapel, handed it to the audio man, and said, "Working some leads."

"For this story?" Muldoon asked. "Because I could use you for some voice-overs. I've got some studio time up at the university."

"It's for a story," Jake said. "Something I'm working on."

When that didn't seem to be enough, Jake lied and said, "Katz knows all about it."

Muldoon closed his mouth and nodded, then turned away.

Jake headed for Otisco, a small hamlet of homes — some barely more than shacks overgrown with weeds — clustered on the north end of Otisco Lake. The road ran in and out of steep valleys, sometimes cutting through rolling farms with milking parlors that kicked their ferocious stink out onto the highway, anointing passersby with real-life country living. As he drove, Jake rolled up the windows and called in to the office to ask one of the researchers at the news desk to have them find everything they could on Tarum Jakul International.

"What project do I assign this to?" the young woman asked.

"What do you mean 'assign to'?" Jake asked.

"We're not supposed to research anything that's not assigned to a specific approved project."

"Since when?"

"Well, they cut our staff in half to save money. The businesspeople in LA thought we were wasting too much time doing research that wasn't vital to the show."

"Put it to the bunker-man story in Syracuse," Jake said.

"You're sure, right? Because I have to get approval from the producer, too. That's Muldoon, right?"

"Forget it," Jake said. "Thanks anyway."

He called the house and got Sam.

"Want a job?"

"Yeah."

"Tarum Jakul International," Jake said, spelling out the names so Sam would get it right. "Find out as much about it as you can. Also, the name, Tarum or Jakul. See if either one is Albanian."

"Is that my mom's name?" Sam asked, his voice pumping energy through the phone.

"I doubt it. It's a clue. Maybe. It might have nothing to do with your mom. When you do a job like this, man, most of it's pretty boring and most of it is dead ends, so cool your jets."

"You got it," Sam said, but his voice was still charged. "Call you back. Wait."

"Yeah."

"How about LexisNexis? You got an account? That'll help."

"How do you know about LexisNexis?"

"All the big libraries have it."

Jake gave Sam his account number and password and told him to go easy on it because they charged by the minute.

On the last leg of the drive, Jake got behind a slow-moving blue compact. He fought the urge to lean on his horn and was glad he hadn't when the car turned in at Dorothy Cakebread's address. The driveway went down toward the water to a small red camp wedged into a row of similar places, all nestled up snug to the shore. When the compact stopped, an overweight fiftysomething woman with frosted hair got out and glared at Jake as she sidestepped toward the front door, fumbling with her keys.

Jake hopped out and called to her. "Mrs. Cakebread? My name is Jake Carlson. I knew your husband."

Before he could say another word, the woman slipped inside the house and slammed the door. Her pale drawn face appeared in the picture window before the windmill of her arms yanked the curtains closed. When Jake knocked softly on the door, she began to scream.

"Go away! Leave me alone!"

"Mrs. Cakebread," Jake said, shouting through the door. "I knew your husband. He helped me adopt my son, Sam. I'm looking for his records."

"I'm calling my lawyer," she shouted.

"Mrs. Cakebread, please. I need your help."

"Leave me alone!"

Jake heard a noise. Two doors down an older man with a full gray beard stood staring at Jake from his front step.

"You heard her," he said. "Should I call the police?"

"I'm not hurting anything," Jake said.

The old man frowned and shook his head. His small dark eyes bored into Jake and he stood there, with his arms crossed, muttering to himself, until Jake went away.

13

Jake headed back into Syracuse. He hadn't eaten all day so he parked his car and walked up the block for fish and chips and a beer at Kitty Hoynes, the corner pub. He sat at the bar and while he waited for his food, a promo for that night's *American Outrage* came on the wide-screen TV suspended from the ceiling. He watched Nancy's face go from somber to jovial as she teased the lineup for the show. A doctor who had massacred his wife and two daughters, an exclusive interview with the owner of Russell Crowe's latest canine victim, and a flotilla of drunks in Lake Michigan. Around the bar, half the people were focused on one another or their drinks, but the other half stared vacantly at the screen.

Jake told the bartender that he'd changed his mind and moved so he could eat at a small cocktail table by the window. He took his pint and had sat down with his back to the TV when his phone rang.

"Nothing," Sam said, sounding glum. "It's not a corporation for sure, unless it's in Delaware. They aren't on line, but I've got a number I can call tomorrow. I'm gonna call the county clerk there tomorrow, too. You're in Onondaga, right? And see if it's a DBA. The name isn't Albanian as far as I can tell. This doesn't do any good, does it?"

"It takes time, Sam. It takes time. What are you reading?"

"*Return of the King.* Why?"

"It's good, right?"

"Yeah."

"Go read that and don't worry."

"Yeah, right," Sam said, "you're not going to call me if I can't find things."

"I'll call you," Jake said. "There'll be more."

"Sure?"

"Sure, man."

"I'll go look again. The Department of State has a Web site, but I know it's not there."

"Read your book. Then get to bed."

When he finished eating, Jake strolled back toward the hotel. The night was clear and balmy, and a breeze whispered through the new leaves on the trees. The block of refurbished brick buildings held a dozen bars and restaurants. They called it Armory Square after the fortress that loomed on the south edge of the block. Jake peered through the windows at the people talking and laughing together. He cut through an alley that led to his hotel, but instead of going inside, he put his hands in his pockets and kept going toward the office building where the agency had been. He hoped to prove to himself that he hadn't lost his mind completely. Once he got out of the Armory area, the sidewalks were empty except for an occasional bum foraging in the shadows. The business area was a ghost town after six.

Jake walked past 220, craning his neck for a look inside. The security guard's lectern stood empty. He let himself in and pushed the elevator button. Nothing happened. Jake looked around the narrow lobby and found the stairwell door. Its handle wouldn't move. He looked around and listened, then took the driver's license out of his wallet. He slipped the license into the space between the frame and the door, sliding it up and down, fishing it in and out and turning on the knob. After five minutes, he returned the rumpled and twisted license to his wallet. He thought about kicking the door in, but ran his hand over the metal frame and decided against it.

He peered through the glass front door, scanning the street before he walked out onto the sidewalk and headed for the hotel. His steps were quick and with every few, he'd check the empty street behind him.

Inside the hotel, he hunkered into the back corner of the bar and ordered a drink from the kid with the stutter. He was the only patron. After his third drink, he took a deep breath and let his shoulders relax. He pulled out his BlackBerry and opened an e-mail from Muldoon with an attachment, the itinerary for tomorrow. When Jake had finished going through his mail, he opened his cell phone and began to scroll through the stored numbers, looking for someone he could call.

A couple times he actually hit the send button, but ended the call after the first ring. He fished the wedding ring from his pocket and looked through it up at the TV. A pretty brunette read the news. He put the ring up to his lips, holding it with both hands and running the smooth round surface over his skin.

During a commercial for a blood pressure drug, two men walked in wearing three-quarter-length coats, sneakers, and jeans and sat down at a small table in the far corner. Jake put his ring back on and presented them with his back. He examined the men as best he could in the bottle-lined mirror. They didn't talk or signal to the bartender, who finally walked out to them to take an order.

Jake watched the bartender load up two pint glasses with ice, then pick up the soda hose and fill them with Coke. He brought the sodas out to the men and said something Jake couldn't hear. If they answered, Jake didn't hear that either. Jake ordered another drink and finished the one he had while he watched the kid make it. The bar seemed suddenly warm. He reached inside his shirt and scratched his chest. When the drink came, he knocked it right down and paid the bill. When he turned, the men stared in his general direction without eye contact or expression. Neither of them had taken off his jacket.

Jake stood and turned, slowly tucking away his wallet while he assessed them directly. Both wore their hair short with blunt cuts that looked homemade. One was thin with a sharp nose. The other was stouter and taller with darker skin and jet-black hair. He smiled at the men on his way out but they let him pass without even looking up. There was a light on in the office beyond the front desk, but no sign of anyone. Jake glanced over his shoulder. The sharp-nosed man looked out at him. Jake stepped around the corner and backed into the elevator.

When he got to his room, he turned the lock and fastened the chain, then went to the window, thinking he could watch them leave. When he pulled back the curtain, he saw a glass door that led out onto a tiny concrete balcony. A small metal chair barely fit in the space.

The room didn't face the street. Three stories below, a small brick courtyard with a pool had been wedged into the space between the adjacent buildings and their alleys. A dark green pool cover stretched across it, outdoor furniture stacked off to one side. Jake tugged the glass door shut and turned the deadbolt.

The message light on the phone next to the bed was blinking. There were three messages. All of them were just silence for a minute before the call ended with a click. Jake laughed quietly, shaking his head. He took off his suit, brushed his teeth, put on a pair of shorts and a T-shirt, and got into the bed. It was early, but he was tired, mentally as well as physically. He turned off the light and blinked at the white beam shooting in through the curtains. When he got up to draw them tight, he heard a tiny beep and a click and turned toward the door. He stared at the handle and the sound he had just heard registered as a card key opening the lock.

The handle slowly turned. Jake's eyes shot up to the chain, stretched taut between the frame and the door.

When the door began to open, Jake yelled, "Hey! I'm in here!"

The door stopped and Jake realized no light was coming in from the hall. He picked up the phone and dialed zero. It rang and rang.

He stretched the cord so he could see the door.

Something glinted in the opening. A coat hanger with a small hook at the end. Still no answer.

"Hey!" Jake shouted.

The hanger wavered and rattled against the door before it hooked one of the links in the security chain. Then it went wild, snapping this way and that, rattling the chain.

Jake let the phone drop. He turned, threw the bolt, and yanked open the balcony door. The front door rattled and banged, and Jake stepped up onto the chair and balanced himself on the railing. The door inside burst open. Two dark shapes tumbled in. An orange tongue of flame flashed and something zipped past Jake's ear.

He jumped.

14

Jake hit the middle of the pool cover and it gave way with a muted splash. He scrambled across the undulating surface with his arms extended for balance, hit the brick wall, and scaled its rough face before he could even think. He kept low and tight to the wall, running along its length until he reached the side of the hotel where he knew he couldn't be seen from the balcony. He stopped there, breathing hard, and his knee began to throb. He realized that his feet were bare and that he must have scraped the skin off the tops of them on his way over the wall.

It had all happened so fast, he had to reconstruct it in his mind to be certain that the two men really had tried to kill him, that the flash and the angry zip past his ear really had been a bullet. It took only a second to compute. He hobbled as fast as he could between the hotel and a parking garage until he came to the sidewalk. He looked both ways, then sprinted with a sidewinding motion across the street, where he ducked down between the parked cars.

Even in the shadows of the cars, he felt naked just staring at the hotel entrance, so he positioned himself in such a way that he could look in one side of a car and out the other. Crouched down with only his eyes above the level of the car door, he felt safe enough to watch the hotel. In less than a minute, the two men walked out. They stood on the sidewalk for a minute, scanning the street, then rounded the corner, going back up the alley Jake had just come out of.

Jake crept through the parking lot, bracing himself on car bumpers and half dragging his leg. He got to a spot where he could see down the alley, just as the dark shapes of the men disappeared out the far end. Jake stood and staggered back into the hotel lobby. Again, there was no one at the desk. He slammed his hand on the silver bell over and over, leaning over the desk and grabbing the phone.

A young woman came out from the back, yawning and tugging at a tangle in her hair.

"What are you doing?" she asked.

"Calling the police," Jake said.

He glanced out at the street.

"Are you a guest?" the woman asked.

"Two men just walked into this hotel while you were" — Jake looked her over, then glanced out at the street again — "sleeping, and tried to *kill* me."

"Huh?"

"I'm calling 911."

The dispatcher talked calmly to Jake and listened to his story. The girl behind the desk watched, wide-eyed and openmouthed.

Soon the street outside began to flash red and white, and a black-and-white car bumped up over the curb and screeched to a stop. One uniformed cop jumped out, scanning the area with a hand on his gun. The other talked into the radio for a minute before putting on his hat and following. Together they walked into the small lobby, hands on guns, their heads swiveling from side to side.

"This way," Jake said, tugging one of the cops by the arm toward the door, "they went down the alley."

The cop shrugged him off and said, "Just calm down."

"They're getting away."

"Who? What happened?" the cop asked, his eyes dropping to Jake's bloody feet.

"He just grabbed the phone," the girl

113

behind the desk said, crossing her arms with a frown.

In tattered sentences, Jake introduced himself and then described the men he had seen in the bar, the door being opened, and his jumping from the balcony when they broke in and shot at him.

"And you're sure it was the same two men?" one cop asked.

"I'm sure," Jake said.

"You saw them?"

"I saw them in the bar. I saw two guys bust in my room, and I saw the same two guys come out after I jumped out the fucking window and ran around the building."

"Easy."

The other cop turned to the girl behind the desk and asked, "Did you hear the shot?"

She shook her head.

Jake snorted and said, "She was sleeping."

"Did anyone? Anyone call?" the other cop asked.

"No," she said, poking out her lower lip.

"Let's take a look at the room," the cop said.

"These guys are still out there," Jake said, raising his voice and pointing at the entrance. "They're looking for me. You could still get them."

The other cop raised his nose and leaned toward Jake.

"Have you been drinking, sir?" he asked.

"Are you kidding me?" Jake said. "That's got nothing to do with it. They're trying to kill me. I'm with *American Outrage,* the TV show."

He looked from one cop's face to the other, but neither reacted.

"I'm investigating a story about an international adoption agency that turned into a travel agency," Jake said, losing his breath. "I've already been threatened on the phone. You can ask the DA's office. They've been helping me. Call Steve Cambareri."

The cops looked at each other, then one said, "Look, whoever they were, they're gone now. Let's take a look at your room and go from there."

"Fine," Jake said.

He turned to the girl and asked for a key to 311. She looked at the cops and told them she needed Jake's ID.

"I was in bed," Jake said. "I jumped off the balcony."

One of the cops stared at Jake for a moment, then said to the girl, "You can give us a key and we'll check his ID when we get to the room."

When the elevator doors opened on the

third floor, Jake was surprised to see that the lights in the hall were on. He hobbled off the elevator.

"Are you all right, Mr. Carlson?"

"Twisted my knee a little," Jake said, "but I'm fine."

He led them to his room and one of the cops knelt down, examining the edge of the door.

"They had a key," Jake said.

The cop glanced at him, then put the key into the door.

"Maybe you should be careful touching the handle," Jake said. "In case there's fingerprints."

The cop pursed his lips and pushed down on the very end of the handle to open the door. They walked into the room. One cop flipped on the lights while the other examined the door and the chain.

"I had that chain on," Jake said, "and they worked it with a coat hanger."

The cop turned the chain over in his fingers, shrugged, and let it drop.

"You say they took a shot at you from here?" he asked, bending down and running his hands over the carpet.

"Yeah," Jake said.

The cop looked up at him. "No shell casings."

"But how hard is that to pick up?"

They asked Jake to get his ID. He found his wallet and took out his driver's license.

"What happened to it?" the cop asked. "I can't tell if this is you."

"I was trying to open a door," Jake said, looking at the twisted corner of the card and his mangled picture. "I locked myself out of my house a few days ago. Here."

Jake handed over his press ID. The cop put the two of them together and looked them over. Jake turned to the other cop. The curtains billowed in a small breeze while he examined the curtain and the glass. The other cop pushed past him and walked out onto the balcony, where he leaned out over the railing.

"Pretty good jump," he said, looking back at Jake.

"That's what happened to my knee," Jake said, squeezing his lower thigh.

"So where were you when they shot at you?" the other cop asked.

"When I saw the coat hanger, I opened the door and went out. I thought I could make the jump. It was instincts. I wasn't sure I was going to do it, really, but I saw the gun flash and heard the bullet go right by my ear and I just did it. I barely remember how I landed and got over the wall."

"Why do you think they shot at you?" the cop asked.

"To kill me. They threatened me on the phone yesterday morning."

"No, how do you know they shot at you?"

"I saw it," Jake said, his voice rising. "I heard it."

"The gunshot?"

"The bullet."

"But no gunshot?"

"I don't know. Yes. No. Maybe they — they must have had a silencer."

"And they took just one shot?"

"I jumped and ran."

The cop looked out over the railing again, then back into the room.

"It was dark," he said. "You couldn't really see who it was."

"I saw two men," Jake said. "Jesus."

"Mr. Carlson," the other cop said, taking out his card. "I'm going to suggest that you get some rest and come down to the station tomorrow afternoon and fill out a report."

"What are you, kidding me? You know who Steve Cambareri is?"

"Sure."

"I'm working on something with him here. He's a friend. He knows the deal. Call him if you think I'm crazy."

"We'll let him know what you're up to,"

118

the other cop said, "but you get some sleep first. You've been drinking and this whole thing may look a lot different to you in the morning."

"I just jumped out a three-story fucking window."

"We know you did, Mr. Carlson. Get some rest."

The cops pushed past him and let themselves out the door, one of them muttering something about a code six. Jake stood there for a few minutes, then he locked the door, set the chain, and pushed the bureau lengthwise in front of it. He washed the blood and dirt from his feet and patted the tops of them dry with a towel, wincing.

From the shadows of the curtain, he looked down into the courtyard. Nothing moved, and he had to stare hard at the rumpled pool cover to make out the impression from where he'd landed. He closed the door to the balcony and drew the curtain closed.

When the lights were off, he lay down and stared up at the ceiling.

15

The alarm woke Jake up in another hotel. He had to remind himself about limping out of the place he was in and finding a new hotel near the university, where he paid in cash for a room. He showered and yanked a custom-tailored Zegna suit out of his bag, then put on a shirt with no tie and called down for his car. He gave the valet a ten, remembering what a crappy job that was from his days as a teenager working weddings. Instead of pulling away, he sat with his hands gripping the wheel, scanning the lobby to see if anyone followed him out.

No one came, but when he pulled out onto the road, a black Ford F-350 with a shiny chrome grille pulled immediately away from the curb and rumbled up behind him at the next light. Jake signaled right, and so did the truck, but when the light changed, Jake took a left, stomping on the gas. He kept his eyes in the mirror. The truck turned the other way.

Jake turned his attention back to the road just in time to see that he was running a red light. Car horns blared. Tires shrieked. Jake swerved and made it through, then gave it more gas.

He climbed the ramp to the highway and eased up on the speed as he wove his way into the thick pattern of traffic. His phone rang and he answered it gruffly. It was Sam.

"I got it," Sam said.

"What?"

"Well, the county clerk was open at seven-thirty, but they didn't have a DBA by that name. The Delaware office opened at eight and that's where it is, arum Jakul International."

"That's great," Jake said, trying to pump some enthusiasm into his voice the way his high school wrestling coach had done before they faced a team everyone knew would slaughter them.

"Only problem is they wouldn't tell me anything more about it," Sam said. "I ordered the certificate of incorporation, that's what they called it. It won't give us much, just the date it started and shares or something, but they said it'd have the address in Delaware on it. I ordered a fax and they said I might get it by this afternoon.

So, we can go from there, right?"

"We'll see," Jake said. "Hey, everything's okay around the house, right?"

"Like what?"

"Nothing. Louie's good? You guys remember to put the alarm on when I'm gone, right?"

"The alarm? Yeah. Juliet does. I always hear it beeping."

"Good."

"Dad?"

"Yeah?"

"You okay?"

"Of course."

"You're sure?"

"Why?"

"You just sound weird."

"I'm fine. Good job on the Delaware stuff. Keep me posted."

Jake hung up and followed the directions from the e-mail on his BlackBerry. The bunker man had lived east of the city. Jake stopped only once to fuel the car and buy a thirty-two-ounce cup of coffee. No one followed him in.

The crew's van and two rental cars were jammed into the rutted driveway of the dingy little saltbox house. Flecks of faded red paint had peeled to reveal the rot of gray wood. Small square windows with dirty glass suggested something closer to a fort than a home. Scrubby lines of stunted trees and brush separated the next-closest houses, a shit-brown ranch with dark green shutters and cardboard in one window on one side and a sagging pale blue trailer home on cinderblocks on the other. Out on the road, a sheriff's car rested on the shoulder. Jake pulled up behind it.

The crew had the cameras and lights set up to the side of the house where the new grass showed the bulge of the bunker below. Jake automatically checked his face in the mirror. He'd forgotten makeup. Even with ten minutes to spare on his watch, he had to hurry. He removed the small emergency makeup kit from his briefcase and quickly covered over the circles under his red eyes and the perpetual raspberry on his left jaw line.

As he walked up to the set, the PA whose car Jake now drove handed him a script. Jake took out a pen and went through it, making small changes, then handed it back. Muldoon slouched in a canvas chair, busy examining the shot in a monitor. He wore a faded blue denim smock with a red bandanna tied around his fat neck and he didn't bother to look up. Jake said hello to the crew and got on his starting mark to run through the script. Halfway through it, out of the corner of his eye, Jake saw Muldoon get up from his chair and move toward the camera.

When Jake finished his rehearsal, Muldoon said, "How'd it go last night?"

"How'd what go?" Jake said, glaring.

"Your project," Muldoon said. The beginnings of a smile were on his lips.

"Fine."

"Well, you look like shit. What happened?"

"How did you know something happened?" Jake asked.

"What did?" Muldoon said. "I didn't know, you just don't look good. Your eyes are all red. You look sick."

"Shitty night," Jake said. "You want to shoot this, or not?"

"Are you limping?" Muldoon asked. "I was going to have you do a walk."

"I can walk."

"I think it'll help hide the red in your eyes if you're moving. You got a crease right through the center of that jacket."

Jake looked down and tugged at the expensive suit coat to no avail and said, "So shoot it tight."

As they worked, Jake kept an eye on Muldoon. They got the shots he wanted of the grassy bulge created by the underground bunker, then went into the house, where

Jake did a stream-of-consciousness as they moved through, a handheld camera following him and zooming in over his shoulder on things like an empty birdcage bearded in mold and a refrigerator with a hole punched in its face. The floor was filthy. Empty cans, old newspapers, and dirty dishes covered the shelves and tabletops. The furniture was torn, sagging, and broken. At regular intervals, peeling paper hung limp from the walls. Triple lines of police tape kept them from going inside the bunker or even down the basement stairs, but the feeling of depravity and filth was powerful enough even upstairs to make Jake sick to his stomach.

Just as they finished, Muldoon's cell phone rang. He spoke heatedly into it, then snapped it shut and cursed.

"Well," he said, eyeing Jake. "Time for you to work your magic."

"Meaning what?" Jake said.

"That was that Catherine Anastacia's mom," Muldoon said. "She's canceling on us."

"Until when?"

"Until never."

"She's the reason we're here," Jake said.

Muldoon looked at his BlackBerry as if he weren't all that concerned and said, "Well, good thing we got a backup story for sweeps."

"What's that?"

Muldoon looked up and with a straight face said, "Jessica Simpson's bodyguard is writing a book."

"What kind of shit is that?"

"He said she caused emotional distress from her singing."

"You're kidding."

"Like I said, time for your magic. If you got any left."

16

"Jesus," Muldoon said, looking at his watch. "Two hours and you're still at it?"

"It's like surgery," Jake said in a low voice, glancing over his shoulder. Catherine Anastacia sat drinking coffee with her mother at their kitchen table. "You rush it, you lose your patient."

"All that crap about you playing the trombone," Muldoon said in a whisper. "The fucking *Music Man*?"

"When she started talking about the time she was Desdemona," Jake said, "that was the only common denominator I could come up with. Did it work? All of a sudden it's her and me, two high school wannabes versus the world."

"Well, can you close the deal?" Muldoon asked. "Jesus, when you got her going about the little sister with the boyfriend who smacked her I thought you had it locked up."

Jake's eyelids drooped and he sighed. "I'm close."

The two of them went back into the kitchen and sat down with the women. Jake made small talk for another five minutes before he gave Muldoon a look.

"Listen," Jake said, reaching across the table and covering Catherine's hand with his own. "You don't have to do this with me, but I want you to understand that it's not about the television show. I mean, this is my job, but I'm friends with a guy in the DA's office and what we're doing here is really trying to work with them to make sure this kind of thing won't happen to someone else."

"They told me not to talk to anyone," Catherine said.

"Steve Cambareri and I go way back," Jake said, taking out his cell phone. "He's the assistant DA. Do you want to talk to him? I can call him at home if you don't believe me."

Jake gave her that smile.

"No, I believe you," she said.

She looked down and drew a deep shuddering breath, then she sucked her lips into her mouth, looked up at him, and nodded.

"I'll do it."

Muldoon backed slowly out of the room

to call in the crew. When the shot was set up, he pulled Jake aside and in a low voice said, "You are back in the saddle, my man."

They put Catherine deep in the shadows of the kitchen. She felt more comfortable in the shadows and her mother told her strangers wouldn't be able to recognize her.

When it was done and they had cleaned up and were walking out the door, Muldoon grabbed Jake and hugged him, clapping him on the back. Jake's smile erupted.

"She still looked gorgeous," Muldoon said with an excited hiss. "You could tell. The shadows made it even sexier. Wait till you see this nutcase we're going to interview now. Wait till you see when I smash-cut the two of them together for this piece. Can I ride over there with you?"

Jake let Muldoon ride with him, and by the time they had finished with the husband of the other victim, Jake had to admit that they had something special.

"We should celebrate," Muldoon said. "Bury the hatchet like you said."

"Nothing against you at all, Conrad," Jake said. "I'm glad we're past all that, but I've got this other thing."

"Sure. So, tomorrow's a light day. All we have is the cop who found them in there. I'll e-mail the schedule."

Jake gave him a nod and got into the Taurus. He checked his messages. Still nothing from Cambareri.

Jake was used to getting the shake from story subjects who didn't want the publicity, but not from people he knew. He was the guy even old acquaintances were happy to see, the good-looking TV star they'd brag to their friends about.

He called the ADA's office. The secretary said Cambareri was in and asked him to hold on.

"I'm sorry, Mr. Carlson," she said after a few moments on hold, "the district attorney just called him in on something urgent. I think something to do with you."

17

Jake left his cell number again, making his voice as pleasant-sounding as he could, and thanked her, then drove twenty minutes to the police station. He planned to follow up on his complaint from last night despite the skepticism of the cops who had showed up at the hotel. Before he went in, he decided to try Cambareri again.

The secretary asked, "Is this you, Mr. Carlson?"

"I know," he said. "I went through a kind of dead zone and I thought maybe Steve tried to call me back."

"Well," she said, "he's on another call right now."

"Look," Jake said, "I know he's busy and I know I'm asking him to do me a favor here, but could you just ask him if he's got the number I was asking him about? I got a call from a restricted phone last night and he was going to check with a contact he has at the phone company to get me the number. Someone made a threatening call to me and Steve was going to help me out."

"I'm sorry, Mr. Carlson, but —"

"He doesn't even have to get on the phone," Jake said. "Would you just ask him, please? It'll save us both a lot of headaches. I hate to keep calling you, but this is kind of urgent."

She put him on hold and he stayed there for a good three minutes before she returned.

"Mr. Cambareri says he already left a message on your home phone earlier today, Mr. Carlson," she said. "And he asked that you stop calling this office."

"You're kidding."

"No. I'm not."

Jake hung up.

He dialed his home number and got the answering machine. The second message was from Cambareri.

"Jake, Steve. Two things. First, the number where your call came from is an Albanian social club on the west side, so whatever you're doing, stop. Word is these guys are part of the group cutting off people's heads up and down the East Coast — Boston, New York, Philly. That brings me to number two. I don't care who's trying to kill you,

you don't throw my name out to a street cop you don't know, because you have no idea who his uncle might be. Especially when you're drunk. Thanks for nothing. Friend."

The click was profound.

The district attorney's offices were in the public safety building on the same block as the police station. He got out of the car, pulled on his rumpled jacket, and circled the station. There was a parking lot on one side of the public safety building and a garage beyond that. Jake checked his watch and positioned himself so he could see across the entire lot.

A few minutes before five, people started coming out. Most of them left through a side door. A few came around from the front entrance. At ten after, the flow of people dropped off to a trickle. At five-thirty, Jake was beginning to think he must have missed Cambareri when he saw his old friend come out the side exit sharing a laugh with another man in a suit. Jake went right for them.

With ten feet to go, Cambareri spotted Jake and his smile faded. He said something to the other man, who stared at Jake for a second, then shrugged at Cambareri before moving on. Cambareri started walking, too, right past Jake, addressing him on the move.

"What do you want?" he asked, eyes forward.

"Steve, what's going on?"

"Nothing."

"What do you mean? Everything's fine and all of a sudden you ask me not to call you? I got shot at last night."

"I'm no sucker, Jake," Cambareri said, taking a set of keys out of his pocket. "Fool me once, shame on you. Fool me twice, shame on me. You aren't fooling me twice so cut the bullshit."

"What are you talking about?" Jake said, putting a hand on Cambareri's shoulder.

The ADA spun and knocked his hand off, drawing back a fist.

"Are you that fucked in the head?" Cambareri asked. "Are you such a scum-sucker that you don't even know the difference anymore?"

"I have no idea what you're talking about. I asked you to get me a phone number. Some guy threatened me. Jesus, last night they tried to kill me."

"And I just got my ass handed to me by my boss. You told me this was about your *son,* not your TV show," Cambareri said.

"It *is* about my son."

Cambareri shook his head and turned

away, unlocking the door to his car. "Save your bullshit for people like Catherine Anastacia."

Jake opened his mouth, but nothing came out.

"Yeah," Cambareri said with a bitter smile, "I heard about what you did out there. The mom called the second the interview was over to say they did it for us, so the next girl wouldn't have to go through that. They wanted us to know that. That's nice, Jake. You must feel real good about yourself."

"That's got nothing to do with this, Steve. That's my job. She agreed to do the interview. That's why we're here in the first place. It's complicated, trust me."

"What's complicated about lying?"

"I told her convicting this guy would save other people from going through the same thing. That's true."

"Yeah, like we need you guys to convict him? We don't want *her* talking."

"I didn't lie."

"You're working with the DA's office? We ought to bust you and your douchebag friend for impersonating an officer."

"I didn't say that. I didn't say I was working for you."

"No, you just hinted that you were, throwing my name around like I'm part of this shit. Forget about last night. That cop you insulted is the chief's nephew. Now I'm the guy in the office who's connected to the TV people who are fucking with one of our top witnesses for the biggest trial in five years. Do you know how pissed my boss is? I'll be back to traffic violations by the time this is over."

"Steve —"

"Then you try to use me to get in on this whole Albanian thing," Cambareri said, getting into his car. "I'm not your friend, Jake, and you're not mine."

The ADA slammed the car door and started the engine.

"What about the Albanian thing?" Jake asked, pounding his fist against the window. "What did you find out?"

The car jolted backward, out of its space. The tires chirped as Cambareri rounded the corner for the exit.

18

Jake's stomach was empty. He found a McDonald's and went in. He remembered the first time he'd been in one as a kid, one with the real golden arches, anchored in the parking lot front to back and sheltering the entire building. The golden arches were a big thing back then, something his parents might take them to three or four times a year and the only restaurant he ever ate at until college.

He ordered fries and the biggest coffee they had and sat at a plastic booth in the corner looking out over all the empty chairs and the women behind the counter whom he caught pointing his way and giggling so hard they had to hold on to their blue paper hats to keep them from falling off their heads. Jake shook his head, took out his BlackBerry, and read Muldoon's report to New York, telling them about how well the interviews had gone and hinting at a ratings spike for sweeps. There were a spate of congratulatory e-mails coming back at them, and one from Katz specifically asking Jake to call and check in.

Jake dumped the last pieces of French fries from the box into his mouth, then dialed Katz.

"You okay?" the executive producer asked.

"Good as I can be," Jake said, sipping coffee.

"Because Muldoon told me there's some other story you're working on that I'm supposed to know about."

Jake's gut turned. He took a deep breath, thinking about how it would all sound. Crazy.

"I just need the guy to lay off a little," Jake finally said.

Katz was silent for a few seconds before he said, "Lay off how?"

"I'm trying to help Sam find his biological mother," Jake said. "We got him from an agency when I was working here in Syracuse. I'm just asking some questions."

"Jake, this is sweeps. This story is your chance to get things right. I understand about Sam and Karen. I can't imagine everything that involves, but do your job, okay?"

Jake ran a hand over his face and shook

his head.

"There might be a story here," Jake said. "I think there's some tie-in with the adoption agency where we got Sam and these Albanian criminals, like an international human trafficking thing."

"This isn't *Nightly News,* Jake," Katz said. "Get me the bunker man."

"Okay," Jake said. "I'm on it. I gotta go, though, I'm getting a call from home."

When he clicked over, Jake heard Juliet, crying.

"Mr. Carlson, I'm so sorry. I don't know what happened. I'm so sorry."

"What, Juliet? What are you talking about?"

"I can't find Sam."

"Where's Louie? Is he walking Louie?"

"Louie is here, Mr. Carlson," she said, sobbing. "I looked everywhere. Sam's gone."

19

"Wait," Jake said. "Did you try his cell phone?"

"It goes right to his voice mail. He's gone."

Jake nearly fell on his face getting up out of the booth, then his knee buckled and he grabbed the table, knocking over his coffee. He pulled a five from his wallet and dropped it onto the table before stumbling out the door. With one hand still holding the phone, he pulled away from the curb. A kid in a Range Rover screeched his brakes and leaned on his horn. Jake kept going, instructing Juliet to call 911 and conference him in. With Juliet's sobbing and Jake's panicked insistence, the interchange with the operator was explosive.

He raced up the nearest ramp to the highway and wove through the traffic with a heavy foot. He was nearly to the airport by the time they were finally connected to the Nassau police. Jake took a deep breath, doing his best to stay calm.

They tried to brush him off as if he were overreacting, but when Jake got a lieutenant on the line and promised that he'd be making the news if someone didn't meet him when he landed, the cop sullenly agreed. Jake got a one-way ticket and raced up the escalator. The security line wasn't long, but Jake cut to the front, showing his ticket to the agent and telling everyone that he was sorry, but it was an emergency. When the checker asked for his ID, Jake took out his wallet and found only money and credit cards. His license was missing, so was his press ID.

Jake tried to explain about his missing son. He even threw the show's name out there and asked for a supervisor. One of the TSA agents recognized him. He began to beg. The supervisor pressed his lips tight and shook his head.

Jake remembered showing his ID to the cops after his jump. He checked the departure board. He could make the last flight of the day to LaGuardia, but he'd have to hurry. He struggled through the airport on his throbbing knee, got his car, and headed to his first hotel. He dug into the pocket of his suit coat and came up with two key cards, one from each of his hotels. He'd never checked out of the first. That, at least, would save him some time. The whole trip, he kept trying Sam's cell phone, but it went right to voice mail as Juliet had said, meaning it was turned off.

When he reached the downtown hotel, Jake asked the valet to wait. He gimped across the sidewalk and into the lobby. The man behind the desk had pomade in his hair and a small beard. Jake put on a smile, said hello, and walked on past, doing his best to stand straight. While he waited for the elevator, he peeked around the corner and into the bar, not expecting to see the two men from the night before, but unable to stop from checking.

The elevator chimed and he stepped on. At the door to his room he fumbled with the lock, putting the key in the wrong way before opening the door and flipping on the lights. He scanned the area. On top of the dresser, resting on the *TV Guide,* were both his press ID and his battered license, right where the cop must have set them down. Jake snatched them up and froze. The blood running through his chest went cold and he took a step back. It was only a small noise, but he was sure he'd heard it, coming from the dark recess of the bathroom, its door open just a crack.

Someone was there.

20

Jake looked at the door to the balcony, which was closed up tight. If he rattled the lock he might have a bullet in his back before he could get out there and jump again. Just the thought of doing that on his bad knee made him wince. Instead, he grabbed the lamp off the desk, wrenched it so that it snapped free from its cord, and flipped it over in his hand so he could smash the intruder's face with its heavy base. He crept toward the dark bathroom, his breathing ragged. He reached for the knob with a trembling hand. The dark crack in the doorway was four inches wide. If he could pull it shut, he could make it to the stairwell out in the hall before whoever it was could get a shot at him.

He raised the lamp high over his head, stepping slowly. Something moved in the darkness. The door was flung open. Jake's heart leapt, and he swung the lamp. Too close. Its base smashed into the frame of the door with a crack, and the figure darted back into the darkness.

"Dad."

Jake staggered, shaking, then he reached inside the door and flicked on the light. Sam smiled up at him, a mouthful of metal braces.

"I almost killed you."

"That would have been bad."

Jake hugged his son to him, gripping him around the dark blue hooded sweatshirt.

"What happened?"

He held Sam's shoulders at arm's length.

"I took the train," Sam said. "I heard someone coming and I wanted to make sure it was you."

"Sam."

"I heard the message from that guy about someone threatening you. I couldn't just sit there. I mean, what kind of kid would do that?"

"Where's your phone?" Jake asked.

"My battery died," Sam said. He stared at Jake for a second before he said, "Oh, I got the fax for you."

He took a folded piece of paper out of the pocket in front of his sweatshirt and handed it to Jake. Jake unclenched his teeth and took a deep breath, letting it out with a hiss.

Sam had circled the address of Tarum Jakul International in New Castle, Delaware.

"Didn't you think to call me?" Jake asked, looking up. "Juliet is hysterical."

"You would've said no."

Jake took out his cell phone and dialed the house.

"How the hell did you get in here?" he asked, waiting for Juliet to answer.

Sam shrugged and pulled a passport from the sweatshirt pocket. Last spring the three of them had taken a family trip to Ireland, Karen's last.

"I showed this to the guy at the desk and said that you told me to meet you here," Sam said.

Juliet answered and Jake told her he had Sam, that everything was okay, and that she should fill Louie's food dish and put him in the kennel, then take tomorrow off and get some rest.

"So, I can stay, right?" Sam said, his dark eyes sparkling. "We should go to Delaware and check out that company."

"You should let me do what I do," Jake said.

"Come on."

Jake shook his head. "You come on."

Sam smiled at him.

"Shit."

146

Sam smiled some more.

"Okay. We'll go down and get my car. You can come to Delaware. I don't know what I'm going to do with you after that, but you can't stay with me. Not if I'm going to do this thing."

Sam had Jake's desk laptop computer with him and a backpack stuffed with clothes. Jake took the computer bag from him and scanned the street from inside the lobby for his Albanian friends before limping out to the car. It was nine o'clock by the time they were back on the road. Even with Sam chattering away at him, Jake had a hard time keeping his eyes open. Just before midnight, they pulled over on the Pennsylvania Turnpike and checked in at a Marriott. Jake didn't even take off his clothes. The room smelled stale and anonymous and as he fell asleep, he could hear the highway traffic zipping by outside.

Somewhere in the middle of the night, Jake woke up to the static of the TV. Sam was propped up on some pillows, asleep, with his face bathed in the black-and-white light. In one hand was the fax from Delaware. In the other was a wallet-size photo of Karen. He held both equally tightly.

21

Gray light leaked in through the curtain. The clock read 7:23 a.m. Jake slipped out of his pants and examined his puffy knee, which looked like a piece of bruised fruit. Sam was under the covers in the other bed. Jake got up quietly and took a shower. When he came out, Sam was up and had a map spread out on the desk.

"We're real close," he said with his metallic grin.

Jake made Sam shower, too, but didn't bother to argue when Sam said his unruly thatch of hair didn't need a comb. He put on his jeans from the previous day, and when Jake suggested a fresh shirt he pulled a big black T-shirt out of his backpack. In small white lettering it read, MY IMAGINARY FRIEND THINKS YOU HAVE SERIOUS MENTAL PROBLEMS. They ate breakfast at the hotel restaurant, and Sam impressed their waitress by polishing off a full stack of pancakes as well as the All-American Breakfast with scrambled eggs and bacon.

"Set?" Jake asked as Sam licked the last crumbs of a blueberry muffin from his fingertips.

Sam wiped his fingers on his shirt.

"You done?" asked Jake.

"What else they got?"

"Not much."

"Then I'm done."

The low clouds spit down thin, intermittent drops of rain, thickening the traffic around Philly so that by the time they reached Old Airport Road, it was after eleven. Warehouse buildings and crooked telephone poles lined the road. Behind them, a rusty chain-link fence bordered a weed-infested runway. Jake pulled into the nearly empty parking lot of the two-story office building.

"What do we do now?" Sam asked. "Just go up and knock on the door?"

Jake stared at the building for a minute, letting the delayed wipers sweep the windshield clean, then nodded and said yes.

"You stay here."

He got out and started across the lot with the fresh smell of rain in the air. The metal door to the building was orange with rusty scars and it looked as if someone had long ago forced it open with a crowbar. Up close, he could see that it listed at a tired angle. He slipped his fingers into the crack and eased it open. The thin gray rug inside was stained and the hallway smelled of old urine and cigars. Jake turned to make sure Sam was still sitting in the car. He gave him a thumbs-up, forced a smile, and went in.

The suite number for Tarum Jakul was 112. From behind the closed door to 108, Jake heard the one-sided sound of someone arguing on the phone. Suite 112 had no marking on it besides the number, written with Magic Marker. Two-thirds of the way down, though, was a mail slot. Jake poked a finger through, then let it clink shut. He ran his hand along the wood door frame and gripped the knob, looking around before giving it a twist. Locked. He removed his battered license and fished it into the seam.

Coming from the entrance, the squeak of a metal door made his heart jump.

22

"Sam," Jake said, exhaling. "The words 'stay here' aren't working."

Sam shrugged and in a quiet voice said, "I got bored."

Jake pursed his lips and nodded his head. "That was kind of the idea."

"You can open it with that?" Sam asked, pointing at the driver's license.

"Guess not," Jake said, replacing it in his wallet. He knelt down and examined the knob, then ran his hand along the door frame. He slapped his palm against the door itself on the top, bottom, and middle. "I've got an idea, a true investigative reporter's trick."

Sam closed one eye and looked up at his dad. "I think I know."

Jake smiled at him.

"Seriously, a Ranger trick I learned in Afghanistan," he said, then turned halfway around and, with his good leg, mule-kicked the door. Splinters of wood flew into the air with a dusty cloud that made Jake cough.

Sam shook his head and said, "How did I see this coming?"

Jake put his finger to his lips so he could hear if the talking down the hall had stopped. It hadn't, and he stepped into the office. It was a small dark space with wood paneling and a single desk and chair. There was a lamp but it had no bulb and its shade was layered in dust. On the window hung a slatternly set of blinds. But behind the door was what Jake was interested in, a small pile of mail.

He scooped it up and set it on the desk, then went through the drawers, but found nothing other than a moldy phone book and some paper clips. With the mail in hand, he took Sam by the arm and hurried him down the hall and out into the fresh air.

"Can we do that?" Sam asked, getting into the car.

"We just did," Jake said, firing up the engine and scanning the mail.

When a clunky old Caprice Classic rumbled into the parking lot, Jake dropped the letters and put the Taurus in gear, leaving quickly and checking his rearview mirror. He waited until they were well away before pulling in behind a Burger King and coming to a stop.

"Mrs. Fagal said it's a federal offense to take someone's mail, you know," Sam said.

"Who's Mrs. Fagal?"

"My social studies teacher."

"I thought you didn't pay attention in school."

"It's hard not to hear Mrs. Fagal," Sam said. "She's deaf and yells everything."

Jake nodded and tore into the mail. There were some advertisements, but mostly bills. Nothing more than a month old, which suggested someone checked the mail regularly. Everything was addressed to Tarum Jakul International, except for the last letter. Jake held it up and examined the return address. Breen & Meese. It looked like a law firm, and the address was 134th Street in the Bronx. The person it was addressed to was Murat Lukaj.

"Tarum Jakul backward," Jake said to himself.

Sam reached over and tilted the envelope toward him. Jake opened it. There was a cover letter from Lukaj's lawyer explaining the notice from the court that was also enclosed for noncompliance with sentencing. Lukaj had failed to satisfy his sentence of two hundred hours of community service and completion of an extensive anger management treatment program. Jake's stomach turned sour, and he folded the letter and stuffed it back in the envelope.

"Why can't I see?" Sam asked.

"It's nothing important," Jake said, "but it gives us a name."

Sam reached into the backseat and put the computer case on his lap. Patting it, he said, "Great. We find a wireless network and I can do a search."

"That's okay. I'll get that later," Jake said, putting the car into gear and pulling back out onto the road.

"My shrink says I have to tell you if I think you're being overprotective."

Jake looked at him for a moment. "He's a counselor, not a shrink."

"Same difference."

"I'm your father, right?" Jake said.

"Yeah," Sam said. "And I'm your partner in this."

Jake cleared his throat and drove for a few minutes. "I'm starting to get that distinct feeling."

Jake nodded at the computer and said, "I've got a Verizon wireless account on that. Just open the network connections and you'll see it. You can access everything through that."

Sam flipped open the computer and got

to work with a flurry of fingers. Jake called Muldoon and was pleasantly surprised when the producer told him that the cop had had to delay the taping until tomorrow, Saturday. Jake didn't even bother to tell him what had happened, only that he planned to head back home for an overnight with Sam and be back Saturday afternoon for the shoot.

They were on 95 heading north when Sam let out a low whistle.

"This guy Lukaj?" he said. "This dude is a badass mother —"

Jake held his hand up for silence. "Just the facts. Skip the editorial."

23

"Dad, this guy was on trial for murder and racketing."

"Racketeering."

"What's that?"

"The main occupation of badass mothers," Jake said. "Extortion, armed robberies, prostitution, gambling, drugs. The business of crime."

"Killing people?"

Jake glanced over. "Can't have one without the other."

Sam nodded and looked down. "This stuff happened in New York City. The Bronx. There's more. Stuff from 1992. Stuff in the *New York Times.*"

Sam sat hunched over the computer, reading. Jake glanced at the screen, but quickly returned his eyes to the road.

After a few minutes, Sam said, "These guys worked for the secret police in Yugoslavia. When the country broke up, they came over here and started taking over stuff the Mafia used to do. Massage parlors."

Jake looked over at him. "You know what that is?"

Sam nodded but kept his eyes looking straight ahead. "You're the one who ordered Cinemax."

"What about parental controls?"

"Give me a little credit," Sam said, and then was silent for a few minutes. "Says the police can't get them because they have a code of silence. They found one guy dead with all his fingernails pulled out."

Jake's knuckles began to ache until he loosened his grip on the wheel and flexed his fingers.

"It says Murat Lukaj was a lieutenant and that after the FBI started watching him, he disappeared."

"To Syracuse," Jake said.

"And the agency where you got me?" Sam asked.

Jake nodded.

"Were they all criminals? You think my mom was with them?"

"No," Jake said. "Albania was a mess back then. It's like Iraq and Afghanistan. Refugees everywhere. People getting killed. Sometimes babies end up without parents or anyone who can take care of them and they need a home. Murat took advantage of that. *They* were bad, but sometimes good things come from bad. Does that make sense?"

"Not really."

"I guess not," he said, giving Sam's shoulder a squeeze before looking back at the road. "For one reason or another, your parents couldn't take care of you, so you needed us, too. Bringing us all together was a good thing."

"But it's wrong that they did it for the money?"

"Wrong if your parents didn't want to give you up, but they had to because of the money."

"How could you sell your kids?" Sam said.

"I'm sure they didn't sell you, Sam. Don't think that."

"The secret police took me?"

"Who knows? It all worked out, right?"

"You had to pay to get me?" Sam said.

"There wasn't any amount of money we wouldn't have given for you, either," Jake said. "Whatever we had."

Sam's cheeks colored and he looked down at the computer.

During the ride back to Long Island, Sam read out loud everything he could find on Murat Lukaj and the Albanians in general.

According to the articles, the Albanians had taken over much of the skin trade in big cities like London, Milan, New York, and Boston, infiltrating the massage parlors with young girls who were little more than slaves. Human trafficking was their specialty, with Albania acting as a distribution point for young women from the entire region, from Poland to Turkey.

"You sure you want to keep reading this stuff?"

"Sure," Sam said. "Why not?"

One small story in the *New York Post* explained the letter Jake had found from Lukaj's Bronx lawyer. Evidently, it was in reference to a charge of first-degree assault in 2003, when Lukaj had allegedly beat a man into a coma with a stick of firewood. Lukaj pleaded to a lesser crime and so was sentenced to only two hundred hours of community service as well as the anger management. According to the letter from the lawyer Jake found, Lukaj hadn't done any of it.

Jake had Sam run an AutoTRAK. Lukaj had a black '06 Porsche Carrera and a blue '01 BMW 740i with a Syracuse street address, 1196 Cole Road. Jake had Sam write it down and then get MapQuest directions to the place. There was only one picture of

Lukaj with any of the articles and it was from back in 1994.

Lukaj's white face was round with small lips, a high forehead topped by wisps of dark hair, and pale vacant eyes. He looked like a student, too young to be an officer in something like the secret police.

"He doesn't *look* so bad," Sam said, tilting the computer so Jake could see it.

24

The red tip of the sun crept over the distant hill and Murat set down his pencil to watch. In his childhood home in the mountains just north of Tirana, the sun always came up red, filtered through the pollution of Tito's industrial machine until it choked and died. His sun now grew into a red melon, banded by the morning haze until it began to shrink and glow hot and he had to look away. His eyes quickly surveyed the small city below, buildings afire now in the sunlight, long morning shadows reaching from the trees before he noticed the glint of dew on the web in the corner of his picture window. It would be a fine day. His shipment of Latvian girls should arrive at noon sharp.

He picked up the pencil and with small scratches finished the accounts for the strip club on State Street before putting the book away in the bulky safe squatting in the corner of his office. The kitchen was on the same floor, but at the opposite end of the house, a walk long enough to leave his very pregnant wife breathing hard. Murat took that walk to make the coffee, listening to the small sounds the house made in the early morning, relishing the expanse of the place. He climbed the back stairs to wake his fifteen-year-old daughter. She slept with an iPod plugged into her ears. Stray hair masked half her face and the parted lips.

Murat reached for her shoulder, then paused. She had his height, more legs than body, long and thin, and his blue eyes, but the rest was Dardana, his wife. Olive skin. A small upturned nose. High cheeks and thick red lips. In the mirror, he studied his own round face and sinking chin, then tightened his gut and straightened his slumped shoulders, raising himself to full height.

His daughter inhaled the smell of coffee wafting up from the kitchen and rewarded him with a smile and a kiss on the cheek.

"Bacon and eggs?" he asked her as she slipped out of bed, covering her nascent breasts with an arm even though she wore a T-shirt.

She wrinkled her nose. "Just coffee."

Murat preferred paca for his own breakfast, a hearty soup made from lamb innards, but he tried to do things in the American way for his children, and so he worked hard to quell his accent at home and he offered the same bacon and eggs to his eight-year-old son when he rolled him out of his X-Men bedsheets.

When he was first sent upstate, after the real trouble, it had felt like Siberia. But it forced him to adapt, assimilate, go outside the Albanian community to expand business and, after 9/11, suddenly that ability became extremely valuable to New York. The raw materials for business, girls and heroin, needed a new way in other than the big-city ports where all eyes were turned. Murat already had just what they needed.

The cleaning woman arrived just as Lukaj was plying his children with toast doctored up with butter, cinnamon, and sugar. Tajik came after that. Like all the most important people in his organization, Tajik was related, a second cousin with a dark cap of messy hair too thick over the brow and the perpetual shadow of a beard on his cheek. Tajik was neither as tall as Murat nor as thin, but sloppy around the middle like their common grandfather. Murat trusted him with all things, even driving his children to their private school each day.

Tajik accepted a cup of coffee as he always did and smoked a Turkish cigarette with

Murat at the kitchen table while the children made their final preparations.

In a low tone, Tajik leaned close and said, "I got call from the truck driver. He will be late."

"You got *a* call," Murat said, glancing at the small orange ball the sun had become and its brilliant beams streaming in through the mullioned window. "A breakdown?"

"He just say —"

Murat scowled and Tajik regrouped.

"He just *said*, late."

Murat exhaled a plume of smoke and squinted through it at Tajik. "Is this the same driver with the red hair? The one from before?"

"I think so."

Murat glanced at the backs of his children, packing lunches with the housekeeper's help, before he leaned toward Tajik and let his face go sour.

"We will check the girls," he said. "If there are bruises, he will pay."

"Money?"

"Not money," Murat said. "If he is stealing, he will pay."

"But these girls are whores," Tajik said, his simple, doughy face showing confusion.

Murat silenced him with a chopping motion and glanced back at his kids once more. "Not until I say they are."

25

Sam grumbled when he heard Jake's plan and he stomped his feet on his way upstairs to pack. Jake reminded him to bring his cell phone charger. From his office, Jake could hear the slamming of dresser drawers. Jake called Don Wall, his contact at the FBI in Washington. For half a case of Wall's favorite wine, Jake was able to bribe him into doing a weekend search of the Bureau files for Murat Lukaj.

They took the thruway north to Albany, then west and up to Old Forge in the heart of the Adirondacks, where the brilliant green leaves of spring were three weeks behind the city and just breaking free from their buds.

"She's weird, Dad," Sam said as they pulled into the center of Old Forge.

Jake just looked at him.

"She's just old. She's your mother's

mom," Jake said. "She loves you and I trust her."

"You don't like her."

"She's family, Sam," Jake said. "She cares more about you than my parents, but join the club."

They turned at the old hardware store and went up South Shore Road in silence, until they came to a little brown shack standing next to a wooden gate. A brown sign, no bigger than a car bumper, in yellow letters read ADIRONDACK LEAGUE CLUB. An old man in a rumpled cap put down his paper and shuffled out of the shack, swatting at the tiny flies. Jake cracked his window.

"Hi, Melvin," he said, thrusting his hand through the small gap and shaking the man's hand. "Jake Carlson, Eva Wright's son-in-law."

"Yeah, she told me you'd be coming," he said, peering in at Sam.

"Rockefellers here yet?"

Melvin narrowed one eye and said, "That wouldn't be your business, would it?"

Melvin shuffled up the oiled road and unlocked the gate, swinging it open and examining something in the trees overhead while Jake drove past. The road wound through the woods until finally they came to an open space overlooking the lake.

Down by the water was the shake-shingled clubhouse, an old hotel really, with brick chimneys and decorative clay smokestacks. The dark water lay beyond it like a mirror, reflecting the wooded hillsides and the colorful late-day sky.

They kept going, past the tennis courts and the parking lot where only a single Rolls-Royce kept company with a handful of Mercedes sedans. The road that snaked its way around the lake was unmarked. Every so often a driveway would branch off down toward the water, but they too were unmarked and devoid of mailboxes. It was still early enough in the season that the foliage hadn't filled in completely, so through the trees Jake caught the hint of an occasional roofline or the glint of a window down near the water.

"How big is this place?" Sam asked.

"Fifty thousand acres," Jake said. "The biggest private tract of land in the whole park."

When he saw the ten-foot boulder with a birch tree growing directly out of the top of it, he slowed and took the next gravel driveway. The road dipped and turned before they passed through the towering cobblestone gateway and into a gravel lot that butted up to the old mansion. The enormity of the green roof made the thick beams of the dark brown house that much more impressive and would have been suggestive of a fort had it not been for the gingerbread gilding of the roof eaves and the balconies.

On this side of the lake, the sun's rays had been gone for the past hour, but the orange glow of lamps and woodwork from inside welcomed them. Parker, the caretaker, was lighting candles in the great room and he stared at them for a moment with his liver-spotted hand trembling over the flame before telling them that *she* was tending to her garden. They walked out onto the front porch and were greeted by the maniacal call of a loon. They tramped at an angle down toward the boathouse, where the raised beds of the vegetable garden made it easier for Jake's mother-in-law to pick her tomatoes and pull her carrots.

Jake felt a black fly crawl up under the hairline at his neck and he pinched it and flicked it away, then swatted at another hovering by his nose. Sam was a dancing windmill.

Bent over with her back to them, in a blue housecoat, was Eva Nelson-Wright of the Boston Nelsons. Even through the veil of mesh that circled her hat, Jake could see his mother-in-law's icy blue eyes and her pale lips tightening. She changed the trowel from one oversize glove to the other so she could offer him a flimsy handshake.

"Goddamn bugs," Jake said, swatting.

"Those are the good ones," she said. "They eat the smaller ones. The pests."

Jake took her hand and bussed her cheek, getting a whiff of the deet she had sprayed all over her face net.

"Good to see you, Eva," he said.

She turned and said, "Samuel."

Sam gripped her limp glove between swats and let it go.

"I appreciate this," Jake said. "Like I said, I'll feel a lot better with Sam up here."

"Still chasing windmills?" she said.

"These days they've been chasing me."

"Excuse me?"

"Never mind."

"Well, the grocery bill's certainly going to go up."

Jake took the wallet out of his pants and split it open.

"Oh, put your money away," she said, turning away and plunging the trowel into the bed of dirt. "Don't be tacky. I meant the boy eats like a horse. You think that matters to me? It'll all be his one day anyway."

Jake let the hundred-dollar bills hang in

the air for a moment before stuffing them back into his wallet. Sam stared hard at him, and Jake put a finger to his lips and shook his head.

"Parker set you a place for dinner," Eva said, dropping a seed into the hole. "I think it would be appropriate that you do that much before you race off to whatever antics you're up to."

"Dinner would be great," Jake said. "Definitely before the antics start. Sam and I will go get cleaned up."

He turned and put an arm around Sam's shoulder and they walked up to the house, chased by the sound of the trowel scratching dirt.

"And you're leaving me with her?" Sam said, slapping his arm and marking it with a bloody skid.

"It's me she doesn't like, not you," Jake said. "But deep down she finds me funny."

"Mom couldn't stand her."

"Just get along. She's family."

Sam looked out at the water and sighed.

"What did she mean, 'All this will be his'?" Sam asked.

Jake looked back at the four-slip boathouse, two stories high with a complete guest quarters on the second floor, then up at the main house. Parker's shape stood in the vast mullioned window. His hands were fluttering over some kind of glass as he polished it, peering out across the lawn, presumably waiting for a signal from Eva in the event she wanted something. Jake took a deep breath and pushed out his cheeks before letting it go.

"Let's talk inside," Jake said, swatting his neck.

Sam's bedroom had a large sitting area with a bearskin rug and its own broad cobblestone fireplace. Parker had lit the fire and the dry wood crackled and popped in the grate. There was a small wet bar by the doors leading out to the balcony, and Jake took a bottle of beer out of the mini refrigerator before sitting on the couch. Sam put his feet up on the coffee table, a varnished crosscut section from a giant tree.

"She's not supposed to talk like that," Jake said, staring into the fire.

"Am I, like, rich or something?" Sam asked.

"She is."

"But I'm not her *real* grandson."

"I'm sensing a theme here."

26

"She said it," Sam said with a nod.

"Jesus," Jake said. "Believe me, that had nothing to do with you and everything to do with them."

"How could Mom even come from someone like that?" Sam said. "That's what I never got."

Jake took a big swig and let it fizz in his mouth before swallowing. "It's the same way with me and my parents. We're nothing alike."

"And they're your real parents, right?"

"You gotta stop with that 'real' crap. I love you, but it's getting on my nerves, man. I'm as real a dad as you're ever gonna get."

"I didn't mean you."

"I know what you didn't mean, but you gotta think about how it sounds. People can't always read your mind."

"Does she have a will or something?"

Jake set his beer down hard on the table

and crossed his arms. "See? This is why we don't talk like that. Life isn't taking some trust fund and figuring out how to spend it. You work. You contribute. That's life. I've seen it the other way. It's never good for anyone. Don't think you can kick it into neutral."

"It's a lot of money."

"Her money. The first thing your mom ever said to me about her was not to trust her."

Sam said he needed a few minutes in the bathroom, so Jake slipped downstairs and found Eva in the big room overlooking the water. Orange light twisted its way through the old panes of glass and there was a musty smell of spruce trees and old Oriental rugs in the air. Eva had a gin and tonic in her hand, and the floppy hat was pushed back off her head, net rolled up, still hanging from her neck by its bow, and giving her a slightly disheveled look. Jake cleared his throat and she sat up straight, undid the bow, and set the hat beside her on the floor.

"Drink?" she asked, raising the pitcher.

Jake went to the sideboard and removed a crystal glass, letting her fill it halfway before he held up a hand. She dropped in a wedge of lime.

Jake sat in the big leather chair opposite

her, extended his legs, and crossed them. He stared at her, smiling, then said, "Remember what you said when you came to visit after we got him?"

"Who?"

"You wouldn't hold him," Jake said, forcing his smile to hold its place. "He wasn't your grandson and we shouldn't count on having him because his real mother could show up anytime and take him back and there'd be nothing we could do about it."

Her eyes narrowed and she pursed her lips before sipping her drink and looking out the window.

"Things change," she said after a few moments. "Don't they?"

She looked at him and smiled, then her face dropped. "Remember when she lost all her hair and you shaved your head, too? Even when your agent said not to because your contract was coming up and they were saying behind the scenes that you better not? No. I wouldn't have changed having her be with you for the world."

Her bottom lip curled up under her teeth and she looked away, sniffed once, and wiped her eyes on her sleeve before turning back, entirely composed.

"Thank you," Jake said, so softly he wasn't sure he'd said it at all.

■ ■ ■ ■

Dinner was calm, and almost pleasant. After her fourth drink, Eva's cheeks took on their usual pink glow and she grew talkative in a girlish way that, although slightly absurd, was always a comfortable alternative to cold steel. When Eva wasn't talking, Jake could see the same jawline in her face that Karen had had and it brought back the memory of a night they'd shared in the big old place before Karen was sick, a night in a thunderstorm when the warmth of the old lamps glowed in just the same way and every so often a tiny moth would flutter around them until it burned. Jake felt his throat go tight and when he looked up, Eva was staring at him. She cleared her throat softly before asking if he'd like a glass of port. Jake thanked her, but said he had to get going. He gave Sam a big long hug and headed out into the dark.

27

Morning sun shone on Dorothy Cakebread's cottage and tendrils of steam slipped free from the damp wood siding. Jake rolled down his window and watched from the roadside. The bearded man who had spoken with him the previous day came out and began scraping paint from his window frame, filling the air with a rasping that reminded Jake of the dentist.

It was nearly two hours before Cakebread's ex-wife emerged wearing sunglasses, her hair tied up into a lime-green scarf. She carried a bag to the car, set it on the passenger seat, then climbed in. Jake ducked down as she pulled out onto the road. He let her get to the bend before he popped up and lit out after her. She drove for nearly half an hour right back in the direction Jake had come from, downtown Syracuse. When she pulled into the parking garage opposite the hospital, Jake took the first spot he found on the street, in a no-parking zone.

Two minutes later, she emerged from the garage and crossed the street. Jake got out and fell in behind her, following her inside the hospital. He kept back, waiting until her elevator doors closed before he moved close enough to see which floor she stopped at. Four. He took the next car up and stepped out into the pediatric unit. He straightened his back and stared intently around as he walked up and down the halls, meeting the nurses' eyes until they looked away.

Dorothy Cakebread was nowhere to be seen. There was one area, however, that he couldn't see into. The small red sign on the door read PEDIATRIC INTENSIVE CARE. Jake went to the nurse's station at the end of the hall and learned that the name of the chief pediatric surgeon was Dr. Carney. He returned to the door with the red sign, looked around, then pushed it open and caught his breath. Six small beds were lined up on the far wall. In each lay a child connected to a series of tubes and wires. Two were attended by small groups of doctors, talking in hushed voices below the mechanical hiss of the life-support systems.

A nurse confronted Jake immediately, and he flipped open his wallet, showing his press credential.

"Hi. We're doing a TV special on Dr. Carney," he said, "and I was told to get a feel for the ICU."

"Oh," the nurse said, the lines in her face relaxing, "you're that guy. *American* something."

"Outrage," Jake said, extending his hand. "Jake Carlson."

"Did something happen?" the nurse asked.

"This is one of those tragedies that turns happy in the end," Jake said, putting on a smile. "Thanks to Dr. Carney."

The nurse beamed back at him, nodding her head and stepping aside.

"Visiting is almost over," she said. "If you need more time than that, I'll have to clear it with my supervisor. Even for Dr. Carney."

"I'll be fine," Jake said. "Thank you."

Dorothy Cakebread stood beside the bed at the far end of the unit. She was crying. In the bed was a baby about eighteen months old in a tiny pink nightgown. Her head was shaved clean and a crimson scar ran from ear to ear over the crown of her skull. A clear plastic ventilator was taped to her mouth. Its lizard sound raised and lowered her chest and blew soft tufts of steamy air out her nose.

Jake crossed the room and stood over her

shoulder, watching the child with a lump building in his chest. When Dorothy Cakebread looked back at him, he cleared his throat and said, "I have a child, too. That's why I'm here, Mrs. Cakebread."

The sad lines around her mouth pulled tight and the wet eyes began to blaze.

"You're that man."

"Please don't look away. I'm not with the police," Jake said. "I'm a father. I have a little boy. I'm trying to help him find his mother. We got him from your husband."

Dorothy Cakebread took a deep breath and let it out, turning her gaze back to the little girl.

"My daughter's little girl," she said, shaking her head. "They think they got it all, but she'll have to have chemo. My girlfriend has a cousin and her daughter had the same thing and she's seventeen now. So, that's what we think about."

They stood there until a nurse came and softly told them it was time to go. Jake walked alongside Dorothy Cakebread and held open the door. Out in the hallway, he asked if he could buy her a cup of coffee. She shrugged and followed him to the cafeteria, where he set two large cups down between them.

"I know you were upset when I went to

your house," Jake said.

"You think this is better?" she asked.

"I'm sorry," Jake said. "I followed you. I wanted to find the right time and when I saw your granddaughter, I knew you'd understand. When your child is hurting, there's nothing you wouldn't do to make it better. I thought you'd understand that."

"What do you want from me?" she asked, looking up at him with pale green eyes, gripping her hands together.

"Your husband had records from the agency?" Jake asked.

Her face closed tight and she nodded.

"Ronny was a dreamer," she said, staring down at the table. "He thought those people were going to make him something. Like if you drove a Mercedes you were someone. It was mostly why we split up. He always cared, though. And he said if they ever bothered me, I should know where the records were and tell the FBI. He gave me money to keep the unit."

"Why didn't you?"

"Tell the FBI? He said it was my red lever and not to break the glass and pull it unless I had to. Only if they bothered me. He said once I told the police, they would try to kill me and my daughter. He said they'd kill anyone. That they didn't care."

"And they killed him?"

"I suppose," she said, taking a sip of the coffee. "It didn't matter if it was him or them. I knew from the start it would end bad. I know things about people, and he didn't listen. He couldn't be happy with a regular life, a regular job. Kind of a curse some people have. I knew that about him, but I was young and I thought he'd change, but people don't."

She was quiet a minute, then said, "You're not going to stir these people up, are you?"

"I just want to help my son find his mother," Jake said. "I won't let anyone know about the records, or you."

"I probably worry more than I should," she said. "Knowing Ronny, he made the whole thing up to make himself important. He was depressed, you know."

"It would mean a lot to me," Jake said. "A lot to my son."

Dorothy Cakebread reached down into her purse and took out a pen and an envelope that she tore in half. On the paper, she wrote down the address of a self-storage facility and the combination to a lock. She folded it in half and handed it to Jake.

"Thank you. I won't tell anyone."

"I know you won't," she said.

The address wasn't far from the hospital. Jake pulled inside the chain-link fence and right up to the unit. His hands shook as he spun the dial on the lock and it took him three tries before he heard it click. Without even bothering to look around, he jangled the lock free, threw open the overhead door, and stepped inside.

28

The space was nearly empty. A spare tire rested against one of the side walls and in the back three old wooden file cabinets stood in a row. Dust on the floor was thick enough to show Jake's footprints, and the smell of damp concrete and musty paper filled his nostrils. He stepped slowly, his feet chafing the concrete floor. The first drawer he opened held files full of junk, business filings and receipts, but in the bottom he found a small handgun with a faded box of bullets.

Jake took the gun and turned it over in his hands, letting his fingers caress the dimpled surface of the grip. It was a Colt .25 automatic, small, but otherwise not too dissimilar from the Navy sidearm his father had taught him to use as a kid. He put it back and closed the drawer.

The rest of the drawers were stuffed with paperwork. Jake looked at his watch and started to dig. The files weren't alphabetical and had no apparent order. Time ticked away. It was in the bottom drawer of the second cabinet that Jake found a folder that had a five-pointed star with a circle around it drawn with a ballpoint pen on the outside. When he opened it, he saw Sam's name.

His heart raced, but as he leafed through it, he didn't see anything revealing. Most of it looked like papers he already had. They deserved a closer look, but his watch said it was time to go or he'd be crossways with Muldoon again. He started for the door, then went back and opened the first drawer, scooping up the Colt .25 and the box of shells and stuffing them into the pockets of his suit. After he closed up the unit he tossed the file onto the passenger seat and took off for the police station in the town of Dewitt and their shoot with the cop who had first discovered the bunker.

Twice during the interview, Muldoon stopped tape and whispered into Jake's ear, asking him why he was so jumpy and to please settle down. Even the cop's descriptions of the darkness and the sobs of the women didn't fill Jake's eyes with moisture the way they normally would have. His mind was on the file.

When it was finally over, Muldoon told Jake he planned to shoot a couple of dramatizations on Sunday, women being abducted, the bunker man coming for them with a rope, and him burying the bodies of the ones who died. Then he'd begin to write. He told Jake that he wouldn't need him until Monday morning at nine.

"They want to do a toss from Nancy to you and I'll have some voice-over work for you by then," Muldoon said. "This thing is going to be our lead story for the entire week. Meantime, you can grab a day with your kid."

"You sound enthusiastic," Jake said.

"I'm not a kid person."

"See you Monday morning."

Jake drove until he came to a Kmart shopping center. He pulled into the lot and parked and began to go through the file again, this time more carefully. There were copies of things Jake already had, the letter Cakebread had sent them, the declaration of abandonment and order of adoption from Albania, the paperwork from the family court in Syracuse. Jake read through the papers, word by word, grinding each one down into all its different possibilities.

After an hour, he threw down the last

papers on top of the folder and slammed his palms against the steering wheel before firing up the engine. When he came to a stop at the first traffic light, he glanced down in disgust. That's when he saw something written in pen on the back of a court document. A car horn sounded behind him, and Jake looked up at the green light. He crossed the intersection, then pulled over to the side of the road. The written name clicked into place, opening a stream of images.

Niko, no last name, just Niko. Jake remembered the burly old lawyer in the rumpled suit who had appeared with them in family court. He had barely looked at them, and when he spoke, it was with a thick eastern European accent. When the judge ruled for the adoption and rapped his gavel, the lawyer gave Jake's hand a brief shake and marched straight out of the court, leaving Jake and Karen to gush over Sam, whom she held bundled in a blanket.

"Car-wall-cow-sick," Jake said aloud, drawing from his memory. "Can't be many of those."

29

Bad things happened in threes. Niko Karwalkowszc knew this. The first thing had happened earlier in the day. Riding back from the golf course across the street in his personal cart, he saw the bloody skid mark and the mass of fur in the gutter. His dog, run over by a car.

He buried the dog in the garden and had a dinner of toast and peanut butter washed down with Absolut vodka. Now he stared out the bay window at the spot, absently withdrew the plastic inhaler from the pocket of his robe, and took a deep blast. Tears ran down his face. Something he had stopped trying to control when he was a small boy and saw the American GIs outside the fences at Mauthausen, staring in with their mouths agape.

Niko peeled himself away from the window and took a hot bath. He dried off and had begun combing the thin gray strands over the dome of his skull when the phone rang. He stared for a moment into the pocked glass, wondering if the heavy sagging flesh of his face looked that way because of what was really inside of him, or if those dark cunning eyes still retained the affability of youth and were simply prisoners in his aging bulk. He wiped the steam from his glasses and put them on.

The phone continued to ring and he crossed the wooden floor in the hall, scooping it up in his bedroom with a grunt.

"Your office. Now."

The phone went dead. The heavily accented words echoed through his mind, sobering him like a blunt instrument. Through the window he could see the towering border of pines on the first fairway of the Bellevue Country Club. Except for the orange glow of the set sun in the west and the blue glow of the streetlights, everything was dark with shadows. Niko heaved a sigh and took a fresh shirt from his closet, buttoning it up, but not bothering with a tie. He always wore a tie with clients, unless it was after hours and then he knew the kinds of things he was expected to do didn't call for a tie. To wear one would seem almost offensive.

As he backed out of the driveway in his

burgundy Buick, he averted his eyes from the stain on the road, knowing of course that in his office at the bottom of the hill he was sure to find the second bad thing.

As he drove downward, the homes grew smaller. Once he crossed Grand they began to crowd one another and fade until he reached Charles Avenue, where they were truly decrepit. Warped wood. Cracked, colorless paint. Rusted mailboxes. It had taken him fifty years to get up that hill, and it was the Albanians who took him the last half of the way.

It came at a price. Late-night calls like this one. Shady deals. Blood. Bodies. Lies. The American way.

After the war, he put himself through college, learning English at the same time. He went to law school at night while he worked at the bus station in Albany. His first clients were his own people, the Poles. Then came the Italians and the Irish working class who were too poor to pay for a will or a divorce from an attorney who spoke without the heavy accent. It was a living, but not a country-club living.

Then came the Albanians, flooding into Charles Avenue from the decay of Yugoslavia. They trusted no one, but needed him. It was the first time in his career that his broken English helped him get clients. He believed they were somehow comforted by a lawyer who knew how harsh it was to be marked as different in this country. And, during the past fifteen years, it was his work for them that had elevated him to the brick house he now lived in across from the Bellevue Country Club. He even had a membership.

There was no shortage of work with the Albanians. Niko had never seen or heard of a criminal group as creative or flexible as Murat Lukaj and his men. Any opportunity that fell their way, they took advantage of. Something as small as a truck of baby formula they might hijack to sell. Or something as big as a shipment of weapons stolen from the nearby Army base they might sneak onto a container ship bound for the Middle East. Nothing seemed too small and nothing seemed too big. They were the consummate opportunists.

In the parking lot of the small corner building that held his office, Murat's long blue BMW was parked at a haphazard angle beneath the street lamp. Next to it was a silver Audi coupe whose side was punctuated with half a dozen bullet holes. Niko shook his head and got out, scanning the empty street. The BMW eased out into the street as if to get its bearings before it roared away up Genesee Street.

Niko frowned, because if Murat wasn't sticking around, it must be bad. He turned to the building and saw a smear across the smoked glass of his office door. When he examined his palm inside the landing he saw that the door handle had also been stained with blood. Niko muttered a curse and heaved himself up the long narrow stairway, one hand on his sloppy gut, the other on the rail, wheezing by the time he reached the landing.

The office door was flung open. Two young men in dark quilted jackets and jeans sat slumped in chairs, hands in their pockets, legs stretched out, staring sullenly up at Niko like hunting dogs in a kennel. The taller one was Shaban, Murat's first cousin and the only Albanian he'd ever seen with long wavy blond hair and a brown Fu Manchu. Niko knew that under the coat would be a sleeveless shirt that exposed Shaban's long lean biceps with their barbed-wire tattoos.

The other was Tajik, baby-faced despite the dark eyes and shadow of a beard, big around the middle, but very powerful. Niko peered into the back room where the slumped figure of a man with curly red hair sat tied to a chair. He'd seen this kind of thing before. Murat had been enamored of the attorney-client privilege ever since one of his people got off on a murder charge in Brooklyn after the gun was ruled inadmissible because it came from the lawyer's office.

Niko clenched his hands and put them in the air.

"He better not be dead," he said, glaring.

30

Niko went to the closet in the hall and took out a bucket that he filled from a spigot in the small tiled bathroom. He dumped in some liquid cleaner, wincing at the ammonia smell and handing the mop to one of the thugs in the chair. He pointed toward the spatter marks on the wooden floor surrounding the unconscious redhead.

"Clean," Niko said, jabbing his finger at the back room and making mopping motions. "You clean it. Get the door, too. There's blood on the handle."

Shaban glanced up and gave him an annoyed look, but nodded his head. He nudged Tajik and, together, they went to work in the thorough way that Niko knew would leave the floor spotless. Niko saw the red light on his answering machine blinking, but before he could cross the room to play the message, the phone on the desk jangled, startling him.

He picked it up.

"I paid your bill," Murat said. "On your desk. You see it?"

Niko picked up the paper bag he hadn't noticed and looked at the banded bills inside. Twenty thousand. It was just the way they did business. Niko got paid for the last job whenever a new job came along, Murat's way of cheating him without saying so.

"Very good. Let's talk about the *other* package," Niko said, eyeing the form in the back room. "Is it past expiration date?"

"No," Murat said. "Still fresh."

"Because it's very messy," Niko said, closing his eyes briefly and shaking his head like a tired schoolteacher.

"It's your mess right now," Murat said. "But we can get rid of it. You tell Shaban, yes or no."

"My mess?"

"Aren't you the one who places the orders with Canada? Shaban. You talk to him."

The phone went dead. Niko eyed the tall blond thug, the mop of his hair swaying in rhythm with the mop on the floor.

He called Shaban's name and motioned him over. The man in the chair groaned. Shaban took a big automatic from his waistband and bopped him on the head before coming out into the office.

Niko closed his eyes again and pushed the glasses up higher on his nose and asked, "Can you tell me what happened? Murat said you would tell me what happened. Sit."

Niko put his coat on the back of the chair and sat down behind the desk. He took a bottle of Absolut out of the drawer along with two glasses, which he filled. He pushed one across the desk to Shaban, who looked at it disinterestedly.

Niko sipped his vodka while Shaban told him the story of how the man bleeding all over his office had come to be there, how he'd pulled his truck over, gone into the can, raped one of the girls, and gotten rough enough to kill her. How the New York City Albanians expected the driver's head, but how Murat wanted him to decide if the union would tolerate losing a man, since Niko was the one who dealt with the union. Without the Toronto union, there could be no deals with New York or anyone else. Niko considered the situation with the detachment of a brain surgeon who has already removed the dome of the skull.

Finally, Niko said, "They understand reputation, and an eye for an eye. They will have to."

Shaban smiled at him and slapped his palm on the desktop with a firm nod. He got up and walked into the other room.

"Nothing here," Niko said, his voice rising.

Niko winced at the sound of the body thumping on the floor. Shaban marched past him, dragging the man by his ankles while his partner followed, mopping up the tracks. Niko clutched his chest, dug the inhaler out of his pants pocket, and took three puffs.

When Shaban returned, Niko muttered for him to make sure they took the ropes off the chair. While he struggled into his coat, the two thugs emptied the bucket and began rinsing out the mop. While he waited, Niko could feel the draft coming up the stairway. It made him shiver but he resisted the temptation to take another drink. When he forced his eyes away from the bottle on the desk, they instead clung to the blinking red light on the answering machine.

Niko pursed his lips. He fished for the inhaler and when he had a good hold on it, he pushed the playback button, just to get it over with. It had to be bad news, number three.

"This message is for Nicholas Karwalkowszc. You helped me and my wife with an adoption about thirteen years ago through the International Children's Adoption Agency of Central New York and I want to talk to you about it. Please give me a call at 917-555-6601. My name is Jake Carlson. My son's name is Sam."

The voice took hold of him and Niko closed his eyes. He heard the thump of the bucket being put away, then the low laughter, and the sound of footsteps going down the stairs. The plastic shell of the inhaler snapped in his hand.

31

When Jake woke up Sunday morning, he snatched his cell phone off the night table without looking at the number coming in.

"Sam?" he said.

There was silence and the sound of the phone being adjusted before a man's voice replied, "This is Nicholas Karwalkowszc. I believe you called my office last night."

"I'm sorry, Mr. Karwalkowszc," Jake said. "I don't know if you remember, but you helped with the adoption of my son."

The lawyer chuckled and said he was sorry, but he'd done hundreds of adoptions.

"But you have records," Jake said.

"No, you would have to go to your agency for that."

It was silent for a minute before the lawyer said, "Mr. Carlson, are you there?"

"The director of the agency died seven years ago," Jake said. "And I already have his records. That's how I got your name. I thought you might have something more. I thought you might remember. I thought I could show you what I've got and maybe you'll remember something. I'll pay you for your time. Your hourly rate."

"You have agency records?" the lawyer said. "Cakebread's?"

"You remember Cakebread?"

"Somewhat."

"How did you know it was him?"

He stuttered, then said, "You said thirteen years ago. Most of them back then were for Cakebread, so I assumed."

"Can I meet you? Today would be great."

"I have some plans already. Let me call you back. I'll see what I can do."

Jake hung up and looked at his phone for a moment before starting to move. He went to his briefcase and took out the little Colt as well as the box of shells. He loaded the gun and slipped it into his pocket. He wanted to check the building where the agency had been again, and also his original hotel room, places he didn't want to be without a gun.

200

32

On Tioga Street, Murat sometimes held court in his social club, a corner building in a rundown residential neighborhood. Tall, narrow city homes that needed new paint and shingles. Broken sidewalks that fought back gutters lined with grit and garbage pounded flat from a winter of snow. The club, once a bar, had a glass front window and bricks old enough to have struggled free from their rigid lines. Inside the small front room, a beautiful young woman, black-haired and big-breasted, cleaned her beer glasses behind the bar without looking up. She was the only one.

Niko passed through the narrow hallway into the back where the strong smell of coffee overwhelmed its competition, stale beer and burnt incense from the previous night and even the fresh smoke of the morning. From the walls of the room hung rich red tapestries, glowing in the yellow light of candles and a chandelier of tarnished bronze. White linen cloths shrouded each and every table. In a place of honor on the back wall hung the Albanian national flag with its black double-headed eagle.

Behind the big round corner table, Murat laughed with his men through the smoke. His hands hid behind a tall silver coffeepot. From his slumped narrow shoulders hung a russet Versace sweatsuit with sleeves plowed halfway up his forearms, revealing bangle bracelets that gave him the air of a gypsy.

Murat's moon-shaped face rose nearly a foot above the rest. His short hair was light brown, thinning, and whisked to the side. His mirth exposed a small mouth with large crooked teeth, and eyes so pale they could hardly be called blue. The black in the ring around the irises and the holes of the pupils seemed to reveal not simple darkness, but a negative universe within. A small white scar cut through the brow over one of those eyes, but Niko had picked up enough through the years to know that Murat gave most of the scars.

Murat could look at the serial number on a hundred-dollar bill and remember it three months later. He could also pull the trigger on one of his own men if he felt it was in his own best interest. He was a natural leader. Attention to detail and the loyalty of his men kept him from most trouble. He was the only client Niko had ever known to keep his own books.

In the background their strange music groaned, an accordion and their saz, a two-string guitar, yielding a sound that could only make Niko think of a harem. He twisted his lips.

"Niko, you don't like Sevdah?" Murat said, calling to him from the middle of it all and referring to the music as he stabbed out his cigarette. "I tell you, it's about love, Niko."

Murat turned to his men, and smoke leaked out his nose as he said something in Albanian that made them laugh. The social club was the one place where Murat would grow sloppy with his English and let his accent run thick. Niko's eyes lingered on the coffeepot until Murat raised a long bone-thin arm up off the table and snapped his fingers, jangling his gold bangle bracelets and calling for a cup. Another beautiful young woman appeared in a tight black shirt that revealed a muscular bronze stomach. She set the cup and saucer in front of Murat and stayed long enough for him to run his hand up her leg before disappearing into the back. Murat poured the coffee.

Niko sat down.

Murat's eyes lost their smile and he directed the rest of his men out of the room with a word and the twitch of his head.

Niko took a sip of the thick black brew and said, "I got a very disturbing phone call."

Murat waited.

"A man named Jake Carlson," Niko said, watching Murat's eyes for any sign of life. "We gave him a boy, thirteen years ago. He says he got my name from Cakebread's files."

Niko thought he saw a twitch at the word "files" but it was too slight to be sure.

"I already know this man," Murat said, reaching for the pack on the table and tapping out a cigarette so that the cellophane complained. "He's a reporter, on TV."

Niko furrowed his brow.

"The show *American Outrage.* Now he's doing a story," Murat said, lighting up and creating a plume of smoke that forced one eye to close. "How did he find the files?"

"I can only presume through Cakebread's wife," Niko said gently. "You know, Murat, I always told you he had files somewhere."

"Shaban!"

Murat's shout, abrupt and unexpected, made Niko jump. Shaban, Murat's tall cousin with long blond hair, shot in from the bar, stroking his Fu Manchu. Murat motioned with his head, and Shaban bent his ear to Murat's lips. Niko looked away. He knew Murat had been a young officer in his country's secret police before he came to America and that whispering was only a habit, not an insult. After a moment, Shaban nodded and left.

"He said he wanted to find his boy's mother," Niko said. "You think it could be more than that?"

"Does this matter?" Murat said, placing the cigarette in the corner of his mouth, where it dangled as he spoke. "This is America. TV is everything. The FBI? The police? If things are quiet, they will always go away. TV is like a bleating goat."

"I think," Niko said, raising the cup to his lips, "that his boy was one of the ones."

33

It was just past noon when Murat raised the door to the storage unit and Niko walked inside. It was cool, musty, and quiet. His fingers still bore the mustard stain from the hot dog he'd been eating on the tenth tee when he got the call. The metal spikes on his shoes clacked against the concrete as he approached the files. In the dust, he could see footprints he knew belonged to the father.

Murat stayed in the doorway, lighting a cigarette.

"How did he find it so fast?" Niko asked.

"Cakebread's wife," Murat said, peering at him through the smoke. "She has a sick granddaughter."

Niko motioned his head slowly, as if he understood.

"Tubes and wires to make her breathe," Murat said.

"So?"

"Shaban let her know," Murat said. "Those machines, they're delicate, just like her husband's mental health used to be."

Murat tilted his head and said, "I know we paid Cakebread when he found these other babies. Did you ever know where he got them?"

"They were white," Niko said, turning and running his eyes over the file cabinets, "and we got our money. We never asked."

Niko began opening drawers, pulling random files until he had a feel for Cakebread's method of organization.

Murat stood just outside, smoking and gazing at the sky with a look of infinite patience.

One cabinet was filled with business receipts and bills. One was filled with files that were stuffed with the documents given to parents. It was the third cabinet that made Niko grunt. The files in that cabinet had the dirt. Some contained nothing more than Cakebread's handwritten notes. But some had more. Documents. Letters. Photos. Sometimes newspaper clippings. Enough to create serious problems for Niko and certainly Murat.

There was a vague chronological order to the files and within twenty minutes he found what he was looking for. There were copies of the driver's licenses of Jacob and Karen Carlson, their financial information and medical records. But that wasn't what interested Niko. What interested him was the file next to that. It had to do with the boy the Carlsons evidently got. The family he came from was a name people would recognize. There were newspaper articles and a birth certificate.

One sheet had Cakebread's handwritten notes, explaining exactly what had happened and why.

"Find something?" Murat said, stepping in from the sunshine and casting his cigarette to the floor.

"An opportunity," Niko said, showing the newspaper articles to Murat.

Murat nodded and took the folder from Niko.

"What about all this?" Murat asked, nodding toward the file cabinets.

"Very dangerous," Niko said.

Murat shook his head. "If I knew he was so smart, I might not have gotten rid of him."

"I thought that's why you did get rid of him," Niko said.

"Stealing from me is not smart."

Murat rapped his knuckles against the wooden cabinets and looked around. He spied the tire and rolled it over to the cabinets. Opening a drawer, he removed some files and began pulling papers out of it, crumpling them up and stuffing them into the tire. When it was half full, he tipped it against the cabinets and lit the paper.

The paper crackled and before Murat had the door closed, the smell of burning rubber filled Niko's nose. They climbed into Murat's BMW and left a cloud of dust as they sped out through the chain-link gates and onto the boulevard.

34

The office building turned up nothing. Jake went in through the back alley, but saw no one and no sign of anything new. At his new hotel, no one had asked for him and no one was waiting around. Jake grabbed a gyro at a Mediterranean place up the street called King David, then decided to drive out to the storage unit and go through the papers again. Maybe he'd missed something.

He was on Erie Boulevard, a mile away, when a yellow fire truck screamed past him. His eyes were drawn to the black plume of smoke in the distance. He shook his head and said "No way" aloud as he sped after the truck. He knew before he got there what had happened, but he pulled up alongside the storage facility and got out anyway. The air was putrid with rubber and black flecks floated down from the blue sky. Another fire truck arrived and roared into the fenced-in area. Orange flames licked at the roof of the unit where Cakebread kept his files.

Within minutes, the firemen were blasting the roof with a stream of water that turned the black smoke into a haze of steam that was soon big enough to leave its beads on Jake's forehead and upper lip. He looked around, remembering a story he'd done once on firebugs and knowing they liked to watch their work. But then, this wasn't the work of a firebug.

Jake was on his way back to the hotel when his phone rang. It was Karwalkowszc.

"I have some time tonight," the lawyer said. "I can meet you at my office, but not until nine."

He gave Jake the address. Jake recognized it as being very close to the shopping center where Cakebread was found dead in his car. His hand strayed to the gun in his pocket and he almost said something about the storage unit, but he held his tongue and agreed to the time and place. Jake didn't want to wait around by himself, so he dialed Muldoon and offered to look at the bunker-man scripts.

"Thought you were heading home," Muldoon said.

"I got Sam up at my mother-in-law's place in the mountains, so I'm back early."

"Yeah," Muldoon said. "I'd love to have you take a look. I've been holed up in this place all day, and I could use a fresh set of eyes."

When Jake got to the street outside Muldoon's hotel, he fished his hand into the coat and gripped the gun, then studied the area before getting out and going in. He checked the bar and watched behind him while he waited for the elevator.

Muldoon came to the door of his room in boxers and a Raiders T-shirt. His legs showed white and hairy above a pair of blue dress socks. Jake had to step over a tray of half-eaten food, a plate of greasy fries swathed in ketchup and the last two bites of a double cheeseburger.

"Want a French fry?" Muldoon said, nodding at the tray. "I could order you a Coke. Beer if you want."

Jake looked at the cold fries.

"I'm good."

There were papers everywhere and the curtains were drawn. Muldoon pulled a few sheets of paper off the bed and swept some others aside so Jake could sit down.

"I appreciate this," Muldoon said, handing Jake the script.

"Okay if I open a curtain?" Jake asked.

"Sure."

Jake let in the late-day glow, sat down, and started going through the script.

"Good stuff," he said after a while.

"You think?"

"They're going to love the blonde."

"They always love the blonde."

There were other scripts, one for every day of the week. Jake was going through them when he got the call from Don Wall, his friend at the FBI.

"On a Sunday?" Jake said.

"We gotta talk."

"You sound serious."

"I am serious. You gotta stop what you're doing."

"What?" Jake said, eyeing Muldoon. The producer's fingers were moving across his keyboard, but Jake could tell by the angle of his head that he was listening. He got up and gave Muldoon a sign that he'd be back in a minute, then let himself out into the hall.

"It doesn't matter what," Don Wall said. "Just stop. Don't follow these people. Don't ask any more questions. Just stop."

"You sound like the guy who called after they drugged me. They friends of yours or something?"

The line was silent.

"Don?"

"I can't say anything, but you have to trust me on this, Jake. You're not going to find what you're looking for. It doesn't exist. That much I found out."

"Maybe you couldn't find out, but maybe I can," Jake said.

Don huffed and said, "They took these kids from people back in Albania and paid off their stooges in the government to make up phony paperwork for the adoptions. There's no real paper trail to your boy or any of them, so just leave it alone."

"Someone has to know. Someone had to get these kids from somewhere."

"Jake, there was a guy down in the Bronx who crossed these people on a massage parlor deal. He went missing for a while and then the wife comes home and there's one of those bags they carry bowling balls around in on her front porch."

"Let me guess," Jake said. "It was a head."

"I'm not kidding," he said. "That's all they ever found. No witnesses, no evidence, no body. Just the guy's fucking head."

"I don't bowl," Jake said.

"If it ain't your head, it'll be your ass."

"The Taliban used to cut people's balls off and dig out their eyes."

"You're supposed to stop because the

answer isn't there," Don said, "and I'm asking you. As a favor."

"What about my favor? You were going to get me some stuff on this guy."

"This is your favor. Stop."

"Okay," Jake said. "I gotta go. Thanks."

35

Jake walked back into Muldoon's room and said he had to go.

"That other thing, huh?" the producer asked, swinging around in his desk chair, planting his stocking feet on the floor, and leaning over his gut. "You wanna bring me in on that? I know you're still pissed about the FBI agent's wife. I know I get hot sometimes, but my ex-wife says it's because I care. You know. And you like this script I got cooking for the bunker man, right?"

Jake looked at him for a moment before he said, "If it pans out, I'll bring you in. Just try to work with me on the scheduling over the next couple days. I should know by then."

"Because they'll fly me out of here come Wednesday if we aren't working on something else, and I know they got that Jessica Simpson bodyguard thing in the hopper. I'd hate to get out there to LA on a piece of shit like that and have this thing break on you."

"By Wednesday I should know."

"And you'll bring me in? If it's there?"

"Okay."

Muldoon leapt up, crossed the room, and pumped Jake's hand.

"I'm right here," Muldoon said. "Whatever you need."

Jake looked in his eyes for a moment, feeling the coldness of his hand, but thanked him and soon found his car on the street.

The sun had dropped, leaving the sky a deep enough purple to trigger the streetlights. Jake drove onto the highway heading toward the west side of town, then got off in an area where the train trestles were coated in graffiti and the weeds were thick on the roadside and in the cracked parking lots of the abandoned commercial buildings. Human shapes lurked in the shadows of sagging porches and behind the smoked glass of pimped-out cars with their glinting rims. He caressed the shape of the gun through the outside of his coat pocket.

The lawyer's office was just off the corner of Charles Street and West Genesee. On one side was an empty muffler shop, painted bright yellow and frowning with broken windows. On the other side was a small brick building that housed a cookie shop and a florist. Jake sat eyeing the place while he waited for the light to turn green. Behind him, he heard the sudden shriek of tires. In the rearview mirror a pair of headlights rocketed around the corner and headed right for him without slowing down.

Jake braced his hand on the dash just as the brakes squealed and the car bumped his fender. The airbag didn't go off. Jake froze for a moment, then spun around to see someone moving toward him. He gripped the wheel and took his foot off the brake, allowing the car to ease forward.

As the light turned green, two palms struck his window, and he jumped. His foot went to the gas, then he saw the face and slammed on the brake.

It was Zamira.

Jake rolled down his window, stuck the other hand in his coat pocket, gripping the Colt, and said, "What the hell are you doing?"

"They'll kill you," she said, reaching through the window and grabbing a handful of his shirt.

"Karwalkowszc?"

"He told them. Follow me," she said, glancing at the buildings across the street.

"Please."

"Who, Lukaj?"

"They'll see us. *Please.*"

"You just show up here," Jake said, swatting her hand away. "After what you did."

Across the intersection, two men in long jackets came out of the building, pointed at Jake, and started to walk quickly toward him.

"Oh God," Zamira said. She crouched low and ran back to her car.

As the two men moved into the glow of the streetlight, Jake saw one of them draw a gun. He let go of his own gun, spun the wheel, and punched the gas. Zamira's car, a yellow Mustang, turned in front of him. He bumped the side of her door and threw his car into reverse. She backed up too, then shot forward in a cloud of burning rubber, away down the street. Jake followed, glancing in his rearview mirror. The men were sprinting across the intersection. One dropped to a knee in a shooting position and Jake ducked.

He heard the gunshots. Two of them, but nothing struck his car. He fought to stay on the road as he careened around the corner at the bottom of the hill, swerving to avoid a telephone pole, then accelerating to try to keep up with Zamira. When she came to a red light, she never even slowed but blasted through the top of the intersection, scattering a little wake of orange sparks. Jake kept after her as she wove through the decrepit streets of tenements, empty warehouses, and broken-down factories.

Finally, she turned onto an on-ramp and went north on the interstate, slicing through the thin traffic at ninety miles an hour. When they hit a straight section of open road, the wheel of Jake's Taurus started to wobble. Zamira had pumped it up over one hundred.

When her brake lights went on, the car slowed down fast. Jake hit his brakes, too, and nearly lost control as he swerved to make the exit. At the bottom of the ramp she ran another red light, hanging a left and shooting under the bridge, then up a hill before spinning around and coming to a stop in the parking lot of a Motel 6. Jake turned into the lot and pulled up alongside of her, putting his window down.

Her window hummed down, too, but she kept her eyes on the highway and the ramp at the bottom of the hill.

"I thought you were with them," Jake said.

She was breathing fast and though her hands gripped the wheel, her arms were trembling.

"Yes and no," she said. "I don't think they followed us."

"I doubt it," Jake said. "How yes and how no? You can't have it both ways."

She turned her attention to him. "Let's not sit here. Follow me and I'll tell you. I'll tell you what you really want to know, and then you can leave."

Zamira put her window up and the Mustang into gear. Jake followed her for a couple of miles, into a suburban neighborhood to a modest colonial with white siding and black shutters. It stood shoulder to shoulder with similar houses on a tree-lined street. She drove into the garage and he pulled in to the driveway beside a dented white compact. She waited for him in the shadows, asked him to come inside, then closed the garage door behind them.

She unlocked the door to the house, motioning Jake through the small kitchen and toward a couch in the living room. The place was full of furniture, but there was something sterile about it, as if it had all been ordered off the showroom floor.

"Drink?" she asked.

"Vodka if you have it. The whole bottle. Maybe a beer chaser."

She took two Michelob Ultras from the refrigerator and a bottle of vodka from the cupboard along with a glass and set it all down on the coffee table. She sat on the other end of the couch and drew one foot up underneath her as she raised her drink. Jake poured two quick glasses of vodka, knocking them off.

"Stuff like that makes me thirsty." His hands shook.

She held out her bottle. He picked up the other beer and clinked it against hers, took a swig, and waited.

"Better?" she asked.

"Yup. Nice car you have for a secretary," Jake said, looking around. "Nice place, too."

"The car is from a friend," she said. "That would have been stupid."

She kicked off her shoes and put her bare feet up on the coffee table, crossing her long legs. Through the worn and faded jeans, Jake could see their muscular outline. She unzipped the baggy gray sweatshirt and pulled it to the edges of her shoulders. Now, below her snug peach T-shirt and above the low-cut jeans, he could see the bones of her hips and the dark crescent of stomach. With one hand, she undid the ponytail in her hair and shook her head so that it cascaded around her shoulders. One long lock fell across the bad side of her face and she smiled at Jake as if it wasn't there.

"Last time we got to this point, I woke up with a headache and people trying to kill me," Jake said, taking a swig of beer.

"I'm sorry about that," she said, looking down, her voice quiet. "They wanted me to get your extra key."

"Christ, that's how they got in. They shot at me."

"They told me they only needed to go through your things," she said. "I never would have done it if I'd known."

"Guess you made up for it," Jake said, smiling at her until she returned it.

"It's never a good idea to mix business with pleasure," she said, her smile growing.

"You have to be kidding."

"Not yet." She shook her head and picked up a notepad and a pen off the table next to the couch where the phone sat. She scribbled something down, ripped the top sheet from the pad, and handed it to him.

"This concludes our business," she said. "So, now you can relax."

It was a name, Van Buren.

"How's it done?" he asked, holding the paper up in the air.

"Sam's family," she said. "That's them."

36

"How do you know? Sam came from Albania. What's this name?"

Zamira shook her head.

"I heard them talking today," she said. "When they shut down the office, they moved me to a small office over the social club. Sam came from a very important family. The Van Burens. *The* Van Burens."

"What about you?" Jake asked. He realized now what was wrong with the place. There were no pictures on the walls. No knickknacks on any of the shelves. No books. No magazines. It reminded Jake of a set. The only lights on were the ones in the room where they sat. Beyond the windows and even in the hall to the front of the house, everything was black.

"To get out of my country, you had to work," she said. Her fingers strayed to her face and she ran the tip of a finger down along the thin white scar. "A girl can work for seven years in a jerk shack, a massage parlor, and then she's free in America. That's what they tell you."

She made a motion with her hand.

"I get the idea," Jake said. "And you?"

She shrugged. "My parents and my two brothers were all killed. I was thirteen. We didn't have much, a small house outside Tirana. Some goats and chickens. But my father, he pounded it into my head, that for a girl it was better to be dead than a prostitute.

"So I'm stubborn," she said. "I got here and I wouldn't do those things. They thought they could beat me into it. Finally they took it. That's when they cut me. But a whore who won't do what she's told isn't worth a nickel. They would have killed me sooner or later, except that everything else, I would do. No matter what it was, I did it and I did it well and they kept finding things that needed someone like me to do, a young girl who wasn't afraid. After a few years, Lukaj brought me to Syracuse. They gave me a place. I worked hard and never had any problems."

She looked him in the eye and said, "One of my jobs was to get the babies, from Tirana. They had the paperwork, and I pretended to be the mother. I was glad. To help those babies. I knew that Cakebread was finding good homes. People with money. People who cared."

"And Sam?"

Zamira closed her mouth and where the scar ran through it, Jake thought he saw a twitch. Her eyes glimmered. She sniffed and turned away, then took a deep breath.

"During that time," she said, "there were some babies that came from someplace else. I remember because I didn't go to Albania for several months. I asked back then if I wasn't getting the children anymore and they told me that Cakebread found an easier way to get babies right here, in America."

"How do you know Sam was one of them?"

"I didn't, until today. I heard them talking about you and Sam," she said, "and I heard them talking about the Van Burens. You know the Van Burens?"

"The political family?" Jake said, his insides tightening. "*The* Van Burens? Are you kidding?"

"On the Hudson River," she said. "Rhinecliff. Some estate. There's no other, right?"

"I have Sam's papers."

"Lukaj could get papers from Albania to say anything. Every time I went over, they gave me a new passport to come back. I'm sure Sam's papers were like the rest, very official. I don't know who, I always met the same man, Amin. He always had the papers."

"What about now? What about you?"

She stared at him, then moved closer and touched his face. Her voice dropped to a whisper.

"You have what you want. No more business," she said, kissing him.

"What about the goats?"

"What goats?"

"Your goats. What were their names?"

"Funny."

She slipped out of the sweat jacket, and through her shirt he could feel the strong contours of her back. She took his hand and moved it up underneath her shirt to the lace of her bra. A hot current shot through Jake's center, making it hard to breathe. She pulled away, breaking the kiss, and took his hand. She led him upstairs and took off his coat.

When she dropped it to the floor, the gun clunked on the wood. Zamira took it from the pocket, held it up, pinching the trigger guard between her fingers and laughing. Jake stiffened.

"Not much of a gun, is it?" she said, setting it beside a hairbrush on top of her dresser.

"Would you think badly of me if I said, 'It's all in the way you use it'?"

She laughed and moved in close, put her hands on his chest, and pushed him back onto the powder-white comforter of a big four-poster bed.

Zamira straddled his hips and leaned over so her hair fell around their faces and her nose touched his. They kissed and she unbuttoned his shirt, then removed her own. Jake reached up and cupped his hands, feeling through the lace while she shimmied out of her pants, giggling as she reached for his.

When he was naked, she lay beside him and he ran his fingertips over the contour of her hip. She put her arm around his neck.

In a whisper, she said, "Be nice."

Jake recoiled.

"What's wrong?" she asked, touching his face with the back of her fingers.

Jake pulled her naked body tight to his, holding her and listening to the sound of his own breathing. He took a deep breath. "Nothing. I'm fine."

37

Twice through the night, Jake woke and clung to her in the softness of the sheets. When he opened his eyes the third time, vertical rays of sun had stabbed their way through the curtains and he slid out of the bed without waking her. He dressed quietly, studying the lines of her face, her full lips and their hint of a smile, the long dark eyelashes, and the scar that marred its perfection the way a jagged crack would ruin a china vase.

Downstairs, he found the pad and pen by the phone and wrote I WILL BE BACK. COFFEE/SHOWER.

He set the note down on the kitchen table where he was sure she'd see it, then got into his car and headed back to his new hotel so he could shower and change for the uplink shot with Nancy. He put on his dark blue suit with a powder blue shirt and a green tie. When he got off the elevator, he cased the lobby before darting through it. He checked the rearview mirror repeatedly on his way to the shoot.

He got there in plenty of time and Muldoon had everything set up. Jake looked over the final scripts and nodded his approval. He did a couple of dry runs, glancing down at the script for help until he had it cold. While they waited for Nancy in New York, Muldoon asked about his investigation. Jake gave Muldoon a conspiratorial smile and said he didn't want to get anyone's hopes up yet, but that things were still on track.

When the shoot was over, Joe Katz got into Jake's ear over the satellite and told him about an important story he wanted him to throw together, quickly. He explained that his own boss, the president of Galaxy Television, had a daughter at Syracuse University who had just won a cell phone movie contest and that she was getting an award that afternoon.

"I guess Oliver Stone is speaking to the kids and he's presenting it, so you can get the two of them together," Katz said.

"I thought you said it was important," Jake said. "Oliver Stone is a dipshit."

"It's the boss's daughter."

"He wrote *Conan the Barbarian*," Jake

said. "Did you know that? A cell phone movie? Jesus, Joe."

"He asked for you specifically, Jake. What am I? Your fairy godmother? Do I have to keep turning pumpkins into gold for you?"

"Pumpkins to gold? What the hell are you talking about?"

"Whatever. We've talked about it too much already. We're going to lose the uplink. Good work on the bunker man. Nancy loves it."

"Oh boy, now I'll be able to sleep at night," Jake said, but Katz didn't even hear him. The audio in his earpiece went dead and he pulled it free, unclipping it from its cable and sticking it into his pocket before unclipping the mike and handing it to Skip Lehman.

He told Muldoon about the president's daughter. The producer nodded as if he already knew and said he'd do the legwork to set it up. Jake asked if Muldoon could give him an hour or two to get breakfast before they did the voice-over work. Muldoon said no problem, they could meet at the sound studio at SU at eleven, then do the interview in the afternoon, so Jake got into his car and headed back to Zamira's.

He didn't expect her to still be sleeping, but he was thinking he could talk her into a cup of coffee, if not breakfast. Even though she had told him she was done answering questions, Jake had a feeling things might have changed.

When he pulled into the driveway, he was surprised to see the front door ajar. He'd come out that way and was almost certain he'd closed it behind him. He pushed it open and stepped inside, then closed it and turned the bolt.

"Zamira?" he said.

The house was still. Jake felt something creep up his spine. He went into the kitchen and examined his note. It seemed to have been moved, but he couldn't be certain. He stuck it in his pocket, chuckled, and went upstairs. The chill returned when he reached the top step, but he shrugged it off and went down the short hall.

He froze in the doorway to her bedroom. Zamira lay spread out in her underwear, face-up on the bed. The sheets and comforter were in a tangle on the floor. Jake felt his fingernails pierce the palms of his hands. His stomach heaved and he staggered back.

The small dark hole in her temple had soaked the mattress in blood. On the wooden floor, a little brass shell casing glinted up at him, and on the night table beside the bed rested the Colt .25.

38

Jake clutched his gut and swallowed with a choke. Acid burned the back of his throat. He stepped into the room and nudged the shell casing with his toe before kneeling down for a better look. It was small, a .25-caliber. He stood and stared at the little Colt. He reached out for it, but stopped his hand before he touched it and pulled away.

From outside, he heard the distant sound of sirens. He thought of the fire trucks and crossed the little hall to the window in the front room. The sirens were getting closer, but Jake stood frozen with shock and disbelief. Through a gap in the curtain he saw a police car pull up. Two uniformed cops got out and marched up the driveway. Their squad car was parked at an angle half in the driveway, half in the road.

He darted back out, across the hall and into the bedroom. He scooped the gun up off the nightstand and picked up the casing off the floor. He went into the bathroom and yanked back the thin frilly curtains on the window. Downstairs, he could hear the knocking and the muffled sound of the men calling out.

Jake heaved the window up, stood on the toilet, and gripped the window frame, then stuck his feet out and wormed his way through. He hung from the sill for a moment before dropping to the bushes below. His bad knee sent a jolt through him. He struggled to his feet and fought through the tangle of brush. When he hit the grass, he sprinted awkwardly around the corner of the house. He paused behind a tree and saw that the cops had gone in, so he dashed down the driveway, half dragging his bad leg. He jumped into his car and fumbled with the key before stabbing it into the ignition. He slammed the car into reverse and swerved around the nose of the black squad car, spinning the wheel so the rear of his own car swung out into the street. Without even looking back, he jammed it into drive and stepped on the gas, surging up the street and around the corner.

There was no one behind him when he shot out of the housing development and onto a main road, but after he rounded the corner, he saw a dark blue sedan that had been waiting to turn in suddenly whip around and accelerate toward him. Jake stamped on the gas pedal. He wove through the traffic of the double-lane road, then fishtailed around the corner at the next intersection, working his way back toward the interstate.

The road he'd turned on was only a single-lane, though, and he quickly caught up to a slow-moving car and leaned on his horn, flashing his lights. The driver didn't budge and Jake swung out into the other lane. An oncoming car blared its horn. Brakes squealed, and Jake flattened the gas pedal and swung back in front of the slow-moving car a split second before the crash. The car he had passed swerved and pulled over, and Jake saw the nose of the blue sedan surging up from behind.

There was a red light up ahead and a row of cars waiting for it to turn. Jake pressed on, swerved around them on the right, kicking up dust and stones and nicking a light pole with his mirror, but making it around the bend, the sound of horns chasing him. He was on another two-lane road now and he wove through traffic, hung a left on a yellow light, passed the Motel 6, and saw the highway down below. The dark blue car was still back there. He rocketed down the hill and shot into the curve of the highway entrance.

When he saw the traffic crawling up the ramp to merge onto the highway, he reacted instantly. If he stopped, they'd have him. He swung the wheel and cut left, driving off the road and bouncing down the embankment. He hit the ditch so hard that his forehead banged the windshield, but his foot was full on the gas and he came up out of it and had enough momentum to carry him out onto the highway.

There was a shriek of tires and horns, but somehow he made it into the stream, weaving through the traffic, tasting the blood that ran down his face from the bump on his forehead, and getting off at the very next ramp. There was a shopping mall there with a parking garage. He careened down into it and found a spot in one of the darker corners. He shut the engine off and sat there, trembling.

He closed his eyes and saw her lying there with blood on the bed, then opened them wide and stared at the jagged fissures in the concrete wall.

He waited, expecting any moment for either the Albanians or the police to rap a gun barrel against the car window. Visions of running through the garage filled his mind, but when he went to open the door, a weight pinned his hand to his lap. He broke down the facts, examining the evidence the way he knew the cops would. The chance that they hadn't connected him still remained. They had a description of the car, but there was no reason to think anyone had gotten his license plate.

After an hour, he found he could move. He got out slowly and walked around the car. Except for the mirror, it wasn't in bad shape, but he'd report it stolen from his hotel after the uplink with Nancy. The gun and the shell casing were the only things that could tie him to the murder. Any hair or fibers in the bed or fingerprints on the beer can or vodka glass could be explained. Zamira had picked him up and they had had a night together.

He felt the bulge of the gun in his pocket and looked around. Cars came and went and people walked in and out of the glass doors that led into the mall's lower level. He knew the lake lay just beyond the railroad tracks outside the mall. He limped up the ramp and out into the sunshine.

Walking as briskly as his knee would allow, he crossed the parking lot, the road, and the railroad tracks until he came to the edge of the green water. After looking around, he heaved the gun as far out as he could, then did the same with the casing before he hobbled back to the mall to catch a cab.

He tried Muldoon's cell phone and got a machine, then gave the cabbie the address of his original hotel, where he thought he might find the producer. Muldoon came to the door in his boxers and holding a peanut butter and jelly sandwich. He winced when he saw Jake and started shaking his head.

"They went ballistic," Muldoon said. "You look like shit."

"Do you know what the hell happened to me?" Jake asked, pushing his way into the room.

"Yeah, you missed the interview with the president's daughter and Katz ripped me a new ass. Like I've got the leash on you. Christ, does that hurt?" Muldoon said, craning to get a better look at Jake's forehead. "You gotta call Katz. I don't know if you can save yourself on this one, Jake, but you gotta call him right now."

Jake sat on the edge of the producer's bed, looked up at him, and said, "Save? We just delivered what's going to be the highest-rated show for the year."

"Just call."

Jake took out his cell phone and dialed the office. Katz got on the phone. His words were wound up and they popped from the phone one or two at a time. Jake told him the story, how he was working a lead on the Albanians, what had happened to him the night before and then this morning, leaving out the fact that the woman who had saved him was dead. He told him excitedly about his FBI contact warning him away and the possibility that the Van Buren family was involved. When he finished, the phone was silent for a minute.

"You there?" Jake asked.

"You done?"

"Done? You need more?"

"We'll pay you till the end of your contract. That's it. I'm sending Sara up to do the rest of the bunker wraps. I'm sorry. Good luck, Jake."

Jake started to talk, but the line was dead. He looked at his phone and cursed. Muldoon puckered his lips and looked away.

39

Eva was half in the bag by the time Jake rolled in. He found her in the big room listening to Frank Sinatra tunes, her pitcher of gin and tonic half empty and glittering on the sideboard by the window in the late afternoon light. Jake wet his lips at her offer of a drink, but said he had a long drive.

"You ought to have one," she said. "You look like you need it."

Jake touched the cut on his forehead and ran his tongue over the chip he had discovered in his tooth on the way there.

"I've got to drive."

"What's the hurry?" she asked. "Spend the night."

"Trouble at work."

Eva raised an eyebrow. Her next question got cut short by Sam, who burst into the room with a .22 rifle in the crook of his elbow and a dead rabbit in his hand, dangling by its back legs.

"Jesus Christ," Jake said.

Sam grinned and held the rabbit even higher.

"Parker's making stew," he said.

"Hunting is a family tradition," Eva said, raising her glass before finishing it off.

"Head shot," Sam said, extending the rifle to Jake. "Grandma said you don't waste the meat. You said get along."

"Every man where I come from can ride a horse and shoot a gun," she said, filling her glass as well as a second she took down from the shelf of crystal.

"Can we get my dad on one?" Sam asked.

"I've been thinking about buying horses. My father rode Arabians."

Jake looked from Sam to Eva.

"Next time," he said. "We've got to hit the road. Get your stuff."

"You're exhausted," Eva said, taking a sip. "Look at you. At least stay for dinner. Sam hasn't eaten since breakfast. He and Parker fished through lunch."

"I'll go fill the pot," Sam said.

"Not stew," Eva said, handing the second glass to Jake. "We're having sea bass, but I can have him grill the tenderloins and braise them with raspberry sauce for an appetizer."

"Eva, I'm serious," Jake said, but he took the glass and had a sip.

241

"So am I," she said, returning to her seat and looking up at him with her chin in the air.

They stared at each other across the room. A little smile tugged at the corner of Eva's mouth and Jake pursed his lips and took a drink.

"I take that as a yes," Sam said, heading toward the kitchen and calling Parker's name.

"Ask Parker to bring your father's bag in," Eva shouted after him.

Jake finished his drink and settled into a low-backed burgundy leather chair. Parker appeared and without a word struck a match, touching it to some paper under a fire he'd built before disappearing again.

"I wonder where Sam is," Jake said.

"I'm sure changing for dinner," Eva said, crossing the room and refilling his glass.

"You got him to change for dinner?"

"He has the makings of a gentleman," she said, walking back to her spot. "I've always thought so."

Jake looked out at the lake and sighed. The mountains rising up around them felt like a protective force. The crackling fire and the smell of balsam and wood smoke made the past few days seem like a bad dream.

Sam showed up at the table wearing a dark green polo shirt and khakis. His hair was still a mess. After dinner, they played Scrabble and Jake and Eva drank fifty-year-old port. Sam made up words like "snarf" and Eva would laugh at them until tears ran down her face. At nine, Parker appeared, cleared his throat, and whispered something into Eva's ear. She spelled "excursion" with the X on a triple score square and claimed victory before she excused herself and wished them good night, giving Sam a kiss on the cheek.

"She takes a bath," Sam said, watching her disappear up the stairs. "I think he doesn't like her to get too hammered."

Jake started to pick up the game and said, "I was thinking maybe you could stay here a little longer."

Sam's face clouded over.

"I thought we were going home," he said.

"You're doing okay here," Jake said, heading up the stairs. "School's almost out. It's good for her."

"What about what we're doing? Finding my mom," Sam asked, following Jake into the guest bedroom.

Jake sighed. "I ran into some complications."

"Part of the job."

"Thanks, Coach."

"Rabbit get to you?" Sam asked, picking a pillow off the bed and throwing it at the headboard.

"Hey, I'm glad. She thinks you've got the makings of a gentleman."

"Bull."

"Look. This thing is getting dangerous."

"Family first, right?"

"What do you mean?"

"Cut the crap," Sam said. "You go home, I go, too."

40

Jake started from his sleep.

The noise at the door made him jump. He thought about Zamira. He thought about Lukaj.

It was only Sam, coming in from the hall.

"What's up?" Jake asked.

"Car's packed," Sam said. "I told Parker to scramble some eggs."

Sam's hair was a mess, and he wore a scruffy pair of jeans and one of Jake's faded old workout T-shirts. Jake touched his bruises and hobbled into the shower.

Eva joined them at breakfast, stone sober and prim in a flower-print dress and a straw sun hat. She drank tea and ate sausages that Parker brought on a salver, removing the silver cover with a flourish. Outside, an oriole sang in hopes of a mate and hummingbirds darted in and out of the red plastic window feeder.

When they got up to leave, Sam kissed

Eva's cheek.

"School ends soon," she said, patting Sam's cheek and directing her piercing gaze at him. "I expect you back for a visit."

When Sam looked at him, Jake nodded. Sam took her hand and told her he would be back.

Jake marched through the newsroom with Sam in tow, trying to ignore all the eyes he felt on his back. He stopped at the desk of Joe Katz's assistant, Penny, and saw the overnight ratings sheet on her desk.

"Nice," he said, scooping them up and reading the numbers. They were twice the normal audience. It was unprecedented.

"The Catherine Anastacia interview run last night?" Jake asked, looking up at her.

"Yup."

"They cut me out of it?"

Penny's face turned red. "Not completely."

"Let me guess," Jake said. "Sara did the voice-overs? The toss to Nancy?"

Penny looked down.

"LA must be happy with this," Jake said.

"Thrilled," Penny said.

"Where is he?"

"Um, downstairs," she said, suddenly interested in her computer screen.

"Control room?" Jake said. "Doing an uplink?"

"Something," she said. "You can wait right here. He should be done any time."

"That's okay," Jake said, taking Sam and starting for the stairs. "I'll catch him there."

"You should probably wait here," she said.

Jake kept going, passing the desks of editors, production assistants, researchers, bookers, people Jake had worked with for several years, all of whom averted their eyes. The only thing Jake could think of was the dead girl, lying on her bed, and that let him share in their revulsion as his feet slapped the concrete steps on his way down the back stairwell.

He could tell by the glow of lights from the bank of screens that something was being shot, but it wasn't until he slipped quietly into the back that he realized that they already had someone in the adjacent studio, auditioning for his job. He stopped before Sam could realize what was going on and in a whisper asked him to wait outside.

The five top executives for *American Outrage,* along with several suits from LA, were crowded together, elbow to elbow, all staring up at the program feed at a kid with straight dark hair and icy blue eyes. Even in an Italian suit it was obvious that he was lean and muscular and taller than Jake. Nancy bantered back and forth with him, simpering in a schoolgirl way that made Jake want to puke. To wrap it up, the two of them exchanged smiles, then a little laugh that caught on with the crowd in the control room, who broke out in a collective giggle.

Joe Katz leaned over and switched on his microphone.

"Thanks very much, Skye. Nancy, thank you. That was great."

The room was abuzz before the lights even came on. When they did, Joe Katz saw Jake by the door and popped out of his seat, ushering him into the hallway.

"Skye?" Jake said, shaking his arm free. "Are you fucking kidding me?"

"What the hell happened to your face?" Katz asked.

"Where'd you get that guy?" Jake asked. "Some modeling agency?"

"Hi, Sam," Katz said with an awkward smile.

"Can I talk to you in private?" he said to Jake, leading him into a greenroom, a place full of overstuffed furniture where guests were kept before an appearance on the set. There was a bowl of M&M's on a sideboard and Katz held it out for Jake.

"I saw those numbers last night," Jake

said, shaking his head at the candy. "Great, now you got Skye. It's like the daily double."

"I thought you were busy with Sam's thing," Katz said.

"Joe, I need to talk to you," Jake said.

"Don't do this, Jake," Katz said, turning away and replacing the bowl.

"Remember the guy who escaped from prison with the warden's wife?" Jake asked. "He wouldn't talk to anyone, then I showed up. Remember the woman whose husband got tossed off that cruise ship? That schoolgirl up in Alaska who killed her mother? Come on, Joe."

"What's done is done," Katz said. He pushed his hands up under his glasses to rub his eyes, then let them fall back into place and looked at Jake. "You'll find something else. Look at you, when you heal up. How about your approval rating with women in our last focus group? I'll get that thing to your agent."

"I'd rather sell cars than sit behind a desk and read the screen," Jake said. "Come on, Joe. I'm no talking head."

"This is beyond me," Katz said, looking down at his desk. "You burned all your chits, and I'm done burning mine."

"What about a freelance job?" Jake said, leaning forward, selling it. "A blockbuster.

You don't pay me unless I deliver. What about the Van Burens? They're the ones behind all this. You know this is my power alley. I'm not bullshitting. This is huge. You'll have Diane Sawyer knocking down your door, *People* and Howard Stern will be crawling up your ass."

"Christ." Katz sat down on the edge of the leather couch.

Jake could see his mind working and he sat in the adjacent chair, leaning toward the producer.

"It'd have to be shocking," Katz said with a faraway look. "I mean something that would gum up the elections. The one brother, Peter, he's still on the Intelligence Committee, right? I'd need the whole family to dance. Him *and* the sister who's married to that movie producer. The mom, too. I'd pay for that."

"One hundred thousand for five two-part segments."

Katz snorted.

"You paid that for Al Fayed."

"That was Princess Di. The bodyguards. The photos with Dodi when they were kids. You're nuts."

"I'm talking organized crime," Jake said.

Katz's head lolled and he winced. "We've seen that."

"White slave trade."

"You're bullshitting me."

"Selling babies."

"Christ," Katz said, the stunned look of a man hit with a board filling his face. "If it wasn't you, I'd say bullshit. Are you serious? What are they doing with Albanians?"

"A hundred thousand?"

"You get that," Katz said, his hand fluttering to rest on his knees as he leaned forward, "I'll pay you a hundred *and* figure a way to get your contract renewed. Your kid's okay with this, right? That's good."

"Sam?" Jake said, raising his eyebrows. "He hasn't got anything to do with this."

"He's the story, Jake," Katz said, sitting back and dropping his jaw. "Don't tell me you don't see that."

"My kid's not a story," Jake said. "He's out of this. It's the Van Burens."

Katz laughed. "He is a Van Buren, right? This whole baby thing. This is what you're doing for Sam. That's the story. Sam."

"I don't know if Sam's theirs," Jake said. "He's not going to be a part of this. He's thirteen. Middle school. The age where kids perfect being mean."

"Jake, you're kidding."

"You're kidding. Are you that fucked up?"

"Why? Because it's you this time? All I'm

talking about is the same thing you get from everybody else. What do I hear you say? It's just a brief window into their world."

"The window's closed," Jake said, getting up and heading for the door.

"Maybe," Katz said from behind him, "but it's still glass."

41

The body was already gone by the time Niko got over to the clubhouse. The somber expressions worn by the police had infected the club's typically friendly staff. Niko walked through the dining room, watching the commotion out on the eighteenth green through the curving bank of windows. A technician knelt down beside the large bloodstain to take a sample. Niko slipped out the side door and inside the yellow tape that kept the media at bay, and approached the green.

He felt a large hand on his shoulder and looked up at the big blond face that seemed familiar.

"You can't be in here, sir."

"I am a member," Niko said, peering at the name on the uniform, then looking up. "Ron Osinski?"

The cop nodded and his grip loosened.

"Niko Karwalkowszc," Niko said, touching his own breastbone. "You're on the other side of the law now. What was it? Shoplifting, I think. Your mother didn't want you to have a lawyer. 'Jail,' she said."

The cop's face went red and he let Niko's arm drop and said, "Mr. Karwalkowszc. Hi. What are you doing here?"

"I'm a member," Niko said. "I had a tee time at eleven o'clock with a client. I guess not."

"No," Osinski said. "I'd say this afternoon but with what we got, you never know."

"A body on the golf course?" Niko said, wagging his head.

Osinski looked around. Under his breath he said, "They don't know if it happened here, but this is where they think the head came off."

Niko sucked in a pocket of air. "Any idea who?"

Osinski shrugged. "They don't tell us. Not me anyway. It's the FBI. Someone said something about some Albanians."

Niko looked in the direction of Osinski's nod and saw an enormous black man in a well-made dark suit. His eyes were hidden behind a pair of Ray-Bans and he was talking to what looked like a detective in a blue blazer and tan slacks.

"Get the paper," Osinski said in a low

tone. "A newspaper guy got a picture last night before they taped it off."

"I'll just go back in this way," Niko said, "so I don't get you in trouble. My job is to get you out of trouble, right?"

"Sure," Osinski said, his face flaring up again.

"Tell your mother hello from me," Niko said. "She must be proud."

Niko went back across the street. His newspaper waited on the step. Niko went inside. Another police car rolled up the street and pulled into the club. He stood in his living room and opened the paper to the local section. Page one had a three-column picture of the dead man on the eighteenth green. The body was facedown. No head. No hands.

Niko changed into his gray suit. With the local section folded on the front seat beside him, he backed out of the driveway and headed up the hill past the golf course. With such a blue sky and balmy temperature, the fairways were conspicuously empty.

It was less than fifteen minutes to the big house on the farm. He passed the original farmhouse and barn, gray and rotted. One of the dark blue silos had fallen and rested at a forty-five-degree angle, crumpling its brother like an old top hat. A quarter mile down the road, Niko turned and passed through a gauntlet of massive pine trees where a man in a leather coat sat on a lawn chair in the narrow strip of grass. The man took one hand off his gun to speak into a handheld radio as Niko went past. The trees spit him out into a twenty-acre clearing, and there it was.

Three stories high. The brainchild of Murat's wife, an Albanian girl who had grown up in the Bronx and been influenced by the neighborhood in Scarsdale, where her own mother had cleaned homes. There was something of a Georgian mansion in its size and stature, but its narrow square columns and a brick façade that adorned only its face missed the note. The bulk of the structure was wrapped in white vinyl siding, like a regular suburban home on growth hormones. To one side of the long straight driveway was a man-made pond in the shadow of a massive gazebo. On the other side, a white rail fence cordoned off a long single-story stable and half a dozen horses no one ever rode.

Niko followed the blacktop around back and parked his Buick under the single shade tree next to a five-car detached garage. Beyond a white picket fence was the Olympic-size swimming pool, where a single faded raft floated back and forth according to the direction of the fickle breeze. Niko walked up the back steps and in through the kitchen. Through the archway that opened into the living room Niko heard Dardana Lukaj's voice, bitching about the swelling in her legs and how the house-keeper had misplaced the special socks she'd ordered off the Internet.

Stepping lightly, Niko cut through the dining room, circumventing Dardana's domain and winding his way through the house toward Murat's study, where he was welcomed by the stale smell of cigarettes and the back of his client's head. Murat sat at his desk, facing the bay window that looked out over the treetops. Niko paused to admire the panoramic view: the entire city of Syracuse, its suburbs, and most of the five central counties in upstate New York. On one side of the vista beyond the city, Oneida Lake lay sprawled between north country trees and a great swamp to the south. On the other, farmland stretched to the big lake, whose shore was marked by a burr on the horizon, a nuclear cooling tower with a plume like the embryo of a cloud.

Murat was on the phone, dressed in a midnight-blue velour sweat suit, but he spun around in his high-backed leather chair to face Niko. Small ears protruded from his moon face that might have been funny if it weren't for the flicker of icy blue eyes and the wag of his head that told Niko to sit down. One wall of the office was lined with bookshelves that bore only a menagerie of souvenirs common to national parks, monuments, and theme parks. A model of the arch over St. Louis. A grizzly statue from Glacier National Park. Mickey Mouse. A trumpet lamp from Memphis. A salmon clock from Seattle. A vial of sand from Venice Beach.

A spectacular plasma screen nearly filled the opposite wall. It was divided into quadrants, and each section flickered with the images from one of four separate television stations. News, an MTV reality show, Maury Povich, and a skateboard competition on ESPN2. The keyboard remote that operated the system rested on the desk between Murat's computer and an open ledger.

Niko set his newspaper down over the top of the remote, knowing that when Murat was finished with the call, his fingers would instinctively seek its buttons to either change the channels or restore the volume. Then he circled the desk to sit in one of two low-backed leather chairs facing Murat and waited for him to be finished.

"He went to the studio?" Murat said into the phone, his eyes passing over the newspaper, finding Niko, and offering up a wink. "Good. Yes. Follow him. I'll tell you when it's time."

When he hung up, Murat opened his arms and said Niko's name amid the jingle of bracelets.

"Is this you?" Niko said, pointing to the newspaper, folded to expose the three-column photo of the headless body on his golf green.

Murat glanced down, smiled, and laughed silently.

"Because that is where I live," Niko said, knocking a fist into his palm.

Murat shook his head and clucked, removing a nickel-plated Glock from inside his Puma sweat jacket and examining it. "This is getting to be a dangerous place, this Syracuse."

"I saw a boy I knew who is now with the police," Niko said. "He told me the FBI is here, in town. He said they are looking for some Albanians."

Murat wrinkled his lips and he leaned forward. "You work for me. When you work for me and you make a mistake, then you should feel what I feel."

Niko felt his stomach tighten. "Is it the father?"

"The father?" Murat said, raising his eyebrows. "No, that's your truck driver. The father has nine lives."

"He got away from you?"

"He's a lucky man," Lukaj said, his lips parting to expose a row of crooked teeth. "I may have even found a temporary use for him."

Then his face turned serious. He looked down the sights of the pistol at Niko and said, "But how long can his luck last?"

42

"How do you know this lady?" Sam asked.

Jake shut his car door and waited for Sam to join him. The lush green foothills of the Catskills crowded the river's byway. Boat hulls crowded the docks and a sailboat puttered out toward the Hudson under the sunny blue sky. When Sam rounded the car, Jake started off across the gravel parking lot toward the tent awning in back.

"I knew her from Syracuse. Her husband flew a helicopter for the TV station I worked for. Now she writes for the Middletown paper. I ran into her by chance a few years ago.

"There was a high school teacher in Poughkeepsie, a woman, who was sleeping with her students," Jake said, searching the plastic tables for his old acquaintance. "The teacher's parents lived in Kingston and she holed up there during all the ruckus. Judy found her before anyone and she called me out of the blue."

Sam looked up at him and nodded as if to say *That's just what people do.*

"She got me that interview before everyone else. Wouldn't take a dime. She's different."

As if on cue, a high-pitched hooting sound burst out from beneath the tent. In the depths of its shadows, Jake was able to make out the flutter of a pink silk handkerchief. When they got to the table, Judy rose to her feet, cackling with laughter and saying "hi" over and over until Jake gave her a one-armed hug.

"Oh, your face," she said.

Jake waved it off and said he fell on an outdoor shoot.

Judy's eyes were as black as her wild head of hair. The skin on her thin face was pale except for two spots of pink rouge and some fiery red lipstick. She wore a flowery silk dress and beside her on the plastic table was a wide-brimmed sun hat. He introduced Sam, who took her hand and surprised Jake when he gave Judy a kiss on the cheek that made her blush.

When they sat down, Judy's face turned solemn. She reached over and put a birdlike hand on Jake's arm, giving it a squeeze and telling him she'd heard about Karen, she hoped he'd gotten her card, and how sorry she was. They made small talk after that and learned that Judy's ex was still flying for Channel Nine and that they got along better now, divorced and two hundred miles apart, than they ever had before.

After they ordered crab cakes and salads Jake said, "So what can you tell us about the Van Burens?"

Judy smiled and took a sip of her white wine.

"The Kennedys of the Hudson Valley," she said. "Closest thing we've got to royalty. I like that kind of thing. I've done six interviews right at Ridgewood."

"That's what they call the big mansion, right?" Sam said.

"Have you seen pictures?" Judy asked.

"On the Internet," Sam said.

"You have to see it in person," Judy said, gazing out at the river. "You can smell the gardens as soon as you're through the gate. Four of my pieces were on Peter. Congressmen have to talk to the press, but I also did one with Jan and even one with Gretta when she sponsored the flower show for the hospital."

"Here, look," Judy said, digging into her purse until she came up with a pen that she handed to Sam. "That's the family crest.

Gretta gave that to me."

Sam examined the crest and said, "Is that a lion?"

"The black-footed lion who brought death to its adversaries," Judy said, taking the pen back and gazing at it. "It also meant that the knight who wore it wasn't above a little treachery. The top half is red to symbolize courage. What do you want to know?"

"Something a little more recent than knights," Jake said. "A woman in the family who might have been pregnant in 1992."

"Pregnant?" Judy said. "You're kind of between generations. The next wave of grandchildren are five or six at the oldest. Babies."

"You're sure?" Jake asked.

Judy shrugged and said, "Not one hundred percent. I got here in 2000, so anything before is just the stuff you'd read in *People* magazine or *The New York Times.* You know what happened around then, though? Clint Eggers. He was the big bass guitar player for Heroin Scream. The guy that made the rest of the band look like Smurfs. He married a Van Buren. She wasn't even eighteen, I don't think. They weren't married much more than a month before he died in a car crash."

"What was her name?" Jake asked.

"Mary, no, Martha," Judy said. "I never heard of her until that happened. He died and it hit the news he was married to a Van Buren, a teenage bride."

"I thought George was the oldest," Jake said. "The state senator."

"Well, she was from Peter's first marriage," Judy said.

"First? Isn't he the spokesperson for that Family First movement?"

"Probably why no one really knew about her before Eggers died. Peter's marriage to Martha's mom didn't last long. They kept her existence pretty quiet. Probably shipped her off to boarding school early on. You never saw her at the family things. I heard she was a little wild. Different. Then she married this rocker when she was seventeen."

"Would the paper's archives have anything on the family?" Jake asked.

"You bet," she said. "They're big news around here, and you should have seen the old coot who used to cover them before me. He died right after I got here. Bonkers over the Van Burens. They called him Van Bonkers behind his back."

"Are the archives on line?" Sam asked.

"Microfilm," she said. "I can get you into our library though."

When lunch came, Jake asked Sam if he'd washed his hands. They argued about it for a minute until Sam gave up and disappeared inside.

"You okay?" Judy asked quietly, glancing at the door Sam had disappeared through.

Jake took a deep breath and let it out slow. "Not really. Karen's death still feels like yesterday. Sam's on this kick to find his roots."

"You've got this crazy light in your eye," Judy said.

"I got shot at, believe it or not," Jake said.

"Over this?"

Jake nodded, but put his finger to his lips when he saw Sam coming and said, "I'm fine."

After they ate, Judy showed them her thirty-two-foot sailboat she kept moored at the docks.

"In August I take it out to Nantucket," she said proudly. "By myself."

They walked through the boat before getting into separate cars to go to the library.

On the drive into town, Sam said, "She's a little out there, huh?"

"Brilliant woman," Jake said. "Used to teach English at Syracuse University. We met through her husband, the pilot. She'd have these fantastic dinner parties with poets and scientists and philosophers, all kinds of fascinating people. Your mom and I would go."

"How'd she end up here?" Sam asked.

"She and her husband split," Jake said with a shrug. "And this is something she wanted to do. She's one of the few people in this world who do the job they do because they want to, not for the money, not for anything else."

"Like you?"

"Yeah," Jake said, "but you want me to be honest?"

Sam nodded.

"It's both. I do what I do partly because I love it, but partly it's the money and the other stuff, too."

"People knowing you," Sam said.

"And living on the beach," Jake said. "The platinum card. I'm just being honest. I always try to do that with you."

"I know," Sam said.

When they arrived, Judy introduced them to the woman who ran the archives. She took them down the back stairs into the basement and set them up in a cubicle with a viewing machine and several canisters of microfilm that included everything from

1992, the year Sam was born.

Jake thanked Judy and asked, "Can I get your cell phone? I had an old number in my contacts. That's why I called you at the paper."

Jake inputted the number into his phone, then Judy left them to their research.

"Can we get another one of those?" Sam asked the woman, pointing to the viewer in the cubicle.

She hesitated, then said, "Of course."

"It's so my dad can help out, too," Sam said, the serious expression never leaving his face.

When they got all set up, they each took a canister and began.

"Let's not waste time right now on anything but the front and the local sections," Jake said after he had a feel for the format of the paper. "We can go through and if we get nothing, we can always go back again, but whatever we need should be in one of those."

"Okay. Just make sure you check the entertainment section on Sundays," Sam said.

"Why?"

"They run this little society column there," Sam said.

"Yeah," Jake said. "That's right. Good work."

Sam never looked up, but he did hold up a thumb for Jake to see to let him know he was on board.

They sat there like that for more than two hours. Sam found three references to the family and Jake found one, but neither had anything to do with a baby. Jake's eyeballs began to ache.

"Maybe we'll knock off for today," Jake said, massaging his tear ducts. "Come back in the morning."

"How about going and getting a coffee while I do a little more?" Sam said, rotating the crank on his viewer and focusing in on a new section.

"You want a hot chocolate? Why don't you come?"

"Maybe later."

Jake shook his head and went back to work. It wasn't twenty minutes before he felt a surge of adrenaline. Then a chill fell over him. He thought about what he'd said to Sam on the way over to the paper, how he tried to tell the truth. There was no way he could hide what he'd found from Sam.

He cleared his throat and said, "Hey, Sam, take a look. I think I found something."

"You did?" Sam said, popping up out of

his chair and crowding into Jake's cubicle. "Let me see."

Jake slid the viewer over for Sam to look at. He closed his eyes and could still see the image. A young girl with long dark hair, her swollen face hidden by sunglasses. The men in black suits. The women with dark hats and veils. Flowers everywhere. And in the middle of it all, a gleaming white casket.

"A funeral," Sam said. "And a bunch of the Van Burens. I don't get it."

Sam took his face away from the viewer and looked at Jake with alarm. "Who died? That rock band guy?"

Jake took a weary breath, shook his head, and grabbed Sam's knee.

"I think. Maybe. You did."

43

"Wait, I shouldn't have said that, Sam," Jake said. "It could all be bullshit, a lie. Zamira, this woman I met. The Albanians. Just because they said it, we don't know."

"You know," Sam said. "You've done this thing a million times. You always used to say that to Mom, about your instincts."

Jake took the viewfinder back and looked at the young woman identified as Martha Van Buren-Eggers. The caption to the small article that accompanied the photo read ANOTHER TRAGEDY. It talked about the death of Clinton Eggers the previous December in a drunken car crash in Vail. It talked about their Las Vegas wedding on Halloween. It said little more about the death of the infant other than that he had been stillborn after Martha went into spontaneous labor at Ridgewood, the family estate.

"There should be a death certificate," Jake

said in a murmur.

"You mean there might not be?" Sam said.

"You're here," Jake said.

"Can we find out?" Sam asked. "Can we get it?"

"County courthouse," Jake said, checking his watch. "We might make it."

They picked up quickly and hustled out of the newspaper office with Jake thanking the woman in charge of the archives and telling her they might be back the next day. The courthouse was five blocks away, a cobblestone two-story colonial building with a white cupola. They dashed up the front steps and yanked open the broad white door. The woman in the clerk's office rolled her eyes at the clock, but Jake knew they had two minutes to spare.

"I need a death certificate," Jake said.

The woman sighed deeply and in a monotone asked, "Are you the parent, child, or next of kin, or do you have a documented legal action against the person?"

"No," Jake said. "It's public information, right?"

"No, it's not," she said, looking up at the clock. "And we're closed."

She put a marker up on the countertop and disappeared into the back.

They walked slowly down the courthouse

steps with Jake dialing Judy and asking her if she had a contact who could get him a death certificate at the Ulster County Courthouse.

"I've got a friend in the DA's office," she said. "Whose is it?"

When Jake told her, the phone was silent for a moment before she asked why.

"I don't think that baby really died," Jake said, looking into Sam's big dark eyes. "If there's no certificate, then we'll know it."

"Is this for TV?" Judy asked. "Because I thought, when I saw Sam, that this was something personal."

"It is personal," Jake said. "I'm not even with the show. I actually got fired over all this."

"See, that's why I have to let my guy know what he's getting into," Judy said. "You don't cross these people. They may have some hundred-million-dollar foundation to help sick kids, but you cross them and bad things happen."

Jake motioned for Sam to sit on the bench, then he walked a few feet away and, speaking softly, said, "I've seen bad."

"Not guns and bombs," Judy said. "A bullet you can dodge. A bomb you can diffuse. The things that happen to these people's enemies ruin your life from the inside out, like anthrax. Odorless. Colorless. You're walking along and then you're paralyzed. Then you're finished."

"You'll get it for me?"

"Did you ever meet a woman who said no to you?" Judy said. Then she cackled and hung up.

There was a Quality Inn not far from the courthouse. Jake got a room for them and they had dinner at Monkey Joe's in the historic Rondout District, built by the Dutch in the seventeenth century.

"We should go see Ridgewood," Sam said while they were having cheesecake.

"Just walk up and ring the bell, right?" Jake said. "Ask for a tour?"

"No, just see it. From the gates. Check it out."

"Look," Jake said, "we don't know if these are your people. If they are, there's a pretty damn good chance they don't want you around."

"Just to see it," Sam said. "You heard what Judy said. You have to see it. It might give you some ideas. Besides, what else are we going to do tonight?"

"Looks like they're setting up for a concert in that park," Jake said, nodding out the window.

Sam just stared at him.

■ ■ ■ ■

After Jake paid the bill, they crossed the river and headed south toward Rhinecliff on a highway that ran along the ridge of the Hudson's eastern bank. Every so often the view would open up, exposing the rolling green Catskills and the orange sunset beyond. The river below lay black and still. When they found the turnoff that Judy had described, Jake pulled over to the side of the road.

Crickets and peepers wailed at them from every direction. The sky above the trees was purple now except for a lone dark cloud with a crimson wound down one side. Sam bumped into him as they walked down the gravel drive, trying to stay close. Ahead, a great wall rose from the gloom and as they closed the gap, Jake could make out the spikes atop the massive iron gates. Through the gates, Ridgewood sprawled atop a rise that Jake knew must overlook the river several hundred feet below.

It looked more like a museum than a home, with its fluted three-story columns and triangular Grecian frieze. Two wings extended off the main body and the glow of lights from dozens of windows illuminated the manicured hedges of the surrounding gardens.

Sam sniffed the air and said, "Do you smell them?"

"I do."

They stepped slowly toward the gates. Twenty feet away, they were blasted by white light. Jake jumped back and put his arm up to shield his eyes. Atop the massive stone gateposts, two different bundles of spotlights glared down. Jake took Sam's arm, tugging him along.

They walked briskly back up the drive and were almost to the road when they heard the sound of a car engine and the crunch of gravel from inside the gates. Jake started to jog, and he didn't have to pull Sam along to keep up. As they turned the corner onto the main road, Jake glanced back and saw the shape of an SUV behind a pair of headlights and the tall gates slowly opening.

"Come on," he said, his heart leaping.

They started to sprint, but could still hear the roar of the SUV's engine and the hiss and clatter of the gravel beneath it as it cleared the gates. Jake's car was still a hundred feet away and he knew he wasn't going to make it.

"Wait," he said, grabbing Sam. "Just walk. You're with me. It'll be fine."

They were halfway there when the SUV's brakes squealed and it skidded to a stop at the mouth of the drive. Jake heard an electric window roll down, then the sound of the truck pulling out onto the road and heading their way. It eased up alongside them as Jake was opening the passenger-side door for Sam.

The beam of a high-powered searchlight suddenly lit up the car. Sam's face glowed, his eyes and mouth wide. Jake turned and blocked the light with his arm. He couldn't see the face of the man inside the truck.

"Can I help you?" the man asked in the deep raspy voice of a heavy smoker.

"No," Jake said, dipping his head for an angle that would show him the man's face. "We were just looking."

"You were trespassing," the man said. "Please don't come back."

"When does the tour start?" Jake said. "Isn't this where they filmed *The Haunted Mansion*?"

The man said nothing, but Jake heard the squawk of a radio from inside the truck and then the man's voice softly saying, "Copy. All clear."

Jake waited, then rounded his car and pulled away, the beam of the spotlight holding on to them until he turned the bend up ahead.

"Shit," Jake said, after they'd gone several miles in the dark, "so much for storming the castle."

"They don't have our names or anything," Sam said.

"A deal like that back there?" Jake said. "They got the plates. They'll have our names, addresses, photos, and my job description before we get to the hotel."

44

Jake walked into the bedroom and saw Zamira. He could hear the dribble of blood as it leaked from the crimson hole in her head. Suddenly she sat up, pointing at him and groaning.

Jake's eyes shot open. The groaning was the pipes from the shower in the next room over. Sam was already up and at the computer. He swiveled around in his chair. Jake rubbed the sleep from his eyes and swung his legs out of the bed. He took a couple of deep breaths and shook his head to cast loose the image of the dead girl. Then he stood up and pumped some joviality into his voice.

"Don't you ever sleep in?" he said, being as casual as he could about removing the chair that he had wedged under the door-knob before going to bed.

"Look," Sam said, getting up so that Jake could sit down and read the computer.

"Worms."

"Worms?"

"The early bird."

The Van Buren family foundation had its own Web site. There was a family tree, beginning with William Van Buren and going for seven generations before stopping at the turn of the twentieth century. Only one of the three brothers from that generation was still alive, Jupp, the youngest, who was now ninety-three. The father of those three was Edward, the governor of New York in the twenties.

There was countless information on the foundation, all they'd done, all they planned to do, attacking poverty, bolstering the arts. There were countless papers from Edward Van Buren's governorship. There was a bibliography on the various books written about the family, its fortune, and its various foundations.

"And see this," Sam said, clicking through several screens before stepping back.

It was the Forbes list of the four hundred wealthiest Americans. Number two hundred seventy-two was the Johann Van Buren family with $1.2 billion.

"I guess they don't clean their own toilets," Jake said.

"See how it says the Van Buren 'family'?"

Sam asked. "That's when the money is in a trust. They can't say it's one person's, so they use the guy's name who made the trust."

"How do you know?"

Sam shrugged and looked from the computer screen to the clock. "I been up since five-thirty."

"Good God," said Jake. "So, who was Johann?"

Sam clicked back through several screens to the family tree and clicked on JOHANN VAN BUREN, 1808–1879. The old photo filled the screen, a dark-eyed Dutchman with a thick handlebar mustache.

"His dad built ships," Sam said, "but he's the one that socked it all away, I guess."

"Enough to build Ridgewood," Jake said.

"And get elected to whatever they want," Sam said.

At breakfast, Judy called to say that her friend with the DA had called the county clerk's office first thing. He'd have a copy of a death certificate for a Joshua Van Buren-Eggers in April of 1992 for them by ten. She said she'd meet them for coffee at a Deising's Bakery at ten-thirty. Jake thought about telling her what had happened the previous night, but decided to roll the dice instead and hope the two ends would never meet. He hung up and stared at his glass of tomato juice.

"So, it's not me," Sam said.

Jake kept staring. He took a drink and smacked his lips.

"Maybe," he said. "But maybe not."

Jake didn't want to say what he was thinking until he found out more. He took Sam back to the newspaper. When they got to the microfilm, Jake went right for the obituary section for the day before the funeral. He had to go back two days before he found it, but there it was, Costello Funeral Home.

"Got it," Jake said, pushing the viewer into the back of the cubicle and getting out of his chair.

When he told Sam where they were going, Sam asked why.

"When someone dies," Jake said, "the funeral director is the one who collects the body."

"I think I'm going to be sick."

"So, I'm thinking that — since there's a death certificate, and since I'm sitting here talking to you — there was no body to collect. Maybe he'll know something."

"From thirteen years?"

"He'll remember," Jake said. "The article says it happened at Ridgewood, and he isn't going to forget a place like that."

Sam shrugged. "It does leave an impression."

The Costello Funeral Home was an elaborate brick Victorian house on Cedar Street with a decorative wrought-iron gate whose pickets were capped with gold fleurs-de-lis. There were several people getting ready for a funeral at ten. When Jake smiled at the woman running things, her face lit up in recognition even before he said his name. She said she was Jim Costello's wife, Jacque. She said she loved the show, that she watched it every night, and she took them right around back.

In her excitement, they walked right in on her husband. Jake looked around and quickly covered Sam's eyes, turning him away.

"Whoa," said the undertaker.

He was dressed in black suit pants and shirtsleeves. An ankle-length white apron spattered with blood covered his front. The body for ten was ready to go, a somber-looking old man in a dark suit already tucked into his casket, but on the table was a middle-aged woman. She was completely naked, with large breasts, fiery red hair, and a blue face. The funeral director was pumping fluid into an incision below her neck while blood coursed out of the same cut, spilling over her shoulder and down the gutter alongside the table.

Costello jumped protectively between them and the draining woman, and herded them out of the room while his wife chattered excitedly about who Jake was.

The wife took them into an office and a few minutes later, Jim Costello came in without the apron and wiping his hands on a paper towel. He gave his wife a baleful look, sat down behind his desk, and asked how he could help. The undertaker looked like a grocer's boy with his straight blond hair and innocent blue-eyed stare. His young wife stood by the door, nodding her head.

Jake smiled at her, then looked at Jim and said, "Thirteen years ago, this funeral home buried a baby, one of the Van Burens. From Ridgewood."

Jim's face grew long and he nodded.

"I took over from my dad about a month before that happened," the undertaker said.

"So you remember," Jake said.

45

The funeral director nodded. "That's some place. Plus, that's a sad thing. It's always sad, but, you know, a baby like that."

"Does that happen much?" Jake said. "People having babies at home like that and you have to get a stillborn?"

Sam studied his shoes. Jim shrugged and glanced at the clock.

"We got time," his wife said.

"You get them both ways," Jim said. "Most people have their babies in the hospital, so home is a little less common. They were set up like a hospital though. It wasn't one of these midwives-in-a-bathtub deals. They had it all."

"The Van Burens?"

Sam looked up.

Jim nodded. "Old Doc Randalls was there in a mask. It was like a hospital room and they had her, the mom, sedated."

"Is the doctor, Randalls, is he still

around?" Jake asked.

"No, I buried him two years ago. Cancer."

"What about Martha?"

"I have no idea."

"And, I know this might sound like a strange question," Jake said, "but it's very important. Did you see the baby?"

"Sure."

"Was it blue?"

"Blue?"

"The baby. Stillborn, they aren't getting blood."

"Well," Jim said, stroking his hairless chin, "I can't say, now you ask. The baby was pretty well wrapped up. The blanket was all bloody, and I just took it and put it into a container we use."

"A casket?"

"There's a molded plastic container that goes inside a casket like that," Jim said.

"And once you put it in there, does any-body look at it again?" Jake asked. "The coroner or something?"

"No," Jim said, raising his eyebrows. "You got the death certificate from the doctor and there's no real need with something like that. It's kind of messy and you don't have to embalm them, not like Mrs. Higgins in there."

He nodded toward the back room where

the voluptuous redhead lay. Sam's face turned pink.

"Jim," Jake said, "I'm not trying to say anyone did anything wrong, but is it possible that there wasn't a baby wrapped up in that blanket?"

"No, I felt it," Jim said. "There was blood, too."

"But, I'm not saying this is the way it was, but is it *possible* that it wasn't a baby in that blanket? I mean, could it have been a doll wrapped up?"

"The blood."

"There's a lot of blood when a woman has a baby. They could have mopped it up."

Jim's wife sucked air through her teeth. Sam sat wide-eyed, and Jake tried to keep his eyes on the undertaker.

"Sure," he said. "I guess."

There was nothing more that the undertaker remembered, so Jake thanked him and his wife. On the front steps, she asked if she could have a picture with Jake. Sam rolled his eyes, but Jake smiled and said of course. Afterward, she pressed a business card into Jake's hand with her cell phone on it in case he ever needed anything at all.

As they walked to the car, Sam said, "Why do people do that?"

Jake shrugged. "When people see you on

TV, they feel like they know you. There you are, every night, or once a week, in their house with them sitting on the couch."

"You're not on the couch."

"But they're with you," Jake said. "The magic box."

"Not to me. It's all phony."

"Not all of it," Jake said. "The good stuff is real. This story's real. I've done things like this for the show before, all the time with NPR. Our job now is to chase down every lead we have. You never know which one is going to spring the truth."

"What story?" Sam asked as they got into the car.

"Yours," Jake said, sliding behind the wheel. "All this. A rich woman has a baby that she gives away, but maybe she thinks the baby died. Maybe it wasn't her who gave the baby away, maybe it was the family. Some old doctor goes along with it. That's all real."

"You think she didn't know?" Sam asked, his dark eyes shiny.

Jake started the engine and pulled away from the curb. "You heard what he said. She was loopy. How could she know?"

Sam stared straight ahead and nodded. "Then maybe she didn't give me away."

"Maybe. But I'm betting no matter who

was responsible, we're going to find some connection to the Albanians. They're not all stirred up over *American Outrage* doing a generic piece on organized crime. There's something there. The next thing to do is find her."

"My mom?"

"Martha Van Buren. Whether she's your mom or not, we don't know, but we need to find her."

"I'm going to have a lot to talk to Dr. Stoddard about."

"Is this bothering you?"

"Nope," Sam said, grinning, "it's a real education."

46

The bakery was also in the historic district, just up the hill from the public pier where the ferry to New York City rumbled to a stop, spinning the brown backwater into dozens of whirlpools. They parked in front of the old brick Maritime Museum, where an ancient tugboat was being refurbished in the yard. The small breeze offered up a whiff of sewage. The sidewalks had been rinsed off by the shopkeepers. Jake and Sam skirted the stagnant puddles as they crossed the street to climb the hill.

Judy sat under the protective wisps of a tall fern with her back to the window, dipping a bag of green tea. Jake ordered a coffee, while Sam wandered to the counter and pointed out two big pastries behind the glass. The death certificate lay open on the small round table, and when he returned Sam spun it around with powdered fingers so he could read it.

"Any idea what happened to Martha Van Buren after the funeral?" Jake asked, sipping from the big ceramic mug.

Judy spooned up the teabag and choked it on its own string, extracting the flavor. "Funny, I never thought about it. I have no idea."

Sam's eyes were glued to the certificate, his head tilted so that his shaggy hair shielded their expression. "Did you know Clinton Eggers was from Kansas?"

"Nothing at all?" Jake asked. "Not even a guess? Some family vacation home? A flat in London or something?"

"I told you," Judy said, "she was, not a black sheep, but a little, I guess, on the edge of the family circle."

She watched Sam.

"You can hang on to that," Judy said.

Sam clenched the copy of the death certificate in his hands and stared out the window as they drove from the bakery back to their hotel.

"You okay?" Jake asked as he pulled up in front of their hotel.

Sam nodded.

They went up to the room, and Sam plugged the computer into the cable for a faster connection.

291

"Square one," Jake said.

He sat down and punched in his Au-toTRAK log-on name. He was denied. He tried again.

"They shut me down," Jake said.

"Don't you know anyone else's code?" Sam asked him.

"Never needed it."

"Slide over," Sam said, taking the seat at the desk and looking at the screen. "Are all the log-on names like this? First initial and the last name?"

"Probably."

"What's that Muldoon guy's first name?"

"Conrad?"

Sam started typing.

"Yeah, but you need the password," Jake said.

"A lot of people just use their log-on name for their password," Sam said, typing, then frowning and shaking his head before typing again. "Or their first name or their initials. Sometimes a number, like Conrad One. Mostly people use one."

Jake watched all Sam's attempts get rejected and said, "You don't just guess someone's password, Sam. That's why they're passwords."

"Doesn't Muldoon drive some old Cadillac convertible?" Sam asked, looking up at him. "That big brown El Dorado thing I saw when you met him that day at Shea Stadium?"

"Yeah."

"He's got something goofy on the license plate, right? Assman or something?"

"Newsman," Jake said, chuckling. "He spells it N-W-Z-M-A-N. You were close. Assman would be good for him."

Sam turned to the keyboard and pounded something out, then hit return. He looked up at Jake with a grin.

"We're in."

Jake laughed and shook his head.

"I told you, you need me," Sam said, without looking up from the computer.

He typed for a few minutes, then said, "There's three Martha Eggers in the entire country. One is eighty-seven, one is sixty, and the third is my age."

"So, try Martha Van Buren," Jake said.

Sam typed, waited, then said, "There's a bunch. The closest are three in New York and one in Connecticut."

"No Van Buren-Eggers?"

"No," Sam said after another attempt.

"Her birth date should be somewhere around 1974 or five," Jake said. "That would make her eighteen when you were born."

"Here, 1974," Sam said. "Here's her address. Two-thirty-six East Seventy-second Street. What's this, Dad?"

Jake looked where he was pointing and said, "Associated addresses are like where someone works or has some kind of business. A place they're at a lot other than their residence."

"So we'll take that, too," Sam said, writing down 165 EAST 69TH STREET.

"One thing you know," Jake said, "either she's not doing too bad or the family is still taking care of her. The real estate on the Upper East Side isn't cheap."

"Can we go?" Sam asked.

"Yeah, but this part of it I need to handle," Jake said.

"We're partners on this," Sam said.

"And partners share the load," Jake said. "Sometimes one partner has to step up and the other steps back."

"She's my mom," Sam said.

"We don't know anything, Sam," Jake said. "We need to go slow. We can't walk in there and say, 'Here's the baby you thought was gone.' I don't want to put you in that situation either."

"What situation?"

"I've seen things," Jake said. "People are strange sometimes. It's just better."

"What things? I want to go."

"You can't," Jake said.

Sam glowered at him while they packed and the whole ride down the Thruway to Manhattan. They found a garage near the Seventy-second Street address. There was a Starbucks on the corner and Jake set Sam up there with a hot chocolate, a piece of marble cake, and a copy of the *Post* someone left behind.

"I'll be back," he said.

"Thrills," Sam said, snapping open the paper and taking a bite of cake without looking up.

Jake sighed and headed out.

The doorman at Martha's building recognized Jake from the show, but wouldn't tell him anything more than that Martha wasn't home.

"Can you just tell me when she's *likely* to come back, so I can check in?" Jake asked. "Come on. Help me here. It's nothing bad."

The man clamped his mouth shut and shook his head.

"So much for notoriety, right?" Jake said, and walked out.

The Sixty-ninth Street address was an old brownstone without any signs or nameplates other than a brass placard that had the street number next to a call box with a small round button that rang a buzzer inside. Jake looked up at the camera mounted in the corner above the door and a woman's voice came out of the call box asking whom he was there to see. Jake said Martha Van Buren.

"Of course. Please come in," she said and the lock buzzed.

Jake swung open the door and stepped into a small foyer with a small Oriental rug, a coatrack, an umbrella stand, and a light fixture hanging from a chain. There was a sterile aura to the place that Jake couldn't figure. To the left was a set of white marble stairs. Ahead, down a short hall, was a wooden door that led to a small waiting room with four wingback leather chairs and some magazines. Behind the glass partition over a counter was a young woman in glasses and a tight hair bun. She slid open the glass as Jake approached and said, "Hi, I'm Jodi. Welcome to Llewellyn House."

She handed him a clipboard, asking him to sign in and provide a picture ID.

Jake checked himself from asking what kind of place it was and began filling out the form. When it came to the part where he was to state his relationship to the patient, he put down cousin. The woman took the clipboard back, checked Jake's driver's license, and came out into the waiting room with a warm smile.

"I thought I recognized your name," she said. "I've heard you on NPR, right?"

"You used to," Jake said, returning her smile.

She led him through another door and into a room with a couch, two chairs, a coffee table, and a fireplace. It was the front room, and the window looked out onto the street through beveled glass and decorative black iron bars.

"Martha will be with you in a few minutes," the woman said. "Can I get something? Evian? Coffee?"

Jake thanked her but said he was fine. She smiled and left.

Jake went to the window and drew the curtain aside. He looked out through the bars at the leafy branches of the tree guarding the brownstone and the people walking past. The door opened and Jake spun around.

Martha Van Buren was pale and thin, giving her big dark eyes center stage in her appearance. She wore designer jeans, closed-toed Birkenstocks, and a thin, dark green sweater. Her dark hair was pulled into the same tight bun that the receptionist wore, only several wisps had escaped and they pestered Martha so that she had to sweep them back several times a minute.

She sat in one of the chairs facing the couch and said, "Hello."

She neither smiled nor frowned, but looked expectantly at Jake while she battled back her hair.

"Martha, I'm Jake Carlson."

"Hello," she said, again.

"I know how unusual this is, but I wanted to talk with you about Ridgewood."

She looked away as if he'd flipped on a harsh spotlight. Her back was rigid and her hands gripped the arms of her chair so that her knuckles went white.

"Martha?" Jake said, but she didn't respond.

Jake looked around the room and decided to wait. After a few minutes, he tried again.

"I'm sorry to ask, Martha," Jake said softly. "I'm not doing this for me. I have a son. I'm trying to help him."

"Did they tell you to come?" she said bitterly, still looking away.

"No one told me," Jake said. "It's just me."

"I don't want to talk about that place."

"Did something bad happen? Is that why?"

She shook her head. Jake waited again.

"Are you happy here?" Jake asked.

"Yes," she said quietly.

"You're lucky," Jake said.

"Now, maybe."

"I used to be lucky," Jake said. "I had a wife and I used to tell people she was the best thing that ever happened to me."

A car passing by outside gave a friendly beep to someone. The ventilation kicked on and Jake felt the air move. Martha remained still, and Jake was getting ready to make his last run at her when she cleared her throat.

"I had that," she said, and Jake let it linger in the air for a moment.

"If you just let me tell you my story," Jake said, "I won't ask you questions. If you just listen and then you want to tell me something, you can. If you don't, I promise I'll leave."

Martha turned his way, her face coiled with anxiety. She looked at him briefly before staring at her feet. It was several minutes before she said, "All right."

"Martha," Jake said, edging forward in his seat and softening his voice even more, "my wife and I adopted a baby boy thirteen years ago. My wife recently — my wife is gone now and Sam — that's my boy — wanted to find out where he came from. I'm an investigative journalist, you might have seen the show *American Outrage*? So, I've found people before and I told him I'd help. I have no idea if you're connected to my son in any way, and I hate to bring up things from the past that you don't want to think about. I know. I've got my own things and I know what it's like when you just want to bury them.

"But I wanted to ask you about the baby you had."

Martha looked up at him, her big eyes shimmering like water down a well.

"I don't know," Jake said, raising his hands and splaying his fingers, "but I think there's a possibility that your baby might not have died."

Martha's lips trembled and she rose to her feet. She took two steps and dropped to her knees.

"My baby," she said, shuddering with pent rage.

Then she reached out and gripped Jake's knees with a sob.

"They never let me *see* him," she said between gasps. "They said he was dead, but I wanted to *see* him. No one would listen. They called me an addict, but they gave me drugs, too. Their painkillers. When I married Clinton, he said he'd disinherit me. Clinton didn't care."

She pulled free from Jake, still clenching fistfuls of his pant legs.

"He loved me."

She said it as if he might doubt its truth, then she began to wail.

47

Sam shoved the rest of the cake into his mouth and licked his fingers. He took a swig of hot chocolate and swished it around in his mouth to clean the cake off his braces, then dumped the rest of it in the trash before slipping out the door. His head jerked this way and that, scanning the street ahead for any sign of his father. He stepped into a crosswalk and a cab blared its horn, nearly clipping him.

People stared, and Sam tucked his chin and plowed ahead. When he reached the apartment building on Seventy-second, he scanned the lobby from across the street. The doorman was a tall black man in red-and-gray livery. A woman walked inside with a shopping bag and stopped for a word before disappearing into the lobby. Sam searched up and down, then jogged through a break in the traffic and huffed up to the door.

The doorman swung it open for him, but Sam pulled up short and said, "Was that Jake Carlson who was just in here?"

The doorman looked up and down the sidewalk and said, "He was, five, ten minutes ago."

" 'Cause I wanted his autograph," Sam said.

The doorman puckered his lips and tilted his head.

"See you," Sam said, and jogged off down the sidewalk toward the second address.

Now he was less careful about looking around, knowing that he was several minutes behind Jake, and not wanting to miss anything. He tripped on a crack, but caught himself and wove his way through a crowd at the crosswalk on Third Avenue. Rancid warm air from the subway wafted up through a grate and he held his breath. When he reached the brownstone, he kept to the opposite side of the street, walking by it before doubling back and ducking behind a Volvo wagon. Through the car window, he studied the brownstone. When Jake appeared at the front window, Sam dropped down. When his heart settled, he peeked up and saw nothing but the curtain.

He took a trembling breath and crossed between cars, mounted the steps, and buzzed in. He patted his back pocket and removed the passport when he went through the next door and saw the receptionist's smile.

"Hi," Sam said, ambling up to the desk and angling his head at the floor as he held out the passport. "My dad's here, right? Jake Carlson?"

"Well," the woman said, taking the passport, "yes, he is."

"But don't say anything," Sam said. "If you could just show me where they are. He said if I could make it to just have me wait outside the door. I know he's with Martha Van Buren. He said outside the door until he comes out to get me."

"All right," she said, stepping out into the waiting room and opening an adjacent door. "They're in there."

48

The side door swung open and a man with a young face, but gray hair at the temples, came in. Jake started to rise, but Martha was wrapped around his knees, groaning. The man knelt down with his arm around Martha and talked soothingly to her, softly murmuring into her ear as a horse trainer will do with his charge. He set a small black case on the table and opened it with his slender fingers. Jake saw several syringes and a bottle of clear liquid.

"Can I help you?" the man asked Martha gently. "Let me give you this. Are you okay?"

Martha looked up, red-eyed, from the case to the man. She shut her eyes and nodded emphatically.

"Good," the man said, petting her arm and preparing his shot.

Martha kept crying, but she looked away when the man injected her arm. She sucked in a deep breath and let it out slowly. The man stood and nodded and helped her back to her chair. Jake shifted in his seat and brushed at the tearstains.

"I'm Steve Warren," the man said, extending a hand to Jake. "I'm one of the doctors. Jodi heard her and called me. We've found that when something like this happens with Martha, we're better off nipping it in the bud."

"Yes," Jake said, nodding, "thank you."

"I hope you were comfortable with that," the doctor said, zipping up his bag. "As you see, it helped."

"What was that?" Jake asked.

"Thorazine. I've seen you before. Are you her brother?"

"No," Jake said. "We're related. Cousins. It's a long story."

The doctor held up his hand. "None of my business. I'm happy you're here to see her. We encourage our clients to have visitors, but Martha's not that outgoing. I hope this doesn't dissuade you. It's important for her."

"Did, did the family, our family, put her here?"

The doctor smiled and reached for the door.

"Everyone who's here is here because they want to be. Treatment is entirely up to the patient. We only recommend things. We never force any kind of treatment or any length of stay. Our clients come to us when they need us. It's the way Llewellyn House has operated for fifty years. It's refreshing, believe me, when you've seen the alternative."

"Can you tell me what's wrong with her?"

Warren gave him a funny look.

"Is she getting better, I mean. Do you think?"

"Treatment gets better all the time," Warren said. "But we're kind of swimming upstream because schizophrenia tends to get worse with age."

"She, like, hears voices?" Jake asked, lowering his voice.

"No," Warren said, glancing her way, "Martha's functional. It's not like that. But sometimes people with mild schizophrenia are worse off. It's not unusual to go undiagnosed for years."

He stooped over Martha and in the patient voice people use to talk with Alzheimer's patients, he asked, "Are you okay? You're all right? Okay. Good. I'm going, but you call me if you need me."

Warren looked at him with an easy smile. "She's okay."

Jake waited for the doctor to leave before

he sat back down and asked, "Do you want to talk?"

Even against the power of the drug, her face twisted with agony. She took several deep breaths and Jake thought the interview was over. Then she began to speak.

"When Clinton died, I didn't have any-place to go. So, I went home."

Martha locked her glassy eyes on him. She no longer swept away the random wisps of hair and they hung limp down her forehead.

"They hated Clinton," she said. Her eyes shifted to the window and the waving dappled sunshine that fell through the leaves. "So, he did some drugs, but he loved me and I was pregnant. My father, he said they could fix that, like it was a disease. After that I didn't speak to him until it was too late for him to make me do something. Clinton was dead and I went home."

She looked at Jake and said, "Do you think my father killed him?"

"Your baby?"

"Clinton."

"I have no idea," Jake said, a shudder passing through him.

Martha hung her head again and mur-mured to herself. After a minute, Jake stood up and held out his hand. When she took it, he patted it gently with his other hand. He cleared his throat and said, "I'm not sure at all if my son is the one. I think we should do a maternity test, and go from there. At this point, we're only guessing."

"He's got to be my son," she said, gripping his hand with both of hers so they were locked together. "My father didn't want me to have Clinton's baby. It was a boy, the oldest of his grandchildren. There's something about it in the will."

"Okay, we'll find out."

Jake let go of her hands and stepped back.

"Will you be here?" Jake asked.

She looked around and said, "Yes. They have oatmeal for breakfast. You can come if you want to."

"So, I'll get the test set up," Jake said. "Okay? I'm going to go, but we'll come back."

"For oatmeal?"

"Maybe."

Jake reached for the door and hesitated. Something told him to go back, to tell her he was sorry, that he knew he'd made a mistake, and that there'd be no test. When he pulled open the door, Sam looked up at him, his face pasty with horror and shock.

"Sam," he said.

Before he could recover, Sam bolted down the hall, threw open the door, and disappeared.

Jake took off after him. When he blew out the front door, Sam was already in a full sprint, heading down the sidewalk in the direction of Central Park. Jake took off but didn't catch him by the arm until the crossing on Fifth Avenue. Sam struggled to get free, but Jake was able to pull him into a bear hug.

"No!" Sam yelled. "Leave me alone!"

Jake held on while Sam thrashed against him. People moved away from them and a cop appeared and asked what was going on.

"Nothing," Jake said, still holding on, "he's my son."

The cop's eyes went from Jake's face to Sam's and he said, "Doesn't look like you. How about some ID?"

"I'm Jake Carlson, officer," Jake said, pulling the wallet out of his pocket and showing it to him with one hand.

"Who's the kid?"

"You stupid asshole!" Sam screamed, turning his red face toward the cop. "He's my *father.*"

The cop stepped back.

"Come on, Sam," Jake said softly. With his arm around Sam's shoulders he led him across the street and into the shadows of the trees in the park.

Jake kept Sam moving until his trembling stopped and they reached the boat pond, where they sat on a bench. Sam stared out at the water, sniffing to himself.

"I'm a freak," Sam said. "I thought those guys at school were all these stupid assholes, but they were right. I'm a freak."

49

Sam wiped his nose along the back of his forearm.

"I'm not a hundred percent sure she's your mother," Jake said.

"Don't say that," Sam said, "because she is and you know it."

"I don't know it."

"How? How do we look all this time and find her and you say now she's not? Then who is?"

Jake shook his head.

"I don't know."

"It makes sense, me being this freak, some heroin baby."

"Cut the crap," Jake said. "You're a normal kid."

"I never should have asked," he said, shaking his head. "I deserve it. I should have left it alone."

"No one gets to go back."

"I don't want to do any test. I want to go home."

Jake fixed his attention on a boat that careened across the pond, tilting in the wind.

After a time, he said, "We can't just stop, Sam."

"I don't care anymore," Sam said, without raising his head. "I don't want to know."

"If they did this," Jake said. "People have to know."

Sam looked up at him with a bitter, tearstained face and asked, "Why?"

"Because it was wrong."

Sam just stared, until he said, "Because of TV. Right?"

"It's got nothing to do with TV," Jake said. "I could have gotten my job back if I was doing this for TV. Did you know that?"

Sam shook his head and said, "I want to go home. I don't want to know anymore."

"When people like this — people with all that money — break the law," Jake said, "a lot of times the only way they get in trouble is when some reporter digs them out. What I do is about what's right and what's wrong, not about getting on TV. It's who I am. I know you don't like it, but those are the facts."

"That's all you care about, right?" Sam

said, standing up. "You're always flying off somewhere to get the facts. But what about what I need? This is about *me*. Remember, your son?"

Sam turned and started to walk away.

Then, over his shoulder he said, "What about that fact?"

Jake launched himself off the bench, grabbing Sam by the arm and spinning him around.

"No way," Jake said. "You're not turning this around on me. You wanted this. You sent me on this. I know it turned ugly, but you're not just walking away with that face. You don't get to do that in life and you're not doing it with me."

"Let me go."

"You're coming with me, Sam."

"You can't make me," Sam said, digging his heels into the pavement.

Jake spun on him. "I'm your father. You do what I say."

"My father's a dead drug addict and my mother is a loon."

"We have no idea who your father is," Jake said. "She's a confused woman, Sam. She's not well. Come on."

Sam hung his head, shaking it, but allowing Jake to pull him along.

"Where are we going?" Sam asked.

"To get that test," Jake said, "and get this thing going before someone finds out and stops her from doing it."

50

There was a DNA Labs collection office on Thirty-fourth Street. They swabbed the inside of Sam's mouth with several cotton swabs before sealing them in three separate envelopes and packing them into a small box. Jake asked the technician if he could take the other kit to the woman they thought was Sam's biological mom. She said it was no problem and together he and Sam drove back uptown to the Llewellyn House on Sixty-ninth Street.

Jake found a parking spot on the street, and told Sam he thought it was best if he went in alone.

"You'll stay this time?"

"I don't want to see that woman."

Inside Llewellyn House, the receptionist was obviously flustered to see him again. She told him Martha was asleep, so Jake asked for Dr. Warren instead. After a few minutes he was shown into a small, windowless office, where the doctor sat at a desk wearing a small pair of reading glasses.

He swiveled around in his chair, and Jake calmly explained why he was there.

The doctor furrowed his brow, whipped off his glasses, and said, "Mr. Carlson, do you think this is good for Martha?"

"I think the truth is good," Jake said.

"Really?" the doctor said. "Was it good for your son to hear that the people you think might be his parents were drug addicts? That was your son in here, right? Your adopted son?"

"Look, we don't know if she's even Sam's mother," Jake said, "but she might be. This test will tell us."

Jake held the box up for Warren to see.

"This is step one," Jake said. "We can get to who the father is later."

"Well, Martha is resting from the Thorazine," Warren said, eyeing the box. "She's asleep. You'll have to come back tomorrow."

As the doctor stood and reached for the door, Jake said, "You said your patients, or your clients, have autonomy. That you let them do whatever they like."

"Everyone here is free to come and go and make their own decisions. The visitor's room is treated like an extension of their own homes. What they do is entirely their business. That's central to the house's mission statement."

"So, if she wants to do this, she can do it. Because that's what she said to me. I'm just wondering about this place. The mission statement and all that."

Warren narrowed his eyes, but nodded and said, "Come back tomorrow, Mr. Carlson. If she still wants to do your test, she's free to do so. She can do whatever she likes."

"And meantime," Jake said, "you won't be trying to convince her otherwise, right?"

"I'm a doctor, Mr. Carlson," Warren said, waving him through the door, underhand, like a maître d', "not a tabloid reporter."

"I'm not here as a reporter," Jake said, stopping outside the door. "I'm a father."

51

Jake told Sam they had to come back the next day, and he asked him where he wanted to eat. Sam said the Italian place that overlooked the Brooklyn piers so they could get ice cream afterward, and that's what they did.

The girl behind the counter with her hair tucked up into a white scarf and a small silver hoop in her nose recognized Jake and asked him to sign a napkin. The older couple two places back in line crowded in saying they thought they recognized him, too. They were from Arkansas and asked him to sign their ferry schedule. The rest of the line looked at him with vague recognition and Jake knew the best thing was to get moving before everyone wanted him to sign things just because the others did.

"That's a pain," Sam said as they walked out.

"It's not too bad," Jake said. "One in fifty.

If you keep moving, you're all right. It's not like people are taking pictures."

"Not like Eminem or something, right?"

"No, my clothes fit too well."

The wind whipped through their hair, melting Jake's pistachio and forcing him to roll the cone around on his tongue nonstop to keep it from dripping. The Brooklyn Bridge loomed above them and a ferry muscled its way into the dock, blaring its arrival before disgorging a hundred tourists. Jake put an arm around Sam's shoulder as they cut through the crowd and sat together on a bench watching the ships move up and down the East River, their lights beginning to twinkle.

"Remember when you and me and Mom and Louie were at Jones Beach that time the waves were like eight feet high and we had those blow-up rafts?" Sam asked, crunching his cone.

"I do."

"Yeah."

The sun dropped behind the island of Manhattan as they finished their cones. Sam asked if they could see a movie. Jake said sure, and it seemed in that moment as though nothing was wrong. They'd drive through the dusk to see a movie, then head home, where Karen would meet them. Sam would go to bed and he and Karen would undress, giggling like teenagers. The ocean breeze would swirl through the open glass and they'd fall into the sheets thirsty for each other's heat and Karen would whisper for him to be nice the way she always did.

There'd be no Albanians. Jake would have his job. Sam wouldn't have any problems in school. It would all be just the way it used to, when it was all too routine for him to fully realize its precious value.

Jake studied the skyline, picking out City Hall with its elaborate design and intricate detail, a wedding cake among concrete boxes.

"They used to make things a lot better than they do now," Jake said. "A lot nicer. Look at that bridge. They don't do things like that anymore. They just slap up some steel and cables.

"Okay, come on," he said, patting Sam's leg. "Let's go."

Even though it was late when they got home, they took Louie for a walk on the beach. They were all in bed before Jake realized they'd forgotten to rinse the sand from the dog's feet.

"Juliet's gonna kill us," Sam said with a yawn, pulling the sheet up to his chin.

Jake lay still and listened as Sam's breathing got deeper and lower, finally turning into a snore. He got up and slid open the glass door, stepping out onto the balcony where the sounds of the house were drowned in the surf and he could think about what he was doing.

He didn't know how long he stood there or the exact time he went to bed, but when morning came, he found himself in the bed with Sam at his side and Louie at his feet. It was too late for a run. He tried to sneak out so Sam would sleep, but when he came out of the shower Sam was already dressed and downstairs eating cereal at the kitchen table.

"I thought maybe you'd sit this one out," Jake said. He tugged the cuffs of his shirt out of the sleeves of the forest-green Zegna suit he'd taken fresh from the closet, then held up his handheld DVD camera. "I wanted to ask her some questions and get it on tape."

"You said no TV."

"It's not for TV," Jake said. "It's for the DA. There's something between Lukaj and the Van Burens, but cops, in my experience, aren't always A players when it comes to connecting the dots."

"Why the suit?" Sam asked.

"You don't see a tie, do you?" Jake said,

tugging at the open collar of his shirt.

"I'm going with you," Sam said, wiping his mouth and putting his bowl in the sink.

"What about wanting me to stop?"

"Who figured out Muldoon's AutoTRAK? Who found Lukaj's Delaware office?"

"You. So?"

"So, you need me," Sam said, "I keep telling you that."

"You can come," Jake said, "but I don't want you meeting her yet. Let's make sure she's your mother before we do that. Trust me."

"Okay, I'll wait outside," Sam said.

"In the lobby, not listening at the door," Jake said.

"You know why I did that, right?" Sam asked.

"No. I don't."

Sam showed him a full mouth of metal and held his arms out to the sides, palms up. " 'Cause I take after you."

52

Traffic slowed to a stop just before the tunnel toll booth and it took them forty-five minutes to go the last half mile into Manhattan. When they finally arrived, it was after ten. Jake circled the area three times before finally putting the BMW into a garage and walking four blocks to Llewellyn House. When they were half a block away, the white van across the street caught Jake's eye, but he didn't think any more about it until he got to the brownstone. They were on the first step when the front door opened and out came one of the guys from Skip Lehman's crew with a coil of cable around his shoulder and a light stand in his hand.

Jake cursed, handed the DNA test kit to Sam, and launched himself up the steps. He blew past the receptionist and burst into the front room. Sitting in the midst of the lights, cameras, wires, and reflective screens were Martha Van Buren and Sara Pratt, facing each other in two chairs. Martha was dabbing her eyes with a Kleenex.

"Get out," Jake said.

"Hey," Muldoon said, striding over from his monitor and holding out a hand to stop Jake. "You use my AutoTRAK account and don't think I'm going to follow up? We're here first."

Jake slapped his arm down and showed Muldoon his fist.

"I'll break your fucking nose," Jake said.

Dr. Warren walked in and said, "You people are sick."

Muldoon took half a step back and Jake went over to Martha, raising her gently by the arm and saying softly to her that he was sorry and that these people had nothing to do with him. The mike had been wired up her shirt and it pulled at her as she stepped away. Jake unclipped it and pulled the wire out through the bottom of her shirt, throwing it so that it dinged off a light pole. Martha stepped tentatively through the tangle of cables. She was still crying, and Jake put an arm around her shoulder.

"You can't do that," Sara said, popping up and sticking her chin out at Jake.

Jake ignored her, but when Sara followed them and grabbed hold of Martha's arm to tug her back into the room, Jake clenched the reporter's wrist and twisted it until she yelped and let go. He shoved her arm and she stumbled on the wires, banging into one of the tripods that supported the light screen. The screen, a large rectangular sheet of canvas, yawed, tipped, and crashed into the window. Sara tried to spin and catch herself, but missed her grab at the wing chair and sat down hard on the floor.

"I'll sue your ass," Sara said, looking up, her eyes squinted tight and her mouth pulled back to show her little white teeth. "Get this on tape, Conrad. Shoot it all. How's *this* story going to look when I run it?"

The cameras turned toward him as he escorted Martha out of the room. Dr. Warren spoke to her in a low voice and put a hand on her shoulder, but she shook free from him, shaking her head and clinging to Jake. Sam was there in the hallway, wide-eyed and holding the test kit with both hands like a holy grail.

"Go," Jake said to him, pointing, "get out, Sam. Go to the car. Now. I'll meet you."

"Sam?" Martha said, following.

Jake turned and waved his hand in front of the camera that was following them until he heard Sam close the door on his way out. Then Jake pointed back at Muldoon and said, "I always knew you were a fat piece of shit, but I didn't think you'd pimp for this little whore."

He turned his finger on Sara, jabbing it at her as he said, "Run *that* story."

53

The cameraman pursued them out to the sidewalk, where Jake flagged down a cab. When he spun around, the camera was right there in his face. Jake splayed his fingers and gripped the lens, covering it and shoving the cameraman back. He fell to the ground with a thud, but kept the camera going, filming Jake's scowl and his backside as he turned to help Martha into the cab.

Muldoon helped the cameraman up and strode over to Jake as he climbed in.

"Think your fans will recognize you without your makeup?" he said, sneering.

Jake tried to pull the door shut, but Muldoon grabbed hold of it and said, "Wait till I get some B roll of your kid."

Jake popped out and punched both hands, palms out, into Muldoon's chest. The producer stumbled backward, tripped on the curb, and went down hard, ass first, on the concrete.

Jake took half a step toward him, drew back a fist, then jumped back into the cab, slammed the door, and told the cabbie to go. Halfway down the block, Jake took out his ticket and gave him the address of the parking garage. He asked Martha if she was all right. She was huddled in the corner, but she nodded that she was.

"I want to see him," she said after another block.

"Martha, we don't know Sam's your son. That's why we have to do this test. He might not be."

She looked at him, her eyes red and swollen, and nodded.

"So, I need you to just be cool with him," Jake said. "Okay? I'm going to get the test kit from him and ask him to wait. You and I can do the test and talk."

The cab dropped them at the garage and Jake gave them his ticket. Sam arrived just as the attendant pulled the BMW up out of the garage. He had the test kit under his arm. His hands were jammed into his pockets and he was looking at his sneakers so that the unruly bangs covered most of his eyes.

"Sam, Martha," Jake said, ushering Sam into the backseat. "Martha, Sam."

Sam never looked up. Martha got into the

front seat and Jake started driving uptown.

"There's a quiet place in Central Park. Up on 105. The Conservatory Garden?"

"I know it," Martha said. Her eyes were locked straight ahead.

After a few minutes, she began to make small sniffing noises. Jake glanced and saw a tear roll down her cheek. He checked the rearview mirror. Sam was clutching the test kit to his chest, head down.

"I'm sorry," Jake said, not to anyone specifically.

He parked on the street and went around to open the door for Martha. After he helped her out, he leaned over the seat and told Sam that it might be a good idea for him to wait. Sam looked relieved, and he handed over the kit without looking at Jake.

Jake gave him back some money and said it was okay to find a diner if he was hungry, but to keep his cell phone on.

"She seems nice," Sam said.

"I'm sure she is," Jake said.

Jake and Martha passed through the Vanderbilt Gate, a massive decorative stone arch that once was an entrance to that family's mansion. They settled on the edge of a fountain, side by side. The brilliant pink blooms of the crabapple trees shed their petals in swirling clusters.

Jake opened the DNA kit and explained to Martha how to swab the inside of her cheek.

"They use cheek cells for the analysis," he said, opening one of the envelopes for her to deposit the swab. "Totally painless."

When he had all three he put them into their individual bags, then back into the box. He sealed it up and affixed the mailing label before setting it aside. Then he removed the hand-size DVD camera from his shoulder bag.

"I'm just going to put what you say on DVD, Martha," Jake said. "Not for TV, I'm not with those other people. This will be for the police."

He reached out and gave her arm a squeeze. She offered a weak smile, but sighed and began to talk. She was bitter, recounting her childhood as a little girl no one wanted; then her face brightened when she described meeting Clinton Eggers at a beach party on Martha's Vineyard. He was everything her family hated, wild, irreverent, a big, burly, drug-using musician. She loved everything about him, and all her prayers were answered when he loved her back.

Her father was in China, and for a month, she spent every minute with Clinton. But

September came, and he had a tour. She was going to finish school in January and then he promised they'd be together.

"I was on the pill," she told Jake, her eyes slipping out of focus. "When I met Clinton, I stopped. I wanted to get pregnant. I wanted to have his baby and have him take me away from my family.

"I was back at school when I found out and he came to get me. I'd just turned eighteen, so they couldn't really stop us, but we had to run. When we got married in Las Vegas, it was in the papers. My father, being a politician, he had to just go along like it was okay. That's how it is. On the outside, everything's always okay.

"I stayed on the road with Clinton and his band," she said. "It wasn't easy, but I was free. Then, he died, and I did, too. Inside anyway.

"They brought me back. I tried to kill myself, but they pumped my stomach. That would have been too embarrassing. They gave me tranquilizers. I was a zombie, but part of me knew my baby was coming and it was the one thing I started to hope for. I started to think about him as part of Clinton. I remember going into labor, but it's all fuzzy. I think they gave me something. It was all like a dream, a bad dream, and then there I was, in bed, and my baby was gone."

Martha winced and dropped her head. Jake reached over and touched her arm. Behind her, pink and white petals from the crabapple blossoms swirled in the breeze and one rode it far enough to lodge in her hair. Jake brushed it away.

"When you say he was gone," he said, speaking softly and smoothly, "do you mean because he died during the delivery?"

She sniffed and raised her chin, tears welling in her eyes.

"We had the funeral, and I, I went through it all, drugged," she said. "That's how they kept me. So it's just a fog. But inside me, there was something, something that kept saying my baby wasn't in that coffin. I kept having this feeling that they took him, and did something, and now I think I know what."

"What do you think they did?" Jake asked.

"They gave him away," she said, her composure and her words crumbling. She looked down and shook her head. "They didn't want me to have him. There's something about the will and something vesting and him being the oldest. I think he would have inherited a lot of the family money. There's this trust."

Then she raised her head and stared hard

into the camera, her hands clenched into knots, and said, "They said I was crazy. They'll say it now. But I'm not crazy. They're evil. They are *so* evil."

Jake took a deep breath and quietly thanked her as he switched off the camera. Martha moved closer to him and wrapped her arms around his neck, hugging him tight. He held her and stroked the back of her head and told her it was all right, even though it wasn't.

54

Gravel crunched and popped under Niko's tires as he rolled around the broad circle in front of Ridgewood. He looked up at the roofline, three stories high, and the endless rows of shuttered windows, and thought of Versailles.

Niko pulled to a stop behind a black Suburban, and when he got out a man emerged from the truck and marched toward him. Niko stiffened. When the man introduced himself as Vick Slatten, Niko hesitated before giving his own name and saying he was there to see the congressman. Slatten said he was head of security for the Van Buren family and he spoke in the bullying manner of a camp guard. Niko tilted his head, saying that he was a lawyer whose client had business with the congressman.

Slatten bared his teeth. "We know why you're here. Come on."

Niko followed Slatten up the stone steps

and into a great foyer with two grand marble stairways curving their way from opposite sides of the space to a balustrade on the second floor. A massive crystal chandelier filled the space above them. Slatten broke off to the right, down a long broad hallway, and into a room lined with books and looking out over a two-acre garden. They crossed a thick Persian rug, passing through a pair of leather couches to a mahogany desk, and sat down facing it. Slatten looked at his watch and gave Niko a brief, false smile before tugging up the legs of his slacks, crossing his legs, and settling into his chair.

After twenty minutes, a door among the bookshelves opened and the congressman came through giving orders to a young man who swam in his wake the way a pilot fish will trail a shark. The young man took notes about a dinner the congressman wanted to have and the precise order in which to invite the guests, changing his mind three times between the doorway and the desk, where he sat and intertwined his fingers. He reminded Niko of an accountant, with his thin face, frameless glasses, and bowtie.

"And you're Mr. —" the congressman said, picking up a sheet of paper and wrinkling his lips, "Karwalkowszc."

The right corner of Van Buren's mouth gave a little twitch, as if it had been tugged at with a piece of fishing line.

Niko cleared his throat and patted the courier envelope under his arm.

"My client asked me to give you this, Congressman," Niko said.

The congressman nodded at Slatten, who got up and extended his hand. Niko hesitated, then handed over the file, which Slatten delivered to the congressman.

Van Buren snapped off the rubber strap and began removing the papers. Slatten circled the desk to observe over his shoulder. As Van Buren read, a tremor ran through the papers in his hands. His lips stretched tight.

Niko cleared his throat and said, "It's everything you agreed to with my client?"

Van Buren looked up with clear brown eyes, startled. He took a check from the top drawer of his desk and gave it to Slatten, returning to the papers before the check was in Niko's hands. One hundred thousand dollars in a Cayman banknote made out to a corporation in Cyprus. Niko took a breath and let it out slowly before standing.

"Wait," Van Buren said to him. He looked up with a blink, his mouth twitched and tightened into a smile that revealed the tips of teeth too white and too perfect to have been his own. He touched the yellow bowtie.

"Tell him I want the boy. There's a million if he brings me the boy."

Niko steadied himself, gave half a bow, and left the room.

55

When they dropped Martha at Llewellyn House, Muldoon and his TV crew were nowhere in sight. Martha opened the car door, then turned toward the backseat. She reached over and touched Sam's cheek. Her lower lip disappeared beneath her top teeth. Sam hung his head and turned away. She didn't say anything, she just sat there for a moment before jumping out.

"One week?" she asked Jake.

"I'll mail this out right away," Jake said.

Martha nodded, glanced at Sam, then hurried up the steps without looking back. Jake watched the door close, then asked Sam if he wanted to move up into the front seat.

"I'm okay," Sam said quietly, but he pulled the hood of his sweatshirt over his head, hiding his face in its shadow.

Jake put the car back in gear and headed for the FDR Drive. On their way to Kingston, Jake made two calls. One was to Judy, asking her to dinner and to bring all the information she had on Ridgewood, especially any kind of maps or information on the family's cemetery. The second call was to the undertaker's wife, whose tone took on a high-pitched giddiness when she realized it was Jake.

"I know it's a strange question," Jake said, "but would a coffin for an unborn infant like that be sealed in like, some concrete containment or something?"

"No," she said, sounding uncomfortable with the shop talk. "There's no concrete or anything. It's all sealed in the container. Nothing gets into those things."

"So, it's just, like six feet of dirt?" Jake asked.

"Not six feet," she said. "They used to do that before embalming. No one gets buried more than a couple feet these days."

"Like two feet? Three?"

"Closer to two."

Jake thanked her and glanced back at Sam. The hood was down but his eyes met Jake's in the mirror.

Jake pulled into the fire lane at Home Depot and left Sam sitting there. He was in and out with a shovel, a can of bug spray, and a flashlight in five minutes, and then they were on their way back to the Quality Inn. They checked back in, then headed for dinner. Judy met them in the Rondout District at a redbrick, three-story restaurant called Ship to Shore. She had a photo album that included some shots she took during her tour of Ridgewood for her flower show article as well as a copy of the funeral photo from the paper's archives. Jake let the waiter fill their wineglasses before he starting digging in to the album.

Judy was halfway through her glass with a purple tint on the fine hair above her lip when Jake pointed to a photo at the top of the page. Beyond a trellis bursting with pink roses lay a company of tombstones in manicured grass. When Jake asked Judy if she could draw him a rough map of Ridgewood and where the cemetery plot lay, she finished off her glass before she said she'd try. With the tip of her tongue peeking out between her lips, she went to work on a notepad that Jake removed from his briefcase.

When she handed it over, she said, "You're not getting me into trouble, right?"

"Would I do that?" Jake said, studying the map. "Does the wall go all the way around the property?"

"Jake," she said, watching him refill her glass, "what are you doing?"

"Filling your glass. A toast. Here's to the truth, however we find it."

After she took a sip, Judy said, "Do you mean *however* we find it, or however we *find* it?"

"Both."

"You're honest, anyway," she said.

"That's what he always tries to do," Sam said, taking a bite from an onion ring. "He says."

"Don't talk with your mouth full," Jake said. "It makes you sound insincere."

"If you go to the very back of the estate, the side facing the river," Judy said, "there's a terrace with stone steps leading to a grassy outcrop where they have weddings and things like that."

"Good."

"What are you going to do there?" she asked.

"Just checking some things."

"Not with him, right?" Judy asked, nodding at Sam.

"I'm going," Sam said.

Jake looked at Sam, his hands resting on the table balled into fists and his dark eyebrows knit tight.

"He can stay with me," Judy said. "The

NBA playoffs are on."

"I hate basketball."

"Actually, I think I'll need him," Jake said. "There's not going to be any trouble."

As they rode across the Kingston-Rhinecliff Bridge to the other side of the Hudson, Sam said, "She'd be a good mom."

The tires thumped a steady rhythm over the sections of concrete. Jake looked out the window at the sleeping mountains that lay alongside black water below. Somewhere downriver a buoy winked back at the stars overhead.

"Yes, she would," he said, cracking his window and letting the musky smell of water and trees fill the BMW.

"What does she care if I go with you, though?" Sam said above the howling air.

"Just a nice person," Jake said, raising his chin and sitting up straight in the seat.

"What do you need me to do?"

"You'll see," Jake said.

They left the bridge behind and with it the broad canopy of stars. The road they took twisted southward through a dark tract of trees planted close to the road when it was only a carriage track. They passed through the hamlet of Rhinecliff, a cluster of diminutive nineteenth-century houses built into the hill overlooking the river, and continued south on Route 85. They were several miles out of town when Jake drove past the massive stone gates to Ridgewood without slowing down. Sam swung around in his seat, craning his neck for a view of the towering gates. Jake drove for nearly a quarter mile before he pulled a U-turn. They passed the gates again, going another quarter mile before pulling off the road and easing the car down the slight bank and into some pine trees.

When they got out, Jake sprayed his suit coat and pants with bug repellent as if he were wearing the same sweatshirt and jeans as Sam. He slung the camera bag over his shoulder, hoisted the shovel, and scooped up the flashlight. As they walked back up the road toward the gates, a creepy glow showed itself above the trees, light from the Van Buren mansion that made Jake think of dying embers twisting with worms of orange light.

56

They kept close to the trees, and were able to see well enough without the flashlight. It wasn't until they turned toward the river and plunged deep into the woods that Jake flipped it on. The dense wood made the going rough, especially with a shovel and camera bag. Jake twisted and ducked through low branches and tangles of saplings. Finally they came to the stone wall and the six-foot buffer of tall grass between it and the woods.

Jake played his light up the side of the rock wall, ten feet to the top.

"Too bad we didn't bring a ladder," he said.

"How would you get it through those trees?" Sam said.

"Good point."

The tall grass was already damp, but the going was much easier. Jake flicked off the flashlight. Enough light spilled over the wall from the mansion that they could make out the swath of grass as a pale green strip between the blackness of woods and wall. After a time, Jake's knee began to throb. The Ferragamo shoes rubbed blisters into his heels. When they reached the back corner of the wall, the topography dropped off quickly. The grass swath ended and the trees on the slope hugged the wall. Jake flipped his light back on. Dirt and rocks skittered down the embankment as they moved along the base of the wall toward the outcrop, clinging to the trunks of the trees for support.

They were breathing hard by the time they climbed over the low stone balustrade surrounding the terrace. To their right, the tar-black river lay in the valley below, mutely reflecting the wash of stars overhead. Jake set the shovel down and told Sam to catch his breath as he climbed the stairs and scouted the territory beyond the main terrace above them. A great lawn opened up between the terrace and the mansion with a long reflecting pool in its center. On either side of the pool were elaborate gardens with flower trellises, sculpted shrubbery, statues, and fountains. Nearly every window in all three wings of the massive building was lit, enough light to cast long black shadows beneath the broad old trees.

Jake took Judy's map from his pocket and in the light of the stars got his bearings according to the placement of the reflecting pool and the position of the house. From where he stood, Jake couldn't see the front of the place or the garages where any cars might be parked. He didn't see a sign of any kind of guards patrolling the grounds, and suspected that the man he'd seen in the Suburban by the gates focused his attention on that spot since that was where any vehicles would have to go to enter the estate.

After five minutes with no sights or sounds to warn him off, Jake retrieved Sam and the shovel and quickly ducked into the shadows of the trees to make his way to the family cemetery. The scent of cut grass laced with a hint of lilacs began to tickle his nose.

Jake felt his heart quicken at the sight of the headstones. From the photo in the newspaper he and Judy had guessed that Martha's baby — or the coffin that was supposed to contain it — was buried in the southeast corner of the plot. He crouched low and searched through them. When he clanged the shovel's spade off a granite headstone, Jake dove to the grass and pulled Sam down too.

"Wha—"

Jake clapped a hand over Sam's mouth and whispered in his ear not to make another sound.

When his heart began to slow, he peeked up over the stone they were hiding behind and scouted the area between them and the mansion. After a minute of seeing nothing, he started to creep forward again. Instead of using the full beam of the flashlight to read the inscriptions, Jake held it inside his coat, pointing it at the liner before he flicked it on, keeping his body between the house and the stones. In the dull glow he could just make out the words engraved on the stones. The fifth one he came to bore the name JOSHUA VAN BUREN-EGGERS.

Sam ran his hand absently along the edges of the smooth granite surface while Jake removed the DVD camera and turned it on.

"Don't get excited," Jake said in a low voice. "I'm going to turn the camera light on."

"They'll see it."

Jake looked up at the house. It was still nearly two hundred yards away.

"Someone would have to be looking right out at us," Jake said. "And with all the lights on inside, the reflection should be like a mirror."

"What if somebody's outside?" Sam said.

"If this was easy," Jake said, holding the camera out in front of him and flipping on the light, "everyone would do it."

Sam winced at the light and turned his head away, shading his eyes in the bath of electric whiteness.

"Jeez, Dad."

"Can you come here and hold it right there?" Jake asked. He shot the inscription, then zoomed out so he could clearly see the headstone and the plot of grass in front of it.

"Okay," Jake said, handing it over.

He left Sam with the camera rolling, stepped into the light, took up the shovel, and began to dig. The shovel's new edge cut into the turf with a sharp scratching sound that punctuated the tumbling dirt clods from the previous spadeful of dirt.

"You can't dig a grave," Sam said.

"It's not a grave," Jake said. "Not if it's empty."

"Jesus, how do you know?" Sam asked in a high-pitched voice.

"Trust me," Jake said, attempting an authoritative tone that came out sounding angry. "I just know. It'll prove they took her baby. Whether it's you or someone else, this will prove it."

Adrenaline flooded Jake's veins, spurring

349

his work into a pace that filled the beam of light from the camera with a swirling cloud of dust. When the shovel struck the casket, he dug faster still, nipping at the earth without bothering to dump out the dirt, until the lip of the container was exposed. He slipped the edge of his spade underneath it and used the shovel as a lever, leaning on the handle, forcing it up and down until the casket popped loose. Jake knelt and pulled it out of the ground, setting it on its side.

He fidgeted with the clasp for a minute, then let go, stepped back, and raised the shovel. He hesitated for a moment, then set his mouth and swung the blade, busting the latch and partially spilling the contents onto the ground. Tossing the shovel aside, he knelt and separated the lid from the container. The ragged blanket was stained dark brown and he gingerly peeled away its folds, wincing at the stale-smelling rot, his throat constricted so tightly that he gulped for air. The light from the camera wobbled.

Then he froze, and gasped. Protruding from the remains of the blanket was a small dusty white bone.

57

Instead of turning away and giving in to the surge of bile in the back of his mouth, Jake tore into the blanket, pulling aside the tiny bones until he raised a skull from the smelly mess. He held it up to the camera and rotated it in the brilliant light.

"Not human," Jake said, swallowing and choking back a gag. He glanced at Sam's wide-eyed face, staring at him in disbelief from the edge of the light. "I think it's from an animal, maybe a small dog. Look at the teeth."

Jake stared grimly into the camera for a moment, offering up the elongated skull. Then he stood up and took the shaking camera from Sam's hands. The sudden darkness was so complete after the glaring light that Jake could see nothing. He sensed Sam, however, his bulky shape moving close to Jake, reaching out and touching his arm. Jake felt for him and pulled him close, into a rough hug.

"I told you," he said.

His eyes hadn't fully adjusted when he heard the shouts of people coming from the direction of the house. Over Sam's shoulder he saw the swaying beams of light from several flashlights stabbing at the darkness and moving toward them.

"Come on," Jake said, pushing Sam away, shoving the camera back into the bag, and swinging it over his shoulder.

Sam was bent over the shovel and as Jake scooped up the skull and jammed it into his coat pocket, he told Sam to leave it, grabbed him by the arm, and dragged him toward the terrace in a full run.

When they reached the terrace, Jake looked back. The lights had reached the cemetery and the shouts rang out clear. Spotlights burst alive, blazing from every corner of the mansion, bathing the entire grounds in white light. Jake blocked the light with his arm and heard the high whine of an ATV before it shot around the corner of the mansion and headed their way along the reflecting pool.

He and Sam scurried down the steps and hopped the low wall, scrambling along the steep bank and back the way they'd come. Jake was afraid to run along the wall, so they plunged into the woods, pushing through thicket after thicket, always keeping the glow of Ridgewood to their backs and off to their right.

As the woods began to open up and their way became easier, a giddy refrain of laughter bubbled up out of Jake's throat.

"Those lights are gonna get us right back to the car," he said, grinning at Sam, even though they couldn't see each other's faces.

"What's that?" Sam asked in a hushed tone. "Shh."

"What's what?" Jake said.

He held his breath and his smile faded. He heard it, too. The sound of baying dogs.

58

"Come on," Jake said, tugging at Sam and probing the woods ahead of them with his light as he ran.

Every few seconds he'd glance back in order to keep his bearings in the darkness. The sound of the dogs grew closer. Sam tripped and fell and Jake yanked him up. They both huffed for breath. Then, at its farthest edge, the flashlight's beam caught something flat and gray.

"The road," Jake said. "There it is."

The dogs sounded even closer. They broke through the trees and Jake shined his light up the road one way, then the other. They were closer to the gates than he'd expected.

"Run, Sam," he said.

He pulled at Sam, who was doubled over trying to catch his breath. They started up the road toward their car. Jake swung his light along the edge of the woods, frantic for a sign. Fifty more yards and the beam reflected off the taillight.

"There it is," he said.

The sound of the dogs exploded from the woods, a maniacal snarling punctuated by eager yelps as they hit the road. Jake looked back and saw their snapping white teeth, two of them, big and dark, Dobermans or rottweilers. He fished for the keys in his pocket without slowing down, found them, and hit the remote door lock. The car lights blinked on.

"Get in!" he screamed at Sam.

Jake got to the car first. He flung open the door. Sam dove in. Jake started to slam it shut, but the dogs were fifteen feet away. He jumped in on top of Sam and yanked the door closed on a snapping muzzle. The dog shrieked, but didn't back off, even though its jaws were wedged in the door. It snarled and spit, and the sharp teeth worked open and closed as best they could.

Jake held the door with both hands, knowing that if he let go, the dogs would be inside and tearing them to pieces.

"Sam!" Jake yelled, not even knowing what he wanted his son to do.

Sam wormed an arm out from under Jake, made a fist, and hammered the dog square in the nose. The dog shrieked again, this time pulling free from the door. Jake yanked it shut. He shucked off the camera bag and tossed it in the back, then squirmed off of Sam and into the driver's seat.

Outside the dogs circled the car, snapping, snarling, and roaring. Jake fired up the BMW and spun his tires, kicking up rocks, sticks, and grit as they fishtailed out of the woods, up the bank, and onto the road. He never let his foot off the gas until he almost lost it on a bend, looked down, and saw that he was doing over ninety.

He slowed some, but kept an eye in the mirror, expecting any moment to see headlights closing on them. When he did see a pair of lights, his throat tightened, but he kept his speed steady. The car, whoever it was, wasn't chasing him. Instead, it kept its distance. He was gauging the distance between them and the car behind them when he blinked and out of nowhere saw a swath of white light rolling up the road. He realized what it was the moment he heard the staccato sound of the helicopter. He cursed out loud.

An instant later, their car was awash in the light. The beam wavered, but stayed locked on them. Jake forgot about the car behind him. He floored the accelerator. The light stayed with them as they sped for the town of Rhinecliff.

"Dad?"

Jake's mind whirred. He fished the cell phone out of his coat pocket and handed it to Sam.

"Take this, and get the camera up here," he said. "There's a train station in Rhinecliff."

"So?"

"You take the DVD out," Jake said, his hands clasped to the wheel and his jaw set. "When I stop, you stay down. I'm going to run and when the light goes with me, you wait. Count to twenty and then get to the train station. Here, take money out of my wallet. Take a credit card, too. Get a ticket to Poughkeepsie and get on that train. I'll have Judy pick you up there. Dial her number for me. Do that first, then get the DVD."

Jake told Sam where he stored the number. Sam found it, then dialed, and handed the phone back to Jake. He got voice mail, left a message, and tried again. Judy answered. Jake told her what he needed and she said she'd be there.

Route 85 ran through the center of the little town. Up ahead, flashing lights from a cop car were headed toward them. Jake saw a side street, figured to pass it, then changed his mind, spinning the wheel. His cell phone banged off the window and thumped to the floor. The car screeched around a corner and popped up over the curb. Jake fishtailed in a lawn, then got back onto the pavement and took the side street down toward the river and the train tracks. When he saw the old brick station, he pointed to it.

"See it?" he shouted. "You got the disc?"

"Dad, I don't want to go," Sam said, but holding up the small gleaming disc for Jake to see.

"You gotta do what I say," Jake said. "Buy a goddamn ticket and get off at Poughkeepsie. Stay in the car until the light's gone."

"What about you?"

"Just take the disc and get on that train."

He looked over at his son, slowed the car, and put a hand on his shoulder.

"You've got to do this, Sam. I need you. Just count to twenty."

Sam's face crumpled, but he nodded. Jake pulled over, slammed the car into park, and bolted out.

As he ran up the street, the chopping roar of the helicopter swept up a storm of dust and grit and the searchlight stayed with him. Ahead, Jake saw a police car squeal around the corner, lights ablaze. He ran up a lawn, under some trees, and out of the light. He hopped a fence, staggering from the pain in his knee before he loped across the yard. He scaled the fence in back, tearing a sleeve. The searchlight found him again. He heard car doors slamming out in the street and the shouts of men.

Jake kept going, away from his car, giving Sam time to get out and reach the station. He crossed through another yard, past a house whose porch light flashed on, and across another street into the weedy yard of an abandoned church. Behind him, he heard the scream of tires and brakes, even through the heavy thump of the copter blades. He took half a second to take the skull from his coat pocket and drop it into a juniper bush that was next to the corner of the stone church, then kept going. When he hit the next street, a black Suburban raced toward him out of nowhere, its lights going on, blinding him, and making him jump back so that he tripped on the curb and tumbled to the ground.

He clawed at the grass and scrambled to his feet as the truck doors flew open. Feet pounded the pavement behind him. Jake never looked back, but started to run. That's when something hit him from behind. He felt the air leave his body and saw a flash of light.

59

When Jake shook free from the grogginess, they had stripped off his coat and already had his hands cuffed behind his back. They pulled him to his feet and jostled him toward the state police car, shoving him into the backseat. The trooper slammed the door, then stood talking to a thick-necked man wearing a black windbreaker. He had dark eyes, a concrete jaw, and an iron-gray crew cut. Jake tried to decipher their words. The older man talked the most and the troopers nodded at everything he said.

Out on the lawn adjacent to the one where he'd been taken down, a cluster of neighbors stood talking and every so often one of them would point his way. The helicopter's absence left the little town strangely quiet. Jake watched the man with the crew cut climb into the black Suburban. The same truck had come out of Ridgewood the other night, warning them to stay away.

Two troopers climbed in and when Jake asked, the driver said they were taking him to the station.

"I want my lawyer," Jake said.

The cop in the passenger side turned all the way around to smile at him and said, "This ain't TV."

"No? It might be," Jake said.

The troopers clammed up. They actually passed Ridgewood on their way to the station, and Jake swung around to see if the black Suburban that was following them would turn in. When it didn't, he felt the knot in his stomach tighten.

In low voices, the two young troopers began to speak to each other about the man Jake presumed to be the one with the crew cut in the Suburban.

"Slatten wants to talk with him before we charge him," the driver said.

The other chuckled and said, "Can we just do that?"

The driver shrugged. "I'm not saying no. You can."

"What was he? CIA?"

The driver nodded. "And Army before that."

They pulled into a single-story brick building with a pitched roof that looked more like a modest home than a police station. They led Jake inside and put him in a small white interrogation room, cuffing him to a U-bolt in the metal table that bisected the room. After about ten minutes of Jake hearing the murmur of voices outside the room, the man with the crew cut came in without the cops and closed the door behind him.

Over one arm was Jake's suit coat. In his hands were the DVD camera and its bag. He set the bag and coat down on the table off to the side, turned the camera over in his hands, and popped it open before setting it down and examining the contents of the bag. From the side compartment he removed a new, unused disc. He looked at the plastic seal, then tossed it back into the bag. From Jake's coat pocket, he fished out a smooth round container of skin-tone cover-up that Jake used for makeup in the field. The man popped open the makeup, wrinkled his nose, and tossed it down on the table, where it rattled to a stop.

"I'm Vick Slatten," he said without offering a hand.

Slatten sat down and crossed his arms over his barrel chest. Under his windbreaker, a black T-shirt was stretched taut over his muscular chest. He wasn't tall, but he had the air of a man used to having people get out of his way.

"And you're a reporter," he said, leaning back. "For *American Outrage*. A little face makeup?" He angled his chin at the container.

Jake just looked at him.

"I'm head of security at Ridgewood," he said, sitting forward, his eyes going to the camera bag. He had the angry undercurrent of a man who'd been insulted and had yet to repay the favor.

"And that's like some kind of sovereign nation, right, Vick?" Jake said.

Slatten's eyes narrowed.

"Where's the DVD?" Slatten said.

Jake returned the stare. "Where's the body?"

Slatten didn't blink, but Jake saw his pupils coil. Then he smiled and stood up, circling the table.

"Decency," Slatten said, pausing in his approach. "That's what this family is about. They have a fortune. They share it. They have time. They give it. And then you people come along."

Jake didn't even look at him, but he let his own mouth curl into a smile at the charade.

Slatten's hand shot out and gripped Jake by the throat. An iron finger probed his neck and lanced a nerve. Jake jerked away involuntarily, clacking the handcuffs against their bolt, the legs of the chair squeaking out from under him as it clattered to the floor.

Slatten brought his face close enough for Jake to see the white stubble on his leathery chin.

"I asked a question."

"There is no disc," Jake said, choking out his words. "I didn't have time."

Slatten eased his finger off the nerve and relief washed through Jake, even though the choke hold remained.

"You tell *American Outrage* to sniff for their stink somewhere else. What you did to that grave is a felony."

Slatten let go of Jake's neck and moved toward the door.

"You'll slither out this time, but now you're marked. You cross my path again, you'll be locked up." Slatten opened the door and started to leave, then stopped and looked back. "I'll have a restraining order by noon."

The door closed quietly. Jake sat for another thirty minutes before one of the troopers came in and unlocked the cuffs. He tossed Jake's wallet and keys onto the table next to the makeup.

"Free on my own recognizance?" Jake asked, rubbing the blood back into his wrists and then picking up his things.

"You rather spend the night and see the judge in the morning?" the trooper asked. "I'd be feeling lucky if I were you that these people don't want the publicity."

"Yeah, that's what I hear," Jake said, slipping on the coat and pulling the camera bag over his shoulder. "You know where I can get a lotto ticket?"

The cop huffed and shook his head as if Jake were an idiot. They drove him back to his car and Jake gave them a sarcastic thanks for the lift, waving as they drove away. When their lights were out of sight, he got into the car, set the camera down, and began searching for his cell phone. He went through the entire car, twice, then scoured the immediate area, thinking it might have fallen out when he broke and ran. Finally, he got in and drove the short distance down the hill to the train station parking lot. When he got out, he heard the hiss of the train. He craned his neck and, over the low brick wall, saw the train down on the far tracks, a train headed toward Poughkeepsie.

Jake took off running. He burst into the station and out over the bridge leading to the platform. As he ran, he could see the train was already moving. He slammed open the door and dashed down the steps, but by the time he hit the platform, the last car was nearly a hundred yards away. Jake looked around. Except for the long shadows creeping away from their steel girders, the platform was empty.

Jake pulled the torn suit coat tight and shivered.

He walked slowly back up the steps. The old stone station was empty, too. No one sat waiting on the high-backed oak benches. The vending machines stood silent. The ticket window was dark.

There was a pay phone on the wall. Jake dialed Sam's cell number and got no answer, so he dialed Judy. She babbled something Jake couldn't understand. He raised his voice and told her to calm down.

"I don't know, he's not here," she said.

A surge of nausea washed over Jake.

"The train came through," Judy said, "and they said it would have gone through Rhinecliff at 10:01. I don't know, maybe he missed it. There was a 10:22 to Albany, but that's going the other way. There's also an 11:05 through there to New York. I thought I'd wait for that."

"Well, the 11:05 just left," Jake said, looking at his watch and seeing that it was 11:08.

"Oh, thank God," Judy said. "I'm sure

he's on it."

"Christ."

"I didn't know what to do. I tried to call you."

"I'll try his cell again," Jake said, looking around the empty station. "I'm sure he's on the train that just left. Who knows why he missed the first one. Maybe he had trouble buying a ticket."

"No worries," Judy said. "I'll wait right here."

Jake tried Sam's phone again, but it went right to voice mail. Sam was terrible with his phone, leaving it off, forgetting to charge it, so it didn't mean anything that he couldn't get through. Even though Jake was constantly reminding him, it wasn't unthinkable that he'd forgotten. There was another possibility. Sam could have frozen and might simply be hiding somewhere in the shadows. Jake replaced the phone and walked back down to the platform. He looked both ways, willing Sam's shape to emerge from the bushes, and bellowed Sam's name.

The only sound that came back was his own voice echoing down the tracks.

60

Jake stood for several minutes, thinking, and then realized the distant rumble was another train coming down the tracks from the south. His pulse quickened at the thought that Sam had somehow made the first train, missed Judy at Poughkeepsie, and was now coming back. As the brilliant light from the engine wavered into view, Jake heard the sound of a car door from the parking lot between the station and the tracks.

The ground began to tremble, and when the train sounded its horn, Jake jammed a finger into each ear. The train clacked past, then hissed and squealed to a stop. The doors slammed open and Jake looked up and down the line. A conductor got out way up front. Toward the back, a fat man in a disheveled business suit stumbled off, spilling the contents of his briefcase. Jake watched him, then noticed a different man in black slacks and a black golf shirt wearing what looked like a tan fishing vest. His eyes were fixed on Jake as he walked toward him along the length of the platform. He hadn't come down the stairs from the station, so he must have climbed over the parking lot fence. The man covered one ear with his hand and began speaking into his lapel. Jake backed away. When he turned, he saw the conductor's pants leg as he disappeared back onto the train.

At the same time, around the corner of the station stepped a second man with an identical tan vest. Jake looked at the stairs leading up to the station bridge, a narrow trap if a third person was up there. He spun toward the back of the train. The first man stepped right through the fat man's papers without looking down.

The engine's horn sounded twice. Jake jogged toward the second man and paused outside an open door. The horn sounded again and the doors began to close. Jake waited until they were nearly closed before he shot through sideways.

Only a couple of faces glowed up at him from the seats as he sprinted through the car toward the front where the conductor had been. He saw the shape of the second man flash past, running for the door he had just entered, but the train hissed and lurched into motion. Jake smashed the black rectangular panel that opened the door between cars and darted through the coupling and into the next car before he looked back. The train picked up speed.

He turned and saw the handful of people in the car staring. Jake straightened up and began walking forward again. From the corner of his eye, he saw movement. He turned and froze. The second man was sprinting alongside the train, his left arm raised and bent at the elbow to steady the long black pistol in his right hand. Jake threw himself to the floor instinctively. At the same moment there was a pop and a cloud of shattered glass filled the car.

The passengers burst out screaming, and when Jake looked up he saw a bloody hand clinging to the window frame. The train was running now, but not nearly as fast as Jake's pounding heart. The man's other hand shot into the window, hooking at the wrist and still gripping the silenced handgun. Jake grabbed for the gun, got hold, and started pounding on the other hand with his fist. The man held on.

His short dark hair whipped in the night air and he looked at Jake with the wide burning eyes of a lunatic. He worked slowly against Jake's grip. Jake kept pounding, dumbfounded that the man could hang on even as blood jetted out from the sides of his hand with every blow.

Without warning, someone grabbed Jake from behind and shoved. He felt the wind. Smelled the hot metal. Heard the grinding roar of wheels. Saw his feet rolling over his head as his legs flipped over the top of him. Bolts of pain shot through his back as he bounced and rolled on the ground. Then he stopped, and in the fog he tasted cinders and the blood filling his mouth.

When his vision came into focus, the two men stood over him in the darkness. The second man still held the pistol. The train moaned away down the tracks. The first man grabbed Jake by the shirt with his bloody hand, raised him up, and swung the pistol in a wide arc.

Jake saw stars.

61

The train swayed and bucked. The sound of the conductor's voice squawked down from the speaker that they were arriving in Albany, jarring Sam from his trance. He peeked over the seat, stealing a glimpse of the watch on the wrist of the businessman sleeping with his head against the window, his suit coat for a pillow. It was eleven-fourteen. In the window, he could see the ghost of his own image imposed over the approaching lights of the capital. The events that had landed him there replayed themselves again, a video loop in his brain.

After Jake had sprinted off under the helicopter's spotlight, Sam counted to twenty, leapt from the car, and dashed into the shadows of a front lawn before he turned to watch the progress of the helicopter. It hovered above the houses halfway to the main road. Its broad beam swept to and fro as it cut tight circles in the night sky. Sam touched the mini DVD in his pocket and turned to run when he heard the squeal of tires rounding the corner.

He had ducked down and wiggled into some high shrubs. A silver Audi jammed on its brakes and nearly sideswiped Jake's car. Two men jumped out carrying guns, aiming them at the car and creeping toward it. They hollered between themselves in a foreign language. One yanked the door open and aimed the gun inside. He slid in and began rummaging through the glove box, then searched under the seats before getting out with something in his hand that he showed to the other and then put into his pocket. The two of them checked the trunk, then one of them cursed and kicked the car door shut.

Both of the men had looked around, searching the narrow street with their eyes. One had short dark hair and the other was a scraggly blond. Sam felt his insides freeze as the blond's eyes passed over the bush where he hid. A small noise escaped his throat as the man started walking his way. Sam's muscles tensed and he shifted his head, ever so slightly, looking for the best escape route.

But when the man hit the sidewalk, he had

turned downhill toward the train station. A horn blast suddenly broke the night air, the train from Albany on its way to New York. As it rumbled into the station, the blond shouted to his partner and started to run down the sidewalk toward the station.

The dark-headed man jumped into the Audi, spun around and drove down the hill, shrieking to a stop outside the station. Sam lost sight of the blond. He wormed through the hedge and ducked through the shadows, working his way downhill.

Light flooded the small lot outside the old stone train station. Only a handful of cars rested there. The Audi waited with its engine running. Sam saw no sign of the two men, but he did see the end of the train sticking out from behind the station. The train's horn sounded, twice, then a third time before hissing and slowly gaining momentum. As it clacked away, a man in a suit emerged from the station, then a woman, then an older couple, making their way toward the parking lot.

One by one, the people got into their cars and headed for the blocked exit. The first car, a small Mercedes, sounded its horn at the Audi. Then the man got out and looked around. Another car sounded its horn, too. Finally, the two men came out, their guns nowhere in sight. The man in the Mercedes said something to them, but they acted as if they hadn't heard a word, climbed back into the Audi, and drove away.

Sam had waited ten minutes in the shadows, scanning the area. He saw no one, took a deep breath, and ran across the lot.

Inside, the ticket window was dark. Sam's footsteps echoed off the high ceilings as he crossed the lobby and mounted some steps to the ticket machine. He studied the schedule on the wall. The train he just missed must have been the 10:01 to Poughkeepsie. The last one going south until 11:05. He looked at the clock. 10:17. A train to Albany should arrive in five minutes. He'd be going the wrong way, but he wanted more than anything to get out of Rhinecliff and away from the men in the silver Audi. He looked around, then fed Jake's credit card into the slot. The machine churned out the ticket, then the card. Sam snatched them both and hurried out of the station.

He hadn't waited on the platform, but around the corner of the building where he could watch the lower parking lot. It hadn't been long before the distant groaning of a train grew louder and the ground began to vibrate through his sneakers. He let the train come to a full stop, took one more look around, then dashed across the platform and in through the open doors of the closest car.

He found a seat by the window and pressed his hands and nose to the glass. As they pulled out, the barren platform stayed that way. With the train underway, Sam shut his eyes until a small chirping noise startled him. When it sounded again, he dug into his pocket and pulled out his cell phone. The chirp was his low battery alert, and for the first time all the warnings Jake gave him about keeping his phone charged made sense.

He had dialed Jake's number, but could get no service. He kept trying, frantic to let Jake know what happened and his change in plans. Finally, he got through. The phone rang once, then Sam's phone shut down. The battery was dead.

That was an hour ago.

When he reached Albany, he'd get off and find a pay phone.

62

The train slowed and they pulled into the Albany station. Sam darted through the stragglers and into the station. He ran his father's credit card through the pay phone and placed his call. He got his dad's voice mail.

"Hey," he said, leaving a message, "it's Sam. I'm fine, but two guys were following us and I had to get on the wrong damn train, so I'm in Albany, but I've got the disc. I'm going to cab it back to the hotel. My phone's dead, so don't worry if you can't get me. Hopefully I'll see you at the hotel. Probably an hour or an hour and a half."

Sam hung up and walked through the station, downstairs to the cab stand. Three of them waited. Sam climbed into the first and asked the driver if he'd take a credit card. He said he would and Sam asked if he could take him to the Quality Inn in Kingston.

The cabbie wore a tweed cap and he

turned around in his seat, his eyes glowing white in his black face.

"Boy, you just came from there," the cabbie said.

"I got on the wrong train."

The cabbie snorted and shook his head. "Gonna cost you a hundred and fifty dollars to go to Kingston. We don't go that far."

"That's okay," Sam said.

The cabbie wanted to see the credit card. Sam showed it to him along with his passport.

"It's my dad's."

"You're not running away or anything?"

"I got on the wrong train," he said. "Geography's not my strong suit."

The cabbie narrowed his eyes, but handed back the card and passport and put the car into gear, muttering something under his breath and shaking his head. Sam studied the lights of the capital as they crossed the river, but as they headed south and the road turned dark, he nodded off to sleep and didn't wake until they got off the thruway exit at Kingston.

When they pulled up to the hotel, the driver asked, "You sure you're okay, boy?"

Sam yawned and said, "Yeah. Home sweet home."

He signed the credit card slip, adding a

thirty-dollar tip, and went to the front desk.

A young man with spiked hair and thick eyebrows appeared from the back. He hadn't seen Jake, but he didn't give Sam any trouble about a key once he saw the passport. Sam went up to the room and got on the phone. He had no luck finding his dad. He paced the room until the rumble in his stomach got his attention. He raided the mini bar, grabbing a bag of Gummi bears and a Twix bar as well as a bottle of Sprite to wash it down with. He dug through his travel bag and found his phone charger. Cursing himself out loud, he plugged it into the wall, then turned on his dad's computer and got to work scanning his e-mails. That turned up nothing.

He went to his dad's contacts for Judy's phone number. The clock read 2:03, but he picked up the phone and dialed anyway. It wasn't until he heard the recording saying that the number was disconnected that he remembered his dad had an old number. Her new number was stored in his dad's phone.

Sam paced the room — imagining that each sound he heard in the hallway was his dad coming home — until his eyelids fluttered and he stumbled. First he sat down, then he leaned over. His head hit the pillow.

■ ■ ■ ■

Sometime later, Sam woke with a start. Someone was knocking at the door.

63

The ache in his skull drew Jake's mind up from the dark. He felt for the egg-shaped knot before his eyes even opened, then winced and blinked. He yanked the other hand away from something cold and metal. The steel cuff's chain rattled against a copper pipe. Gray light seeped into the dank space from the seams around a single rectangle on the opposite end of the cellar. He straightened, and his elbow banged off the solid belly of the antique water heater that anchored him to the damp floor. Panic took hold, and in a flurry of movement he jumped up, grasped the handcuff's chain with his free hand, and tried to break free.

His hands were slick and warm with blood before his efforts waned. Along with the sting in his hands and the throb from the knot on his head, his knee also ached. Huffing, he worked his jaw. That hurt, too. A door above him creaked open, spilling a warm yellow light into the old basement, exposing dusty broken fruit crates, barrels, and rusty yard tools. Slatten came down the steps and stood before him, hands clasped behind his back for a moment, until he found a rickety wooden chair, spun it, and sat down so that his arms were propped on its back. He read Jake's face.

"You're okay," he said.

"Are you insane?" Jake asked, raising his hand, the rasp of the cuff against the pipe sounding lonely in the dank space.

"I have some questions."

Jake shook his head. "I told you at the station."

"You didn't tell me about Martha," Slatten said, watching his face. "Yeah, I heard about that after they let you go. What did she say to you?"

"You can't keep this quiet," Jake said.

Slatten raised his eyebrows.

"People are going to look for me," Jake said.

"And when I'm finished, they'll find you. I'll be finished when you answer me."

"Right, you think this just goes away?"

"This?" Slatten said, looking up at the underbelly of the floor above, rusted nail points strung with gray sagging webs. "All this never happened. Not if I don't want it to."

"What are you talking about?"

Slatten grinned. His teeth were faded and set apart, each one seeming to stand on its own.

"You know how it works. He said, she said, and you're running low on credibility right now."

"Where's Sam?" Jake asked.

"Where is Sam?" Slatten said, his voice singsong, hitting the high note in the middle of the sentence.

Jake stared at the cold, bloodshot eyes and the flat line of Slatten's mouth.

"Martha told me she thought her baby was never dead. She thinks Sam is her son. I'm his father. All I'm trying to do is help Sam find where he came from."

Slatten let out a thin stream of air.

"You're a reporter."

"Not on this."

Slatten's left eyebrow went up solo. "Why the camera? Why the grave?"

"The truth, that's all I want."

"Do you know how demented that girl is?"

"No. How?"

Slatten stared for a moment, weighing Jake's tone. "This is the kind of family that keeps our country strong. You've been to

Iraq. You know the kind of things that are out there."

"Same things that are in here."

Slatten got up and started for the stairs. "You're pathetic."

"Are you fucking crazy?" Jake said, kicking the water heater, his voice rising out of control. "You think you can just do this?"

Slatten snorted without turning around. He mounted the stairs and shut the door, leaving Jake blind until his eyes could adjust.

64

"Sammy boy," Muldoon said with a wink and a grin.

The producer stood in the hotel room doorway wearing jeans and a snug white T-shirt under a full-length leather coat. A black felt beret rested at a jaunty angle on his head. He pushed open the door and strode right into the room with a duck-footed walk that left his snakeskin boots pointing at opposite walls. He made a show of looking around.

"They told me you guys were checked in here. Not too many hotels in Kingston, you know. Dad not around?" he said, swinging his head around with a smirk.

"He's out," Sam said, blinking at the sunlight that was already warming the room and stirring up its musty smells.

"Something happen to your dad, Sam?" Muldoon said, sweeping back his coat and putting his hands on his hips.

Sam glared at him.

"Guess so," Muldoon said. "I heard about the cops arresting him last night. Yeah, local hack here saw the police report. It already hit the wire and our overnight editor got it. I already talked to the cops. They took him back to his car at the train station. Funny thing, though. It's still there, and no one's seen him."

"I'm sure he's fine," Sam said, swallowing and biting the inside of his lip to keep it from trembling.

"Or heard from him," Muldoon said.

"What do you know?"

"I know there was some Albanians up in Syracuse who weren't too happy with him," Muldoon said, his eyes sparkling. "Relentless suckers."

Sam stared at Muldoon's boots.

"Question now is, what are you going to do about it?" Muldoon asked.

"The police will find him," Sam said.

"Find him?"

"If he's gone."

Muldoon guffawed and stuck a finger in his ear.

"Good one," Muldoon said, examining a hunk of wax on his pinky.

"What else am I supposed to do?" Sam asked.

Muldoon directed his eyes at Sam and his voice changed. "What do you think Jake would do?"

"Go to the police."

"Oh, right. Your dad? I'm sure he's got deep admiration for Kingston's finest. Did you know about the story your dad and I were working on with the wife of the FBI agent who's missing?" Muldoon asked.

"The one where you screwed him out of the interview?"

"You know why that woman finally talked?" Muldoon asked.

Sam shook his head.

"Something your father taught me," Muldoon said, opening the mini bar and helping himself to a can of nuts. "Police are like every other government employee. They punch in, nine to five, and do the minimum amount of work to keep from getting fired and collect a pension. It's human nature.

"You want them to work for you? You gotta get their attention. That woman was the *wife* of an *FBI* agent, but they weren't doing shit for her.

"Okay," Muldoon said, holding up a Brazil nut as if it were a classroom pointer. "What happens if we run this as a story? People see it. Wives, mothers, politicians, bosses, the bosses' wives, you get the point. People start asking why the hell aren't the police finding the bad guys. Where the hell is Jake Carlson, the freaking hero who uncovered those war crimes in Iraq? You don't get people upset and asking questions, the cops wait for the crime to solve itself, which it never does. You hear what I'm saying?"

Muldoon popped the nut into his mouth and began chewing.

"I hear, but I don't know what you mean," Sam said.

Muldoon moved closer to him and lowered his voice. "We go to the police, of course, we need them. But we make them hungry. We make them put finding your father on tip-top of their list. We break this story, the national media will be *all* over it. It'll be a race between the FBI, the police, the state troopers, everybody, to see who can find your dad and reel this thing in. Trust me."

Sam looked him over and said, "My dad didn't trust you."

Muldoon stopped chewing. "Look, your dad and me, it's like two male tigers pissing on each other. Yeah, we growl and spit, but the end of the day, we're both wearing stripes. If your dad were here, Sam, I know what he'd want you to do. I'm a newsman. So is your dad. Media attention. That's how they found the Boston Strangler, Son of Sam, BTK, all of them. What the hell do you got to lose?"

Sam thought for a minute, then said, "Just so we're straight, I know what this is all about, but sometimes good things come from bad."

Muldoon cocked his head.

"What do you want me to do?" Sam said.

"What did Martha Van Buren tell your dad?" Muldoon said, eyeing the computer on the desk. "He got any notes? Stuff I can use to juice this thing up."

Sam took the mini DVD out of his pocket and held it out to Muldoon.

"I give you this," Sam said, "you sure as shit better use it to get my dad back."

Muldoon reached for it, but Sam snatched it back.

"This is Martha *and* my empty grave," Sam said.

"What?"

"We dug it up. The family cemetery. Me and my dad. The only bones were a dead dog."

"Jesus," Muldoon said, reaching. "This is so freaking big. Everyone with a pulse is going to be looking out for your dad."

Sam gave him the disc.

"So, we're in this?" Muldoon said.

"You got the disc."

"Let's do it right, then," Muldoon said. "We've got to think ahead. We should be running this thing every night, new developments, keep it burning hot. There's a couple other things we can do, and your dad would kill me if I didn't do this right."

"What?" Sam asked.

"You," Muldoon said, adjusting his beret.

"What about me?"

"Come on," Muldoon said, "get your bag. I'll explain in the car. We're going to New York."

65

Muldoon explained how things were done. The story would break that night. During the day, they'd have Nancy do an interview with Sam that they could tease for the following day. After the show ran, the media storm would hit and Muldoon would parse out little snippets of Sam's interview and clips from Martha Van Buren that every other news outlet would run so they wouldn't appear to be out of the loop. When Sam asked about the police, Muldoon gave him a sideways look.

"Come on," Muldoon said, "I'm the master. We go to the best. I got a guy at the FBI who'll tee this thing up with helicopters, dogs, wiretaps, you name it. He's got contacts at Interpol and the CIA. We'll have everyone and their brother looking for your dad. You don't go to some local-yokel cops for something like this. You need like a *Bourne Identity* operation here."

That satisfied Sam, enough anyway that he planted his cheek against the window and kept quiet.

Muldoon parked in Katz's spot near the garage elevator and escorted Sam up to the greenroom, assuring him that he'd get the FBI people there right away. Muldoon set Sam's bag down on the other couch, then walked out the door. Before he closed it, he peered through the crack and waited for Sam to sit down. Then he hurried up to the empty offices. He waved to the overnight editor and went right into Katz's office, where he shut the door and slid Sam's DVD into the player.

It was more than he had imagined, more than he had hoped, a once-in-a-lifetime opportunity. He clutched the disc in his hand, ran down the back stairs to the greenroom, and peeked in. Sam sat with his computer open on the coffee table. Muldoon shut the door and took out his cell phone, dialing up Connie Hines, one of a dozen PAs, production assistants, glorified gofers who got paid nothing and would do anything just to get a shot at the business.

Connie answered in that perky tone that always conjured up an image of the big breasts and the long tan legs for Muldoon. Connie was twenty and red-hot.

"I need you to go out and use your credit card to get an Xbox," Muldoon said. "I'll reimburse you. Pick up some bagels with stuff on them and a couple orange juices. Get me a goddamn gallon of coffee, then get your ass over here, quick. Oh, and wear something, you know, nice."

"Jesus, Conrad."

"You look nice all the time."

"I know, but you don't just say it."

"I got a kid you need to keep an eye on. It's huge. Every newsman in this town is going to be looking for this kid by seven o'clock tonight."

"He's a kid?"

"A thirteen-year-old boy. You know what they like," Muldoon said. "It's the story of a lifetime and I need to lock him down. I don't want anyone talking to him but me. After I get him on the set with Nancy for a one-on-one, I'll get you a suite at the Pierre and you can take him there. You see how important this is?"

"There's a Best Buy on Lexington and a Pick a Bagel down the block."

"Good," Muldoon said, then hurried back upstairs into Katz's office and shut the door. He took out his BlackBerry and found the number of Ed Lurie, his top contact at the FBI.

"Chance of a lifetime, my friend," he said.

"What are you talking about?" Lurie asked. He was chewing something.

"You got ambition, my friend," Muldoon said. "That's why I'm giving this thing to you and not John Gamel out of the Boston office."

"Giving me what?"

"A monster," Muldoon said, then explained the Van Buren story, telling Lurie what he had on DVD, explaining the Albanian connection, Jake's disappearance, and how he was going to break the thing wide open.

"It's yours," Muldoon said, "but you gotta work with me. I got the kid locked down and I need you to keep what you find exclusive to us."

"Nothing hard about that," Lurie said. "I'm your source."

66

Muldoon went back downstairs until he could pass his vigil over Sam off to Connie, then sat waiting for Joe Katz in his office, drinking coffee, going over the DVD, and starting to flesh out the story. At ten, Katz walked in.

"What the hell?" he said, with a look of amazement. "Did you hit your head? You parked in my spot."

Muldoon sprang up out of Katz's seat.

"I'm sorry. I'm sorry," he said. "I lost it. Jesus, Joe, you can't believe what I've got. Look at this. Just look."

Muldoon came out from behind the desk with the remote in his hand. He plunked his backside down on the corner of the desk and went back to the beginning of the disc. He played the Martha Van Buren part, then rolled right into the grave.

When it ended, Muldoon stood up and said, "And I've got the kid."

"Sam? Where's Jake?"

"No one's seen him. I think the Albanians got him."

Katz just stared with an open mouth, shaking his head.

"Relax, I've got the FBI on their way," Muldoon said. "An agent I trust. He's not going to comment to anyone else until we break this thing at six-thirty. The kid gave me the disc, and he's gonna talk. I've got Nancy's interview already written."

"What about Jake?" Katz said. "Your guy with the Feds? He's good?"

Muldoon stared for a second, opening and closing his mouth in confusion before he said, "The best. Doing everything they can."

Katz nodded and rubbed the side of his head.

"You can't put the kid on without his dad's permission," he said.

"The dad is missing."

"We gotta get permission from someone," Katz said.

"Not legally," Muldoon said.

"No, but Jake will sue our asses off. He told me point-blank he doesn't want his kid on air. Think, will you?"

"We're trying to save his life."

"Right."

"I think there's a grandmother Jake leaves

him with," Muldoon said. "I'll work on it. The kid knows the deal. He wants his dad back."

"Okay, do the interview, but get some kind of okay from the grandmother and let's wait for the official word on Jake. He might turn up. We can run the kid tomorrow.

"And you gotta corroborate some of this other stuff. We need backup on this baby thing."

"Van Buren is a public figure," Muldoon said. "We can say almost any goddamn thing we want."

"Saying he committed a crime goes beyond almost," Katz said.

"We're not even saying it. She is."

"I know," Katz said. "We still have to do *some* homework. Have someone get a copy of the death certificate and get somebody to talk to the doctor and the undertaker. I want two sources on this crazy shit. We can't just air it. We got to at least show we investigated, and I want something on these Albanian characters that Jake kept talking about. Get someone, I don't know, an FBI spokesperson to talk about who the hell these people are. Where's the kid?"

"I've got Connie babysitting him in the greenroom. I had her buy an Xbox. I told her to expense it. You got me on that, right?"

"Of course," Katz said, standing up. "Maybe I should talk to him. Is he okay?"

Muldoon held up both hands. "I think just leave him, Joe. Let's get him on tape, and get through tonight's show. I've got him right where I want him and, no offense, but I don't want anything to jar him, give him any crazy ideas. Jake can't have been saying good things about you to the kid after you canned him."

"What are you? His best friend?"

"No," Muldoon said with a shrug, "but I got this kid this far. He's all set. You just get Nancy in here ASAP."

"She's got a lunch with the Olsen twins' publicist," Katz said.

"Screw that."

Katz shook his head and said, "Easy, killer. The word is one of them may be going back into rehab."

"This is Emmy material," Muldoon said.

"Relax. We'll get it," Katz said. "She can do this after her lunch. Even if I could get her to cancel it, she'd be such a bitch it wouldn't work. Let her do the lunch and we'll shoot the kid at two-thirty."

When Ed Lurie showed up, Muldoon reiterated their agreement, then led him down to the greenroom. Sam was bent over his computer, reading something with his brow knit. Connie sat next to him on the couch playing Xbox. When she saw Muldoon, she dropped the control and leaned closer to Sam, peering over his shoulder.

"What are you doing?" Muldoon asked.

"Research," Sam said, eyeing the agent. "Albanian organized crime. Lukaj. He's got a place in his name in Syracuse. I think they should go there first. You with the FBI? What took you so long?"

Muldoon turned and introduced Ed Lurie.

Lurie spent half an hour interviewing Sam. Muldoon sat next to the agent on the couch facing Sam. He kept notes of his own so he could revise Nancy's interview with anything new. Connie stayed next to Sam with a sisterly hand on his leg, patting him gently every so often until he swept it away.

By the end, Sam's voice was strained and his eyes looked red and glassy.

The agent assured Sam that the Bureau would bring all its resources to bear in finding Jake and getting him back, and agreed that someone needed to get out to Lukaj's place to take a look.

"Trust me, though," Lurie said. "Guys like these aren't going to have him locked in the coat closet."

Sam just bit his lip and nodded.

"You got a card?" Sam asked as Lurie stood to go.

The agent handed him his card. Sam asked him to put his cell phone on the back.

"In case I find anything," Sam said, nodding at the computer.

When the agent left, Sam said, "I gotta use the bathroom."

"You know where it is?" Muldoon said. "Next door down."

Sam nodded and got up. Muldoon gave Connie a look that grew angrier as Sam got farther from the couch. When he went out the door, Muldoon popped up, stabbed his finger at the door, and spoke in a furious whisper.

"Go with him!"

"To the bathroom?"

"Every goddamn where he goes," Muldoon said. "What part of that don't you get?"

Connie stuck out her lower lip, but got up and followed.

Jake couldn't feel his hand beyond the metal cuff. A bead of sweat fell from his brow, striking his cheek before he tasted its salt. His shoulders ached in the pits of his arms. His joints trembled and throbbed. The tip of his middle finger just tickled the handle of a rusty pipe wrench. He knew that was what the vague shape and the feel of pitted metal had to be.

The wrench lay along the wall behind the water heater. With all his might, he'd been unable to unseat the heater or the pipes that flowed from it. The wrench, if he could reach it, would allow him to attack the joint where the pipes met the tank.

His breath filled the silence in short puffs. His mind went red and he bellowed with rage, pulling until something popped in his wrist, splitting his anger like a thunderbolt. At the same instant, the distinct sound of metal grating against concrete rang out in the darkness. Jake's eyes watered from the pain, but he stretched again, this time feeling the lip of the wrench handle, this time gaining a purchase. The wrench scraped the floor.

Jake wrapped his fingers around the cool heavy tool. He checked himself from smashing the side of the tank and sat cradling the wrench until his breathing slowed and the pain in his wrist receded to a dull throb. With his fingers and his eyes, he examined the contours of the pipe. Where it hooked into the tank, he fixed the mouth of the wrench and tried to wriggle it on. The teeth bit. It was too tight. He fumbled with the barrel that adjusted the opening. Rust powdered his fingertips. It was frozen.

He slammed the wrench on the floor, showering himself with concrete splinters until the pitch changed. Again, his fingers worked the barrel. This time, it moved. He widened the mouth and wedged it onto the pipe. It fit. He grabbed the end of the handle and pulled, groaning. It didn't move.

With the handcuff rattling against the pipe, he stood, braced himself, and put a foot onto the wrench. He stood on the handle with both feet and bounced. The wrench screeched and moved, so he kept bouncing. There was a snap, and his feet went out from under him. He fell to the floor, still cuffed to the pipe. Tepid water stinking of sulfur sprayed out of the opening, soaking his clothes.

Jake recovered and slipped the cuff off the broken end of the pipe. When he was halfway up the stairs, the water in the tank quieted to a trickle. Jake stepped carefully and tried the door. It was locked. He slipped back down the stairs and made his way to the weak source of light, scooping the wrench up out of its puddle on the way.

He rolled a barrel over beneath the window and climbed up. A board had been awkwardly fitted into the stone frame covering most of the glass. Jake lifted it away, sputtering from the dust. Corrosion had frozen the latch, and when Jake applied the wrench, the window handle snapped off like candy. He banged on it for a moment before simply smashing the glass and using the wrench to dislodge the jagged edges. A tangle of shrubbery awaited him. Thick stems of lilac and forsythia.

Jake heard footsteps crossing the floor above him. He plunged into the opening and fought with the thick undergrowth, squirming through, wincing at the scratches. From the other side of the small house he heard shouts. His hands broke free from the shrubs and found tall grass. He flailed, pulling himself through into an overgrown yard bordered by woods. He could smell the fresh dark shadows beneath the trees, but took only one step before someone tripped him and he tumbled to the ground.

"You're a mess," Slatten said in his gravelly voice. He pitched the butt of a smoking cigarette toward the trees.

The grass swished in front of Jake. One of Slatten's men, wearing sunglasses and the same tan utility vest from the night before, stood ready. Jake slowly got up, ready to launch himself at the man. He felt he had nothing to lose.

"Relax, Clark Kent," Slatten said. "I'm here to invite you to dinner. The congressman wants to see you."

68

By two-thirty, Muldoon's story for that day's show was coming together. They had a copy of the death certificate, and the undertaker had confirmed that he never saw the body of the baby allegedly buried in the Van Buren family cemetery. Nothing so far had disproved Martha's contention. No comment had come from Van Buren, but that in itself was worth something. Muldoon spoke to Sam's grandmother, beat around the bush, and didn't get a refusal to let Sam appear. That was enough for Muldoon to stretch the truth and tell Katz they had the green light. The show's lawyer was still concerned, saying only permission from Jake could guarantee they wouldn't be sued, but Katz knew the story would pull huge ratings and keep their momentum from sweeps going right through the summer, so he was willing to take a chance.

Muldoon left the edit room with specific

instructions on some final cuts, then went downstairs. Sam was in the makeup chair, fussing about the girl brushing gel into his lashes.

"Hey," Muldoon said, "your dad does it."

"That's right," Connie said.

Sam stopped fidgeting.

"Nervous?" Muldoon asked, leading him down the hall toward the studio.

Sam shrugged, then messed the part they'd given him out of his hair.

"I could use something to eat," Sam said.

"Didn't you get bagels?"

"They're gone. How about some pastrami or something?"

"No problem," Muldoon said. "Goddamn it, Connie, I said take care of him. Hey, the minute we're done, we'll get you something."

Sam nodded.

"Nancy's great," Muldoon said, and Connie nodded in agreement. "It'll be like talking to your . . . to someone you know."

Muldoon held the studio door open for Sam, then followed him into the cool, cavernous room, where a hundred different lights clung to the steel grid hanging from the ceiling. Orange, yellow, and blue light washed over the rich wood of the set and two white spots shone down on an interview area where the overstuffed furniture had been arranged to look like someone's living room. The stage manager sat Sam down and an audio man wired a microphone up under his shirt. Connie stood off to the side.

Nancy arrived with a flourish, talking on her cell phone, followed by her personal assistant, two PAs, and the show's publicist. The makeup girl orbited her with hair spray, darting into the group to spray and pat, then darting out. Nancy stepped up onto the set and stopped at its edge to finish her call. Sam stood up and shifted from foot to foot, looking mostly at the ground. While she spoke, Nancy made a kissing motion at Sam and waved with the tips of her fingers. When she hung up, Muldoon introduced them.

"Your father's an absolute superstar," Nancy said, taking Sam's hand, her words gushing. "And you? You're just gorgeous. Look at the size of you. Thirteen? You look like you're ready for college."

She smiled once more at Sam and looked at Muldoon.

"We're ready?" she asked in a flat tone.

He handed her the script and she took out a pen, slashing here and there, more for effect than anything, before she handed it back to him without looking up and turned to the makeup girl.

"I don't want bags under my eyes today," she said with a smile that didn't match her tone.

Sam gazed up at the lights, some glowing dully like jewels, some glaring white, all of them shining down like nearby stars. The set seemed to float in darkness, a fragment of an upper-class living room torn free and cast into the Milky Way, an outpost in space. Three cameras orbited the set, robotic satellites, one swinging from a long black boom, the others sliding along the concrete floor, massive pieces on an invisible chessboard.

Sam's face grew hot under the spotlight's glare. His eyes watered. The makeup on his cheeks dried, contracted, and itched. The gel in his hair smelled like the hair salon his mother used to drag him into before he was old enough to be left home alone. A bead of sweat trickled free from his armpit and ran down into the waistband of his underwear. Sam shifted and moved his tongue around on the inside of his mouth, searching for moisture.

A stagehand asked him if he felt okay. He nodded. The same man asked if he wanted a drink. The words stuck in his throat so he shook his head no. Nancy cleared her throat and read a few lines into the camera, then started over, introducing him with words like *desperate* and *bewildered,* words that made him sound like something he wasn't.

Sam found himself staring into the show host's eyes, looking for a handle in the bright blue color to hold on to, but he couldn't make a connection. The pupils didn't contract or dilate. The irises didn't shift except to pick up the next question off the teleprompter strapped onto the camera hovering over Sam's shoulder. He told himself this was the right thing to do. He told himself the media attention would help find his dad.

"Sam," Nancy said, her voice softened with practiced compassion, "tell us who your father is."

Sam opened his mouth and wrestled his tongue free from its knot. A noise came out. Nancy smiled patiently and nodded. She wore a mask of kindness. Sam gulped and took a breath.

"Jake Carlson."

"Our Jake Carlson, right?" she said softly.

"Yes, *American Outrage.*"

The show's name squeaked out of his mouth and his cheeks grew warm.

"I know your father has been working on an important story involving organized crime," Nancy said, as if Sam's breaking voice were part of every interview. "Can you tell us what happened to him?"

"Well, a few days ago, someone tried to kill him," Sam said. He stopped and looked around, expecting something to change, some kind of reaction, but they all just kept floating in space.

"Tell us about that," Nancy said.

"The district attorney left a message on our home phone telling him to be careful. There's these Albanians that are pretty bad."

"The Albanian mafia?"

Sam shrugged. "Yeah."

"Are they the ones who have your father?"

"I don't know. He's gone and I know they're after him."

"And you'd like us to try and help?"

"And the FBI."

"Of course, and we'll do that. Now how does Martha Van Buren fit into all this?"

Sam took a deep breath. Something inside him loosened and the words began to spill. "I was adopted. My dad was helping me look for my biological mom. My own mom, my real mom, she died. So, my dad was up in Syracuse, doing the bunker-man story for the show and that was where they got me, from an agency there. Where my mom and dad got me. Back when my dad first started in TV. So, he went to where the

410

adoption agency was and started asking questions, you know, investigating, and he ran into these Albanians. We found out that they were taking babies from their country and bringing them over for people here to adopt."

"But it turned out that you weren't from Albania, isn't that right?" Nancy said.

"We thought I was," Sam said. His words weren't doing justice to the way he felt so he began to talk faster. "But then we found out that there were a couple babies who were from here. One of them, we think, was Martha Van Buren's son. They had a funeral for her baby, but it was a trick. Her baby didn't die."

Muldoon retreated to the control room, where he gave Nancy's changes to the teleprompter operator. He stayed in the back and swallowed down a sixteen-ounce cup of coffee, watching while Katz and the director walked Nancy through the interview, feeding her questions and instructions through the clear plastic IFB plugged into her ear.

Muldoon listened, but he realized early in the interview that it would end up as filler more than anything. It would be difficult to build an entire segment around the kid. On camera, his awkward size, braces, messy hair, and natural glowering expression all worked against an audience's natural sympathies.

Nancy's final question to Sam was, "Do you think Martha Van Buren is your mom?"

Sam's eyes glistened and he swallowed, shaking his head in confusion. "I don't know for sure. But she thinks she is."

Nancy let that one stand for a moment, then she quietly thanked Sam for his courage and said she'd do everything she could to help Sam find his dad.

When it was over, Katz turned and looked up at Muldoon and gave him a subtle thumbs-up.

Muldoon pursed his lips and nodded. When he returned to the set, Nancy passed him on her way out, berating the publicist for the two-page spread in *Us* when she'd been promised three. She ignored Muldoon and disappeared with her entourage, leaving the studio suddenly quiet. Muldoon took a weary breath and forced a convivial smile onto his face. The audio man was removing Sam's wire. Connie was right there next to him.

"You did good," Muldoon said, patting his shoulder.

He told Connie to take Sam to get his makeup taken off and that he'd meet them in the greenroom. Muldoon watched them disappear down the hall, and he walked in and sat down on the couch, pinching the bridge of his nose between a thumb and forefinger and fighting back a yawn.

He took a couple deep breaths, thinking about his next move, when he heard a phone ringing softly. It was a cell phone, but not his. It was Sam's, lying on the cushion of the couch where he'd been sitting. Muldoon glanced at the greenroom door, stood, and scooped it up. The caller ID read DAD.

Muldoon swallowed and clamped a hand over his chin. Finally, he flipped it open.

69

Slatten fit his key into the handcuffs and snapped open the lock. He slipped them through his belt without looking. The skin had swollen around the metal band circumscribing a purple canyon around Jake's wrist.

"You did that to yourself," Slatten said, shaking his head and biting back a grin. "You think you're Superman or something?"

"Fuck you," Jake said, returning the older man's stare.

Slatten turned and pushed through the grass, rounding the old farmhouse and climbing up into his Suburban. Jake followed and stood at the passenger door. Slatten's man shadowed him.

Slatten rolled down the window. "Get in."

Slatten's man climbed in back.

After a moment, Slatten said to Jake, "What the hell else are you going to do?

414

Run off and rub two sticks to make a fire?"

Jake opened the door and got in, but he didn't look at Slatten. The rutted road bounced them along the edge of the clearing, then dipped into the trees. Several times they crossed streambeds over the backs of soggy logs, once backing up to start again with their tires chewing off soft orange splinters. Branches whipped the window and snapped the radio antenna, its twang accompanying the thud of rocks on the undercarriage. For thirty minutes they wove through the woods, twisting, turning, veering both right and left at various forks. Jake began to think they were going in circles until they rounded a bend and came out on a country road that spit them onto Route 85, where they headed north. About ten miles later, they passed under the stone entrance of Ridgewood.

Jake shifted in his seat, damp suit pants, dress shirt, and coat clinging to his skin. They pulled around to the back of the mansion. Slatten got out and led Jake into a service door. They climbed three flights of stairs.

"I'm guessing you wouldn't mind cleaning up," Slatten said, showing Jake into a bedroom suite and swinging open the door to a large marble bathroom highlighted by gold fixtures.

"I wouldn't mind if you let me go," Jake said, touching the puffy skin around his wrist, feeling for the groove.

Slatten turned to Jake and tilted his head. "You can go."

"Right. You kidnap me, fucking handcuff me in a dungeon, and now I can go."

"As far as whatever ordeal you've been through," Slatten said in the steady tone of a practiced liar, "the police are looking into the men who grabbed you from the train. When you're tired of our hospitality, I'll call the police and have them arrest you for coming here a second time after you were warned. They can process you, I'm sure it won't take you more than a day to get bail worked out, and you're on your way."

"That's how this works?" Jake said.

Slatten flattened his lips together and nodded, then invited Jake into the bathroom with a sweep of his hand. "There's a robe in there. If you put your clothes in that laundry chute there, they'll clean them up pretty quick. Most of the staff is third generation, some fourth."

"I need to call my son," Jake said.

"There'll be plenty of time after you speak with the congressman."

"He doesn't know where I am," Jake said.

"He's with a friend and she doesn't know where I am either."

"Don't the cops give you a phone call after a couple hours? Just let me know."

Jake shook his head.

"Can you get me some goddamn Advil, anyway?"

Slatten grunted, then turned toward the door, pausing after he opened it to say, "Oh, did I forget to tell you? Dinner is at eight."

Slatten closed the door and Jake heard the sound of a bolt sliding home with a definitive click.

70

"Jake?" Muldoon said.

"Who is this?" said a voice in a thick accent.

Muldoon's heart took off. He crossed the room and shut the door tight.

"My name is Conrad Muldoon," he said, tightening his grip on the phone. "I'm a friend of Jake Carlson's."

There was a pause. "Where is the boy?"

"With me," Muldoon said.

"Let me speak to him. He wants to know about his mother. We will tell him."

"He's not here," Muldoon said.

"You're fucking with us?"

"No," Muldoon said, holding up his hand as though he was calming them.

"Get him. He will want to know about his mother."

"I can work that out," Muldoon said. "We can meet you. Just tell me where."

Muldoon could hear the distinct sound of

the man with the thick accent covering the phone. He glanced at the door and started to pace, motioning his hand in little circles to hurry them.

The man finally uncovered the phone and said, "There is the Salt Museum in Liverpool. You bring him there. You wait on the stone pier behind the museum."

This was it. Muldoon asked, "When?"

"Now."

Muldoon thought he heard voices in the hallway.

"I'm four, five hours away," Muldoon said, talking fast. "I'm not close."

"Okay, ten," the man said. "You be there. You bring the police, you die very fucking bad."

"Salt Museum in Liverpool at ten p.m.," Muldoon said, but the phone was already dead.

"What's up?"

Muldoon spun around.

"Just business," Muldoon said, forcing a smile and holding Sam's phone out to him. "Hope you don't mind. I left my cell phone in my office. I just remembered something about a shot up in Syracuse. Follow-up for that bunker story. This is my top priority, but I got other work going on, too. Hey, don't look at me like that."

Sam took the phone and opened it, punching the buttons. Connie stood behind him with her hands on her hips, shaking her head as if to say Muldoon was an asshole.

"Bullshit," Sam said, looking up with hatred in his eyes. "You asshole. It was my dad!"

Muldoon held up both hands and said, "It wasn't. Sam, listen to me. It was the Albanians. They're looking for *you*."

"With his phone? They have him?"

"I don't know."

"Call Lurie," Sam said, digging into his pocket for the agent's card.

"That's what I was going to do," Muldoon said, concocting a story. "I didn't want to get you all excited, but I'm thinking Lurie can triangulate where the call was made from."

"So where are you going? Call him."

"I'll call from the road and have him come by to get the phone from you," Muldoon said, moving toward the door. "I've got a chance to meet these people. If the phone thing doesn't work, I want to get them on tape."

"You're meeting them? The cops can grab them," Sam said.

"You think the cops can sweat these people?" Muldoon said with a crooked smile. "That's the last thing you want to do. You do that, we'll never see Jake."

"So what do you do?" Sam asked.

"I'll give the tape to Ed Lurie. If he can't find them with your phone, he can run their faces through the FBI computer. They find out who they are and maybe where they are. Then they swoop in with a SWAT team before the Albanians know what hit them. This is a lead we can't ignore."

"You can't just videotape these guys," Sam said.

Muldoon grinned and said, "They'll never know. Filament lens. Right in a briefcase. I wire myself for the sound, get a tech in a van a couple blocks away, and I get all they need for a major bust on tape."

"Then let's go," Sam said, rubbing his eyes and scooping up his travel bag.

"No, no, no," Muldoon said. "You're staying here."

"You're nuts."

"Hold it, little buddy," Muldoon said, grabbing Sam's arm.

"I'm not your fucking little buddy," Sam said, snatching his arm free.

Muldoon nodded at Connie and made for the door.

"You wait and give the phone to Lurie," Muldoon said.

"I'm going with you, you fat asshole," Sam said, slinging the bag over his shoulder and following Muldoon.

Muldoon stopped and turned. He put a stout finger into the middle of Sam's chest.

"I know you're upset," Muldoon said. "But whatever you think of me, I am not going to let you walk right into their hands. That isn't happening. That would be stupid."

"My dad," Sam said, his face starting to tremble.

"The way *not* to get him back is for you to walk right into their hands," Muldoon said. "Trust me. You need to stay safe."

Muldoon gave Sam a little shove to move him away. He took a step backward and, with one eye on the boy, felt for the door until he had it open.

"Connie, get Sam that pastrami sandwich," he said.

Then he slipped out into the hallway, softly closing the door. He hustled down the hall. He would call Lurie, but not for about six hours. He wasn't going to let the FBI botch his story. This one was once in a lifetime. When this thing took hold, the whole country would be glued to their TV sets to see the Albanian mob swirling around with one of America's oldest, richest families.

He'd be the newsman right in the middle of it, in the eye of the perfect shitstorm.

When Muldoon reached the stairwell, he looked at his watch and started to run.

71

Sam knew what his dad would do.

Muldoon kept feeding him that bullshit, and maybe he was right about the media blitz, but Jake wouldn't sit with his thumb up his ass because someone tossed him a sandwich.

Connie was nice enough, but she was dumb as a stump. She sat there, clicking away on the Xbox controls, while he booked himself a flight to Syracuse online and Googled the Salt Museum in Liverpool, New York. After a few minutes' navigation, he downloaded a map of Onondaga Lake Park, home of the Salt Museum he'd heard Muldoon talking about. The map included the surrounding landmarks. When he got there, he'd need a place to hide. When the Albanians left Muldoon, Sam planned to follow them.

That brought him to his next bit of business. He found a Syracuse limo company online and hired a town car to pick him up at the airport and stay with him for the night, paying with Jake's credit card. He'd seen his father do the same thing on a trip they once took to Miami, where his dad did a story and took him to SeaWorld in between tapings. You rented a car and a driver and they did what you told them.

The sandwiches Connie had ordered arrived and Sam ate his, a big fat pastrami with golden mustard. His stomach was queasy, but a man had to eat and he didn't want to lose steam later because he had passed up a perfectly good sandwich. He washed it down with an orange soda, belched quietly, and wiped his mouth on the back of his arm.

With everything in place, Sam got onto the Vonage Web site and started up a phone account. It was less than five minutes before he was placing a blocked call to his own cell phone.

His ringer's quiet chime filled the silence of the greenroom.

Connie was leaning this way and that, making little huffing noises as she blasted her way through some alien world.

Sam cleared his throat.

Connie kept playing.

Sam directed his face to the computer

screen and said, "Do you hear something?"

Connie jumped and said, "Damn, they got me. What did you say?"

"Did you hear that?"

"What?"

"I don't know," Sam said, pretending to type.

"Oh, your phone," Connie said.

"Jesus," Sam said, grabbing for it.

He flipped it open and looked at her.

"Hello," he said, then jumped to his feet. "Dad! Are you okay?"

He sniffed, wiping his face, and looked at Connie, who wore a mask of shock.

"No, I'm okay, Dad," Sam said. "I'm at the studio with Connie."

Connie nodded fervently.

"No, she's great, Dad," Sam said. "No, they're not keeping me here. They're helping me."

Connie stood up, wringing her hands.

"Can I talk to him?" Connie whispered.

Sam scowled and shook his head, making a crazy motion with his finger. He covered the phone and held it away and in a whisper said, "He's pissed."

Sam put the phone back to his mouth and said, "She'll take me. No, she's right here. Where? LaGuardia? We'll leave right now. I love you, too."

Sam snapped the phone shut and grinned at Connie.

"He's okay," Sam said. "Don't worry."

"I'm just doing what they asked me," Connie said.

"I know."

Sam closed up his computer and gathered his things. Connie reached for the phone on the end table next to the couch.

"What are you doing?" Sam asked, his insides tightening.

"I'm letting them know," she said.

"No," Sam said, making a furious canceling sign with both hands. "My dad said just go. He said to have you take me to the airport. Let's just go. He didn't even want me to leave the hotel, but Muldoon, he scared the hell out of me. My dad said to trust you, that you'd do the right thing."

Connie hesitated, then set the phone down.

"I guess if he's meeting us," she said. "It's not like I'm not staying with you. That's what they want."

"Definitely."

"Then if Jake says to go, they can't blame me for that."

They walked down the hallway through a flurry of activity. The show went to air in less than an hour and no one paid any attention to them. They flagged a cab out on the street and rode in silence.

When they finally arrived at the airport, Sam hopped out, the thrill of escape flooding his frame.

"Hey!" she yelled.

He glanced back and saw her standing beside the cab's open door. Panic bubbled up in his throat.

"Should I just hold this cab?" she asked.

"Good idea," Sam said.

Then he pushed through the doors and disappeared into the crowded terminal.

72

Across the river, the sun was settling into the arms of the Catskill Mountains. Blood-stained clouds gathered at the horizon, eager for the close of the day. In their shadows, the small city of Kingston moved closer to its final end and another day further from its eminent past. The congressman's private study looked out over it all, the back lawn with its Italian fountains, gardens, and burial ground. His hand massaged the fold of skin beneath his chin as he thought about things present and past and the tendrils of time that connected them in the way that Siamese twins were bound. Bloodlines and nerves that, if disrupted, inexplicably killed them both.

Slatten's peculiar double knock on the thick wood door filled the room and Van Buren told him to come in.

"Congressman," Slatten said, "Channel Six is running —"

"I know all about it," Van Buren said, cutting Slatten off by raising a hand.

"Are you going to watch?" Slatten asked.

Van Buren sighed and turned his eyes toward Slatten and away from the sweeping view.

"In 1777, the British burned this place to the ground," he said, nodding across the Hudson toward the decrepit city. "Everything, on both sides of the river, except Ridgewood and the home of the British commander's mistress.

"The Rothschilds. You've heard of them? For centuries they've ruled, never openly. Jewish bankers. But money, carefully placed, and they not only survived, they thrived, no matter who ran the government, or the armies, or the church. William Van Buren did the same thing. Something he passed down through the generations the way your father probably taught you to shoot a rifle."

Van Buren scooped the remote off his desk and sat down, rocking back in the leather chair and clicking on the TV that rested in a cabinet surrounded by musty old unread books. Slatten stood, military style, at ease, with his hands clasped behind his back. Van Buren folded his hands over the small paunch at his beltline.

"I'll have a Scotch, straight up," Van Buren said.

Slatten stiffened, then got the drink and set it down as *American Outrage* began with its dour notes and dramatic smash-cut images of celebrities mixed in with floods, fires, victims, blood, and guns. Then Nancy Riordin appeared on set with a picture of Van Buren — from a black-tie affair, laughing and raising a glass of champagne — filling the screen behind her.

"Are the Van Burens, one of America's oldest, proudest, and richest families, about to fall?" she said with a pained expression, as the screen changed to a schoolboy picture of Sam Carlson. "This boy may be the key to a scandal involving sex, drugs, stolen children, organized crime, and American royalty."

Van Buren gripped his glass and watched, sniffing from time to time. Somewhere in his brain he realized that the tendons in his fingers had begun to ache. When the segment ended, the glass shattered in his hand. Van Buren sucked the blood from his finger, trying to stem the flow.

73

Jake lay in his shirtsleeves and slacks, staring up at the crystal chandelier above the bed and the rainbow flecks that the dying sun cast across the ceiling. In his pants pocket, he rattled his keys against the makeup container. As promised, there had been a knock at the door and one of Slatten's goons handed in his clothes. The green suit had been cleaned, mended, and pressed. The Ferragamo shoes shined. The shirt had just the right amount of starch in the collar.

Jake had already tried the windows and the door. There was a phone in the room, but it was dead. His was gone. Below, in the yard, he'd watched one of Slatten's boys pacing little figure eights on the lawn.

His gut twisted tighter with every passing minute of helpless waiting. His mind ran down the list of stories he'd broken over the years. A director at the Justice Department with a teenage daughter who turned tricks to pay for his assassination. A woman whose twin sister disappeared after playing a joke on her boyfriend. The wife of a soldier accused of the rape and murder of a civilian in Kuwait. Parents of a teenage boy killed by police after a department store shooting spree with blanks in his gun. People caught unwittingly in a spotlight they never asked for, never imagined, and wanted to get out of.

He wondered if any of the subjects of his journalism would empathize with his situation. He wondered if any of them even could.

At quarter till eight, he got up and began to pace the room. It was just after the hour when the lock clattered and Slatten's face appeared.

"Time," he said.

Jake put on his suit coat and followed Slatten out into the hallway. A crimson carpet ran down its center and several suits of armor stood at intervals beneath the heavy carved wooden beams. Old oil paintings in gold ornamental frames hung every few feet along the paneled walls.

They descended a grand carved wood staircase lined with portraits of men and women in white powdered wigs. Below, Jake caught sight of a maid in a black uniform with a white apron disappearing down a hallway. They went in that direction and stopped in front of two massive hand-carved doors. Slatten slid them apart and waved Jake in.

The room was enormous, longer than it was wide, with thick wooden beams exposed like the ribs of an inverted ship and knobbed with something like acorns gilt with silver leafing. Three towering windows ran along one wall, arched, mullioned, and dressed in twenty-foot velvet drapes. Between them stood Corinthian pedestals bearing white marble busts, quite possibly Rodins.

Jake had seen opulence before in his work. Not the champagne fountains of South Florida drug dealers. Not the glass garages of professional athletes, glittering with the chrome of two dozen classic automobiles. Old money. European castles. Blue diamonds. Money that didn't need an uptick in the market. Money untouched by the IRS, not because it had been laundered or written off to some bogus business expense, but because it had never entered this country in the form of currency, but rather in the form of priceless paintings, furniture, and sculptures.

This was that kind of money.

A huge silver candelabra glittered in the

center of it all, suspended like a radiant star with more than a hundred single flames illuminating the intricate metal filigree. At the head of a long table Van Buren sat, thin and aged, dressed in a dark suit, wrinkled from a day of work, with a burgundy bow tie, and talking on a cell phone. Next to him, on the right-hand side of the table, was a second place setting.

"Go ahead," Slatten said, and slid the doors shut.

Jake focused on the congressman and closed the gap. Light from the candles glittered off Van Buren's glasses, hiding the content of his eyes until Jake stood directly in front of him. Van Buren acted surprised to see him, told the person on the phone that he had to go, and stood, smiling and extending his hand to Jake.

Jake looked at it, long-boned and liver-spotted with thick knots of tendon strapped across the knuckles, then he stared into Van Buren's brown eyes until the congressman blinked. In the air, the congressman's breath hung, plagued by the hint of a broken sewage line. Jake wondered if Van Buren was too arrogant to care, or if his life was simply devoid of anyone who might clue him in to the smell.

"You want to let me use that phone so I

can call my son?" Jake asked.

Van Buren retracted his hand, joining it with the other. Two parallel rows of perfect white teeth disappeared beneath thin, pale lips. He cleared his throat and, settling himself down again, said, "Why don't you sit down?"

"I'd like to call my son," Jake said, drawing back his shoulders and tightening his jaw.

"Everything in time, Mr. Carlson," Van Buren said in a voice rich with guile, the voice of a politician lusting for power or a billionaire accustomed to buying it.

Van Buren motioned to the chair.

"You think I'm just going to go along with your charade?" Jake said. "This guy Slatten? What rock did you find him under?"

"I'm trying to understand you," Van Buren said. "Please, you should sit. You'll feel better if you eat. We can start with the salad."

Jake looked at the glimmering china plate. On it, dark mixed greens were tossed in a creamy dressing. Jake's mouth watered uncontrollably. He sat down, picked up his fork, and shoveled a mouthful in.

"Creamy shallot," Van Buren said, picking up his own fork. "The dressing."

Next to the water glass was a glass of red

wine. Jake took a drink, warming his insides while hints of dark fruit and cinnamon lingered in the back of his mouth. Bald hunger overran his other emotions. He wolfed down the rest of the salad — light and refreshing — and when he finished, Van Buren set his fork down. Within seconds, two stone-faced servants appeared. One cleared the salad plates and the other replaced them with wide bowls of saffron steamed mussels before pouring more wine. Jake's nostrils flared at the scent.

He quickly extracted three of them and had them down before he said, "Okay, I'm eating. Now, what is this?"

"Think of the *Titanic,*" Van Buren said. "There's a lot of noise. It's dark. Maybe one of us has a light and maybe the other knows where there's a boat."

"Maybe I've got a life jacket and a pack of matches," Jake said.

"You mentioned your son," Van Buren said.

Jake swallowed. "And?"

"It's also about this family," Van Buren said. "Which is something that goes far beyond me."

"You're the congressman," Jake said.

"And I have a wife who's in Paris right now," Van Buren said. "Three children, two with children of their own. A mother. Cousins. I'm sure you know Maria, the movie producer, or know of her."

"What about Martha? You forgot her," Jake said, swallowing and taking a drink of wine.

Van Buren scooped out a mussel, chewed it deliberately, and swallowed, then dabbed the corner of his mouth with a linen napkin. "Martha is a sad story. Not her fault, not ours. I used to blame myself. Her mother and I, it just didn't work. I thought that was part of it, our divorce. I did everything I could, believe me. But they didn't know the things they know now. Even if they did, they didn't have the kinds of medication they have today to help people like Martha."

"What do you mean 'people like Martha'?" Jake asked, stabbing another orange-tinted mussel and freeing it from the black shell.

"Paranoid schizophrenic," Van Buren said, setting his fork down. "You know she's ill?"

"You saying nothing ever happened?" Jake asked, tapping the tines of his fork on the plate. "She's not Sam's mother?"

"She's someone's mother," Van Buren said, shaking his head and frowning. "It might be Sam. It might be someone else."

The servants came with the next course

and another bottle of wine, removing the silver covers from the china plates in a flourish of steam, revealing thick veal chops sheathed in pearly fat and oozing the faintest traces of blood.

"You admit that?" Jake said, slicing into the chop with a knife.

Van Buren cut off a piece of his own, baby-pink strands exposed to the candlelight. He chewed it completely before swallowing and taking a long drink of wine. He sighed and looked at Jake.

"She started drinking in middle school and went from there, but nothing like after she met that . . . rock star, drug addict, lunatic, whatever you want to call him," Van Buren said. "When he died, she didn't want that baby, but she was too far along to get an abortion. She tried to kill herself. We tried to bring her around. Have you ever had anyone who was mentally ill?"

"I've seen them," Jake said.

Van Buren worked at his food, his hands performing deftly before moving offstage while he chewed. Jake thought he saw tears welling in the congressman's eyes.

"I was away when she gave birth," he said softly. "I have no idea what she did to get the doctor to go along with this, forging a death certificate, giving her child away. I don't think I want to know. I know she didn't want the baby and, honestly, I never gave her the choice. I told her she had to keep it. I wasn't going to have a Van Buren child just given away."

"So you had no idea?" Jake said.

"Of course not," Van Buren said, scowling at Jake, disgust pulling down at the corners of his mouth so that juice from his veal pearled in its crease. "Digging up a grave? I was ready to cut your balls off. Then I found out you were right.

"If I have a grandson out there, believe me, I want to find him more than you do."

"What about when people find out?" Jake asked. "It's not pretty."

"You mean your television show?" Van Buren said. "Too late to worry about that, right?"

"Too late how?"

Van Buren studied him, then said, "We thought if we could contain you, convince you of what happened, that we could preserve our privacy. Obviously we're too late. Martha was on *American Outrage* two hours ago."

"That's impossible," Jake said.

"I wish it were."

74

The driver waiting at the bottom of the escalator for Sam wore a dark suit. His head was shaved. A small silver hoop hung from one side of his nose but, other than that, he looked respectable. When Sam said hello, the driver flipped the placard bearing Sam's name and examined it.

"This you?" he asked.

"Yeah, I'm Sam," Sam said. "What's your name?"

"I'm Johnny," he said, looking around. "Where's your parents?"

"I'm meeting my dad later," Sam said. "Don't worry. He's an investigative reporter. I'm helping him out."

"Reporter?"

"For *American Outrage.* You seen it?"

"I heard of it."

"Okay, well, we sat on the runway for a goddamn hour, so we better get going."

"It says 'as instructed,' " the driver said.

"Where are we going?"

"Onondaga Lake," Sam said, removing the recorder from its box. "You know where the Salt Museum is?"

"That's not open now," the driver said.

"Believe it or not, you get used to this kind of crap when your dad's in television," Sam said. "We'll park a couple blocks away and I'll walk. How long to get there?"

"Five, ten minutes."

"I got till ten o'clock. Any place to eat around there?" Sam asked. "Something quick."

"Heid's Hot Dogs, I guess."

"Any good?"

"If you like that kind of thing."

Sam flipped open his computer and pulled up the park map, making doubly certain that he knew every detail of the area he could before they got there. Heid's was just inside the village line, two blocks from the museum. The low yellow Art Deco building had big round windows that must have given the place a space-age look when it was built in the twenties. Now it looked like a relic, but the dogs were good enough that there was a line to get them, even at nine at night.

"Want something, Johnny?" Sam asked the driver.

"Thanks. I'm a vegan, man."

Sam paid cash for two dogs and two Coneys, slopped on relish and plenty of mustard, mixed a pint of chocolate milk with a pint of white in a thirty-two-ounce cup, put on a plastic spill cap, stuck in a straw, and carried the mess back to the car. With a mouthful of food, he directed the driver through the village, scoping the area as best he could from the backseat before licking his fingers and pointing out where he wanted the car to wait for him, on a street corner overlooking the lake.

"Can I have your cell number?" Sam asked.

The driver gave it to him.

"You gotta be ready to go quick," Sam said, punching it into his phone. "Probably just a few minutes after ten. We're going to follow some people. You okay with that?"

"What are you doing, kid?"

Sam considered the guy for a moment, then asked, "Does it matter? Look, I'm gonna add on a thirty-percent tip if you get this right."

"It's just weird," the driver said. "I can't do anything illegal."

"Do I look like a drug dealer? Come on. Look at me. I'm a kid."

"A kid with a credit card."

"And that's how you get paid. I told you, I'm helping my dad. I let you know when this thing airs and you can tell your friends. We good?"

The bald driver stared at him for a moment in the rearview mirror before he nodded and said, "Okay, sure."

Sam got out. The faint fog of his breath floated into the glow of a nearby streetlight. He shivered and wished he had a coat. The sun had gone down long ago; only the hint of burnt orange remained in the bruised, purple sky.

Sam hugged the shadows of the sidewalk, making his way down toward the water. He had enough time, he presumed, to check out the area before anyone got there. He stayed on the fringes of the parking lot and its burning lights, circled the dark museum, and picked his way among the thick old trees along the shore where the water licked at the stony beach. He stopped at the head of the pier without walking out onto it in the open.

He looked at his cell phone and cursed at the single battery bar, but hit the driver's number anyway.

Quietly, he said, "Johnny?"

"I thought you said around ten."

"Just testing. Be ready," Sam said.

To his left was the Salt Museum, to his right a marina bursting with fifty or more boats, mostly cabin cruisers, resting in the arms of two stone breakwalls quite similar to those at the pier. Sam walked out onto those and through the docks, searching for a place where he could see, but not be seen. Finally, he decided to board one of the boats, climbing up over its railing and settling in on the bow, tucked under the edge of the small skiff that was mounted there.

It was just after nine-thirty. He rolled onto his back to get comfortable and stared up at the sky, clutching the cell phone. There were no stars to gaze at, only the bellies of high heavy clouds lit from the city's night glow.

Sam listened to the sound of his own breathing as it mixed with the lap of tiny waves. He was thinking about his dad.

75

Muldoon only wanted one man to accompany him. Skip Lehman had spent time as a cameraman in Somalia and in Kuwait during the first Gulf War and although Muldoon never told him, he had a deep-seated respect for the crew manager. Inside their van was everything Muldoon needed to break the case and burn his name into the mind of every television executive for the next two decades.

Using a map, he directed Lehman to the parking garage for the Liverpool Public Library. The library was two short blocks from the lake, close enough for a good transmission, but not so close that the Albanians would notice. Even if they were keeping a thorough eye on the area, the van, tucked inside the garage, would never be noticed. When they arrived, however, a black-and-yellow-striped arm barred their way in.

"Run it," Muldoon said.

"What do you mean?"

"Run it," Muldoon said. "Drive right through. It's wood. It'll break. Don't worry, I got you covered."

"Okay," Lehman said, stepping on the gas and blasting through the arm with a tremendous snap and a loud clatter as it bounced off the concrete floor with a hollow-sounding echo.

Lehman pulled into a dark corner and turned off the engine. The two of them sat there, listening for sirens or shouts or whatever else might be coming. After several minutes, Muldoon looked at his glowing watch and climbed into the back of the van. Lehman followed and took up his position at the desk, slipping on a set of headphones. Muldoon rigged the mike, clipping it inside his shirt collar and running the wire down his back.

"Here," Muldoon said, handing Lehman the transmitter, "tape this to my back. Here's some duct tape."

"Why don't I just clip it to your belt?" Lehman asked.

"Just tape the goddamn thing."

"Okay. Take it easy."

"Don't tell me to take it easy," Muldoon said. "I'm going into the line of fire here."

He hefted the briefcase, opened it, and switched on the camera. Lehman turned on the monitor, and even in the dim light of the van, the green-and-white images of the night-vision lens let them see the backs of the front seats and part of the dashboard. Muldoon turned the briefcase and angled it up toward his own face until he saw his profile image in the monitor.

"This thing is beautiful," Muldoon said.

"Latest and greatest," Lehman said.

"I love the *look*," Muldoon said, angling his jawline and studying it in the monitor. "It's fucking covert. What are you looking at me like that for?"

Lehman shrugged and started fussing with knobs on the control panel.

"What?"

Lehman turned to him and said, "You don't think this is a little dangerous?"

"Remember Dan Rather in Vietnam?" Muldoon said. "Bullets flying all over the place? Him in a helmet? A foxhole?"

Lehman shrugged and said, "I guess."

"Just don't guess getting this all on tape," Muldoon said, swinging open the van door and stepping out into the garage. He left the building with the briefcase in one hand and his map in the other, taking Tulip Street straight down to the water and hanging a left, past the OFFICIAL VEHICLES ONLY sign and along the parkway drive. Across the water, the lights of several smokestacks blinked at him along with their corresponding reflections on the water's rippled surface. The bellies of the clouds above glowed with orange light from the city of Syracuse, but thick black shadows filled the space beneath the trees.

He passed a marina, silent except for the gentle slap of water on the fiberglass hulls. Up ahead, at the end of a turnaround, the Salt Museum stretched out on the grass, a long low building with a steeply peaked roof. Off to the right, the stone pier jutted out over a hundred feet into the lake. At its farthest point, a ruby buoy light throbbed atop a steel post, reminding Muldoon of a dying firefly.

His heart doubled its pace, and he became acutely aware of just the hint of cigarette smoke. His eyes scoured the surrounding trees, bushes, and benches for the glow of an ember or any sign of a person. He saw nothing and remembered the Albanian's words about no tricks and hurried ahead with long strides to reach the pier. Rocks the size of small desks fit perfectly together to create a straight and narrow breakwall that sloped down to the water on either side.

Dead fish and rotting algae overran the scent of cigarette smoke. Out on the pier, the city now glowed and sparkled importantly and Muldoon could make out the mid-rise buildings, the glass shopping mall, the university on the hill and the white sheet of material that covered its domed stadium.

A choking noise escaped his throat when two dark figures materialized at the head of the pier, walking slowly toward him. The briefcase trembled in Muldoon's hand. He crumpled the map and jammed it into the pocket of his jeans, quickly removing his hand and holding it up in the air, fingers splayed so they wouldn't think he had reached for a gun.

Second thoughts filled his mind long before he realized the men wore ski masks, and when he did, an involuntary whimper rang out in the night air. Before he could react, one of the men reached down, snatched his briefcase, and heaved it out into the water with a splash. The second one frisked him, found the transmitter, and ripped it off his back, pulling up two hunks of skin that made him squeal.

The second man threw the transmitter into the lake and the first man gripped Muldoon by the voice box with a gloved hand, bringing him to his knees.

"Where is the fucking kid?"

"I got the kid," Muldoon said. "I'm on the inside. I just want to talk to you guys. Cut a deal."

"We said bring the kid," the man said, squeezing Muldoon's throat. "You fucked up. Bad."

With his other hand, the man removed a pistol with a fat long silencer from his coat and wormed the thick metal nose into Muldoon's cheek. The newsman closed his eyes.

His bladder let go, and he started to cry.

76

The muttering voices were incomprehensible to Sam, but the splash of the briefcase was clear enough. His head felt light and his heart raced when one of the men brought Muldoon to his knees. Sam thought the man held a gun, but didn't know until he saw the small orange flash followed by a metallic spitting sound.

Muldoon fell over sideways.

The man pointed the gun down at him and there were two more flashes. The second man slung down a duffel bag from his back and removed a meat cleaver. The fat blade gleamed and flashed in the dim light, and Sam turned away.

He heard several metallic notes ring out and he lost his tether. Floating six feet above his body, he realized what his father had been saying about these people all along. His stomach churned and vomit pushed up into his throat. He looked back. Both men had walked off down the pier wearing their masks.

Sam rejoined his body, frozen for a minute before the urgency of following them made itself heard. He rolled to his feet, staggered off the boat, and stumbled along the dock toward shore. When he got to the grass, he clung to one of the large trees, unable to embrace even half its circumference.

The immovable trunk and the thick rough bark felt good and solid and he rested his cheek there for a moment until he realized what he had to do next. He peeked around the edge of it and saw the dark shapes of the two men disappearing into the shadows in the direction of the museum. They weren't heading toward the village, but the parkway that ran along the lake between Heid's and the city of Syracuse.

Sam fumbled with the phone and redialed his driver. He kept the phone close to his mouth, swallowing and hissing into it.

"Johnny? Come get me. Come get me."

"Where, man? Are you okay?"

Sam needed to pee. "Go toward the parkway. Don't hang up."

Sam lost sight of the men. He gripped the phone tight and started to run, not directly at them, though. Some force, like a colossal invisible hand, pushed him away from the men, so that his path was neither toward them nor away. When he got to the edge of the parking lot to the museum, he spied some movement under the trees on the far edge. Sam dashed around the edge of the lot, weaving through the shadows of the trees until he came to an open field across from a playground. Now he'd lost them.

The force wouldn't allow Sam to cross the open ground. The image of Muldoon flashed in his mind. He went to his left, toward some buildings that he could hide behind. He made it to the wall of a concrete skating area and peeked around the corner. He saw a car waiting on the far side of some other baseball fields. Maybe it belonged to the Albanians. Sam pressed his palms against the concrete. He closed his eyes, recalling the map and that the only way out from the baseball diamonds was an entrance connected to the parkway.

He brought the phone to his lips and spun around, sprinting up a narrow lane that joined the parkway at its end, right in front of Heid's, where Johnny was headed.

"Johnny," he said into the phone, "go to Heid's. I'll meet you across the street. Stay on the parkway. They're going toward the city. You there?"

"What the hell are you doing, kid?" Johnny asked.

"Just go," Sam said.

He was in a full sprint down the service road, sucking wind, when he saw the headlights round the corner and start toward him. He brought the phone to his lips. He could hear the whine of the car's engine. It was coming fast.

"I told you the goddamn parkway!" Sam screamed. He snapped the phone shut. He wanted to throw it at the car. The time it would take them to turn around could be the difference between staying with the Albanians and losing them, following them to his dad or starting over with nothing.

The car's brakes gave a little chirp as it pulled up short and the door swung open. Sam put an arm up, blinded by its high beams.

"Goddamn it!" Sam yelled, running. "Turn it around!"

He was to the door before he realized the man driving wasn't Johnny. In fact, it wasn't a black town car, but the silver Audi. The heavyset man wearing a leather coat, a short dark cap of messy hair, and a sneering face grabbed Sam by the wrist and twisted his arm up behind him in one smooth motion. Sam's nose and lips smashed into the car window and he saw stars. Before he could react, the man had Sam's other hand behind his back, too.

Cold plastic cut into Sam's wrists as the man cinched down on a zip tie before taking away his phone. The trunk popped open and the man shoved him toward it.

"Hey!" Sam screamed, struggling. "Help!"

Before he could say another word, he toppled over the edge, helplessly dumped into the trunk. The top slammed down. Sam kicked at it, screaming, but after a few seconds he heard the car door slam and they started to move.

Sam bumped around the bottom of the trunk as the car sped away. Ten minutes later, they pulled over and Sam heard someone from the passenger's side get out. When the trunk lock popped he braced himself, but it didn't fly open. The bulb went on and he saw the end of a rubber tube being fished into the crack.

After a minute, the tube began to hiss. A chemical stink filled Sam's nostrils and he fought to rise up, kicking down with his legs, groping with his bound hands. His eyes went wide. He tried not to breathe, but couldn't stop. His lungs tingled and his head swam. Tears filled his eyes as he fell back into the bottom of the trunk, his limbs now numb and useless. His eyes focused on the end of the hissing hose and he thought of a science experiment they had done back in school. School wasn't so bad, really. He was deep in the bottom of a well. The light was fading. He wanted to tell his dad about school and how he would gladly turn over a new leaf.

Then everything went black.

77

Sometime during the main course a fleck of meat caught hold of the congressman's face just beyond the reach of his lips. Van Buren kept on, steaming ahead, working his knife to the bone, as if the first two courses were simply a warmup. Jake tried to keep his attention on the congressman's eyes as the older man unraveled the less private parts of his family history. He tried to decode the pattern of leafy vines that gilded a wall sconce. He tried to count the dozen or so candles the sconce held, each fat as his swollen wrist. But he couldn't.

He couldn't stop his eyes from stealing back to that gray shred of veal and the way it refused to desist. He couldn't stop thinking of all the things a man with as much power and money as Van Buren must not notice. Things too small. Crude things beneath his dignity. His own bad breath. The bruises on the inner thigh of the chambermaid. A fart in church. Jake himself.

That was the real problem, and Jake knew it.

Jake's hunger ceased. His stomach twisted as he watched Van Buren calmly finish his meat, survey the changing of the plates, then tap his spoon edge against the braised caramel shell, breaking its surface before scooping out the supple heart of a crème brûlée.

"I could help you a lot more with what's going on if you'll let me use the phone," Jake said, repeating himself for maybe the fourth time.

Van Buren straightened up and wiped his mouth clean, then pointed with his spoon at Jake.

"Don't confuse my hospitality," he said. "I don't know if your son is the one. Neither do you."

"If he is?"

"Then I'm guessing, because you say your son matters to you, that you're not going to want this thing in the media either," Van Buren said. "I have people working on this, trust me. Your show we weren't able to convince, but the networks are sitting on this thing until all the facts are out.

"Am I right about you?"

"My son is the most important thing in my life," Jake said. "I'm not a TV whore."

"But your employer is."

"I don't have an employer," Jake said, picking up his own spoon and breaking the crust on his dessert without eating any of it. "I got fired."

"So, you want to contain this as much as we do," Van Buren said.

"What if Sam's not the one?"

"Then I have to protect this family. Whatever I say, whatever happens that you repeat outside these walls, I'll deny. If you want to stay with me on this, you'll have to be patient for a few hours. Believe me, the people I have working on it are the best. If you walk out that door, you're on your own."

"Chained up in some cellar, you mean?" Jake said, caressing his swollen wrist.

Van Buren set down his spoon and dabbed at his lips again. "Whatever happens if you walk out of here is between you and Mr. Slatten."

Jake stared at him.

Van Buren got up. "I'm glad we had a chance to talk."

Jake turned on his heel for the thousandth time, grinding down the small flattened circle in the dark blue rug. He continued along his track to the other side of the room and spun again. He believed that Sam was fine, otherwise pacing wouldn't have been enough. He had already looked over the books on a wall shelf, picked one out, and sat down with it, but his eyes roamed over the words without comprehension.

It was just after eleven when someone knocked on the door. Jake tore it open and found Slatten.

"He needs to see you," Slatten said.

"What's wrong?"

Slatten shook his head and headed down the hall. Jake followed him down a back set of stairs, then along another hall, before being shown into a spacious paneled office. Wood polish and leather hung in the air. Van Buren sat behind a broad desk, examining some papers. He had lost his bow tie and jacket, his sleeves were rolled up, and the top button of his shirt was undone. Behind him, the picture window reflected orange globes of light from the Tiffany floor lamps that matched the one on the congressman's desk. When Van Buren saw Jake, he set the papers down and took a deep breath.

"Have a seat."

"What's wrong?"

"I just got a call," Van Buren said. "Do you know who Niko Karwalkowszc is?"

"The Albanians' lawyer," Jake said.

Van Buren nodded slowly and splayed his fingers across the desktop. "They have your son."

Jake gripped his swollen hand, wincing, then twitching the fingers to shake free from the pain. "Oh, Christ. Where is he? They called you?"

Van Buren glanced at Slatten. "I don't know where. Two days ago I paid the Albanians for some documents."

"They're blackmailing you?" Jake asked.

Van Buren nodded.

"What do they want?"

"Nothing I don't have."

"Money?"

Van Buren nodded.

"How much?"

"A million."

"You're going to give it to them?"

"It's money," Van Buren said. "The important thing is the boy. Your son. Sam. Once he's safe, Mr. Slatten can worry about the money."

"When? When can we get him?"

"Now, tonight."

"But the money?"

"The bank."

"It's almost midnight," Jake said.

"The regional manager is already on his way. It's my bank. I own it."

"I've got a friend at the FBI," Jake said.

"It's not about friends," Van Buren said. "It's about efficacy."

"This is my son."

Van Buren scowled at him, staring hard, and said, "And he might be my grandson. I don't know how much you know about these people."

"Enough," Jake said. "They tried to kill me. They murdered a woman who tried to help me."

"Slatten has done exchanges like this for executives in South America," Van Buren said.

Jake looked at Slatten's expressionless face, the furrows of time on his forehead, the corded muscles in his neck. His eyes flickered at Jake.

"Just Sam. We need to keep him safe," Jake said quietly. "I don't care about anything else."

78

A knock at the door revealed one of Slatten's men. Slatten accepted two maps that he unrolled onto a reading table in the corner of the room. He took several books off the adjacent shelf to weight down the corners and removed a Magic Marker from his pocket.

"What are these?" Jake asked.

"It's the Bellevue Country Club," Slatten said. "From a satellite. One overhead, the other at an angle that lets you see the elevation of the terrain. This is a layout of the course. We lifted it from the scorecard. There's a PDF file on the club's Web site."

"It's where they want to meet," Van Buren said out of the side of his mouth as he examined the map. "We go to the first green. They said they'd signal us where to go from there."

"They'll be on high ground," Slatten said. "Here, or here."

Most of the course was cut into the side of a hill with several holes up on top. Slatten's marker left two dots, one on the seventh tee and another on the sixth green. The slope above those two grassy plateaus was entirely wooded with two cart paths cutting through to the hilltop part of the course.

Slatten then pointed out the first green. "They'll be able to see us here."

"What about the street, here?" Jake asked, pointing to an intersection that bordered the lower corner of the course. "They could wait there."

"Isolation," Slatten said. "That's what they want, but also a place they know, and a place they can get in and out of without attracting attention."

The course was surrounded by housing developments on all sides. It was located on the southwestern edge of Syracuse. The Albanians could get into the city or out into the countryside, depending on which way they went from the course.

"Another reason not to involve the police," Van Buren said. "There's no way of knowing who'll be watching and where they'll be."

"So we just go in there?" Jake asked.

"Mr. Slatten will," Van Buren said, placing his knuckles on the overhead map of the course. "He'll take the money and some men."

"I'm going," Jake said.

The two other men looked at each other. Their eyes said something Jake couldn't understand, then Van Buren addressed Jake.

"We thought you might. You'll have to do what Slatten says. That's the condition."

"You'll be there, too, right?" Jake said, looking deep into the congressman's eyes. "You said you don't know, but I do. He's your grandson."

Jake held Van Buren's gaze until the congressman cleared his throat and said, "Of course I'll go."

"We'll all be safe. I'll put shooters here, here, and here," Slatten said, making marks in the trees around the high ground he predicted the Albanians would choose. "They'll go in from the neighborhoods. Rental cars. They'll have night vision."

"When?" Jake asked.

Slatten looked at his watch. "I sent them fifteen minutes ago on a private jet. They'll be in place by one. The exchange is at two. I don't think we'll need them, but it's always better to have more firepower than less."

"The idea is, no fire at all, right?" Jake asked.

"Of course," Slatten said. "But if we need them, the Albanians will be neutralized instantly. They'll mark up and hold on them until we have the boy."

"How are we getting there?" Jake asked. "You have another jet?"

"We have a helicopter outside," Slatten said.

"Fly it right to Bellevue?" Jake asked.

"No, too much attention," Slatten said. "We'll rent a car at the airport and drive. It's ten minutes. If anything, we may want the copter to pick us up after we get the boy, get out of there without giving them a second bite at the apple."

"Have the helicopter fly in once Sam is safe?"

"Exactly."

"You're worried what they could do?" Jake asked. "Once they have the money?"

Slatten looked at him like an exasperated parent. "Most times, you're right. You give a kidnapper the money, you get to go home with your man. But these people? They have no rules."

79

Van Buren studied Jake's face while he
watched Slatten slip the bulletproof vest
over his head, then strap his gun on over
that. Slatten handed the same kind of vest
to Van Buren and another to Jake. They
were in the back room of a two-story detached garage, Slatten's base of operations.
Guns lined one wall. A desk with a computer and phone sat in front of a bank of
closed-circuit television screens. The vests
came from an open closet crowded with
dark clothes and boots. The navy wind-
breakers Slatten handed them had sailboats
stitched into the labels, the same kind Van
Buren had worn as a young man sailing in
the America's Cup.

"I have to use the bathroom," Jake said.

Van Buren had seen Jake eyeing the small
doorway at the far end of the long rectangular room, so he wasn't surprised.

"Hurry," he said, glancing pointedly at his

watch before nodding toward the open door. Then he noticed Jake's eyes seeking out Slatten for permission as well and he smiled at that. They needed the father to do as he was told.

"It might take a minute," Jake said.

Slatten grunted, and Jake walked the length of the room before closing the door. When the two of them were alone, they simply stared at each other. Van Buren enjoyed the game. He had seen Slatten's silent and confident assessment unsettle senators and administrative cabinet members in seconds.

It was more than a minute when Van Buren dropped Slatten's gaze for a peek at his watch. That's when he noticed the red light on the desk phone glaring at him.

"You don't have a phone in that bathroom, do you?" Van Buren asked.

Slatten's eyes followed the path of Van Buren's. They locked onto the phone, but only for an instant before Slatten marched toward the bathroom door. He rattled the handle, then hammered on the door with the meat of his fist.

"Carlson!" he yelled.

Van Buren glanced at the phone. The red light went out and the bathroom door opened. Jake stepped out into the room wiping his hands on a paper towel.

"All set?" he said.

"Who the fuck were you talking to?" Slatten asked, his chin extended toward the reporter, teeth clenched.

Jake blinked at them and took half a step back.

80

Sam's brain pushed against the inside of his skull, throbbing softly with the beat of his pulse. He opened his eyes. They felt crowded by the bone. The smell ate away at the insides of his sinuses. He blinked, rolled to the side, and vomited. He twisted his nose and face against the stink. It was sharp and rotten and somehow sweet.

His feet had been bound with the same plastic zip ties locking his wrists. Every joint, bone, and muscle ached, but nothing more than his throbbing head. Above him loomed the sides of a tall round structure unlike anything he'd ever seen. Artificial light leaked in from above where a massive convex roof pitched steeply upward.

He was wet, and the stench around him was damp, making the air too thick to breathe without taking great gasps. He struggled against his bonds, rolling and bumping into the metal frame of a wall.

When he rolled the other way, he found a mound of whatever was making the stink. He wretched and rolled back to the wall, panting. He lay there, and his own breathing was the only sound he heard until a car pulled up outside, gravel popping beneath its tires. A metal door rattled open, casting a white rectangle of light into the space and filling the rancid air with dancing motes of dust.

The metal ribs, round shape, and stink defined themselves as an old silo. The rotting feed had fermented in the confined damp space. A man with long blond hair and a dirty Fu Manchu stepped inside with a bandanna tied around his face against the smell. His partner with the short dark hair ducked in behind him, coughing and choking back a gag before raising his bandanna to spit out a gob of phlegm. They raised Sam up by the arms, one on each side, and dragged him toward the opening.

The windows of an empty farmhouse gaped at him like the eyes of a skull. The silver Audi rested in the dirt drive with its trunk yawning wide.

"Get in," the blond man said, pushing Sam toward the trunk.

Sam hesitated and his head was pushed down into the space, burning his cheek against the wooly lining. Sam cowered and tumbled in with his hands still bound behind his back. The blond man slammed the trunk and he huddled in the dark cramped space, bracing his legs against the thin rough carpet as they bounced down the driveway. They rode for a time on pavement, the tires humming and Sam drifting in and out of consciousness until they took a series of sharp turns and came to a stop.

The blond man threw open the trunk and yanked him out. They were next to a woods alongside a country road, high on a hill that overlooked the lights of a city. Sam saw the glow of the dome. The man pointed toward the dark woods and told Sam to go. In the faint light, he saw a black entrance into the trees. He shivered, and when they were a few yards inside the woods and the man flicked on a flashlight, Sam could see the puffs of his breath. The light illuminated a dirt path that wound through the trees before coming out the other side onto the fairway of a golf course where the smell of cut grass filled his nose.

There they stood, Sam nervously eyeing the blond man until he heard the high whine of an electric motor and saw the pale form of a golf cart coming at them from the right. The man shone his light on the cart and Sam saw an older, heavyset man driving with a tall thin man sitting beside him. The cart's brakes squeaked as it pulled to a stop. The thin man raised a hand, filling the night with the jingle of thin metal.

The glow of the light illuminated the face of Murat Lukaj.

81

"I didn't hurt anything," Jake said, his stomach clenched around the dinner Van Buren had given him. "I called a friend. I knew she was worried about Sam. She was supposed to meet him."

"What friend?" Slatten asked.

"Just a woman. A friend. Judy Weissman," Jake said, lifting his voice, attempting nonchalance.

Slatten dipped into the bathroom. "Then I'll just hit redial and ask her to keep things quiet for now. You won't mind."

Slatten held the receiver to his ear and watched the readout on the phone as it dialed.

"She's in 845 area code?" Slatten said.

"She lives in Kingston," Jake said, "she was supposed to pick Sam up last night at the train station. I knew if he was gone, she'd be sick. She's not going to say anything. She's a friend."

Slatten glared at Jake and walked into the bathroom, leaving the door open. From where he stood, Jake could hear the rumble of Slatten's voice, but the words were garbled. After half a minute, he reemerged.

"Don't do anything stupid like that again," he said to Jake. "It's your kid we're trying to save here."

"It's fine?" Van Buren asked.

Slatten hunched over the desk computer and punched in some letters and numbers. Jake edged toward him to try to see what he was doing. When he looked back, he saw Van Buren looking over the two of them as if considering the pieces on a chessboard midway through the game.

After a minute, Slatten nodded, spun around, and said, "Yeah, she's what he said."

Jake didn't speak. He shed his suit coat and pulled on the bulletproof vest over his head, then fished his arms through the windbreaker. He offered Van Buren a sheepish smile and gave him a nod.

Outside, they climbed into Slatten's truck and drove past the mansion to where a helicopter sat waiting in the floodlights coming from a small, single-story outbuilding. Before they were out of the truck, the copter's lights blinked on. Its engine sputtered and began to whine. The blades above swung slowly around, spinning faster until they made a steady chop. The night was clear and crisp. Slatten went inside the building and came out with a big black duffel bag across his shoulder. They passed under the blades, Slatten stopping to load the bag into the belly of the copter.

There were four seats in back. Jake got in with his back to the pilot, facing Slatten and Van Buren, who both found headsets and put them on. Jake looked for his, but saw nothing, so he sat watching the two men's lips move as they were lifted off the ground in the deafening roar, glad for the open window that rousted out some of the congressman's foul breath. The craft tilted and surged forward into the blanket of stars. Jake saw the big river, extending like a tar spill to the north and south, the glow of Kingston, and the pockets of light from the various boroughs and villages snuggled into the mountain creases.

Whenever he looked over at the other two, their eyes flickered at him and their mouths slowed behind the black buttons of their mouthpieces. The bags under Van Buren's eyes had deepened and the lines of his face sagged under the weight of a long day. A strand of faded hair hung limp across his wrinkled brow. Slatten's age and the time of night seemed to have no effect. His eyes darted about, his mouth was set, and the lines in his jaw rippled.

The stars were lost in a bank of clouds. Not much later, the copter banked and Jake caught sight of downtown Syracuse, the white dome standing out like a lesion. They were even with the glass tower of the shopping mall on the end of the lake when they began to drop toward the airport. A Cadillac Seville sat waiting next to their landing pad. The copter bumped to a stop and the blades swung to a lazy halt. They hopped down. Jake's ears continued to hum as he crossed the blacktop and got into the backseat. Slatten tossed the money bag in the trunk and took the wheel. He talked in his cell phone as he drove.

Jake studied the night sky through his window. The clock on the dashboard glowed. It was 1:28.

82

Below, a long way off, Sam heard the slam of a car door. Somewhere in the distance a siren sounded and a helicopter chopped the night air. Murat kept the binoculars tight to his face, studying the area where the car door had closed for several minutes before he spoke.

"Good," Murat said. "Call them."

The dowdy old man flipped open his cell phone, dialed, and waited.

"This is Niko," he said, his words thick with what Sam thought was a Russian accent. "Yes, we have him. I will put on a light and you can see."

Niko nodded to Murat, who let the glasses drop to his chest, then reached down and yanked Sam upright. Niko shone the beam of a large flashlight onto Sam, blinding him so that he winced and looked away.

"You see?" Niko said into the phone. "Yes, you can talk to him. Here."

Niko shoved the phone into Sam's face.

"Your father," Niko said, "talk to him."

"Dad?" Sam said, tears filling his eyes.

"I'm coming," Jake said in a low urgent voice. "Don't worry. Everything's fine. Trust me."

Niko snatched the phone away from Sam's face and Murat forced him to his knees before taking up his binoculars. Even in the faint light, Sam could see the Albanian's grin as he turned to Niko.

"He's coming."

83

A sudden choking sound filled the air, followed by a monstrous hissing before, finally, the sprinkler heads popped out of their bunkers, showering the thick fairway grass with fountains of spray. The smell of stale pond water mingled with the heavy scent of cut grass and mud. A bullfrog let fly with a gut-rending croak, breaking into the chorus of early summer crickets. The frog went quiet, making way for the dull chop of a helicopter blinking along over the city below.

Jake ignored it and searched the shadows, deep and fathomless beneath towering maples and oaks.

He suspected that Slatten's hidden snipers were a lie to placate him, but worried that the Albanians might have tricks of their own. His senses strained at every sound, smell, and movement. The grassy ground rose steadily toward the plateau of the upper golf tee. Van Buren slipped on the wet grass. Slatten caught him by one arm and tugged him into place, keeping the big bag of money poised on his shoulder all the while. The spray, the slick grass, and Van Buren's age slowed their ascent. Jake flexed his fingers and held his tongue, stopping every ten feet to look back and check his watch while he waited. A jet of water suddenly cascaded down on him, and he held up his arm as a shield. The water dripping from the end of his nose barely registered.

He wiped the face of his watch clear. Just seven minutes before two. In the distance, beyond the hissing sprinklers, he still heard the beat of the helicopter. He quickly retraced his steps and took Van Buren's other arm. The congressman shrugged him off and straightened his back, even though his breath came now in short wheezing gasps.

"Almost there," Jake said, trying to infuse some pep into his words and angle his nose away from Van Buren's foul breath at the same time.

"You two go," Van Buren said. They were two-thirds of the way up the fairway. Trees blocked sight of the seventh tee, where Sam and his captors stood waiting.

Slatten glanced up the hill, using the break to set the money down and catch his own breath. "Not without you, sir. They've seen us already. If only two come out, it'll be trouble."

Van Buren glared at Slatten, then tilted his nose toward the sky over the city. "I hope you told your pilot to stay clear until we're ready."

Slatten squinted in the direction of the distant copter and frowned but didn't speak. Van Buren gave him a curt nod and a grunt and started back up the fairway on his own. Jake fell in behind him and tried to keep from stepping on his heels. Instead of pushing through the underbrush, they took the long way around the base of the knob where the tee area lay, following the cart path and circumscribing the sixth green.

The path rose sharply, they rounded a bend, and there Sam stood between Lukaj and Niko, hands bound behind his back. Jake's heart leapt into his throat. He checked himself from running straight to his son.

Jake cleared his throat and kept walking, ignoring his companions. Instead of staying on the path, which circled around the tee area, Jake took three leaping steps up the steep skirt of longer grass to reach the plateau of the carefully manicured tee. When he reached the bench and the ball washer, Murat commanded him to stop.

Sam's pale face shone through the darkness, a mask of terror.

"The money," Murat said. He raised the hand that had been resting on Sam's shoulder, and Jake saw that he held a nickel-plated handgun. The gun caught the city's orange glow, reflecting it back at Jake.

Jake froze, numb except for the blooming knot of sickness.

"Niko?" came a voice from beside him. Van Buren, breathing hard.

The lawyer's light flashed on and the beam sprang across the grass before it scaled Van Buren's and Slatten's forms. Slatten's rigid posture bowed under the weight of the money bag. Van Buren braced his hands above his knees, supporting his torso while he sucked air and waved off the light.

Murat grabbed Sam by the hair. Sam's eyes widened. He struggled against Murat and cursed him. Murat shoved Sam forward and kicked at his legs, sending him face-first onto the grass.

"Lukaj," Slatten said, standing with his feet planted apart on the opposite edge of the tee. "Leave him. We have the money."

Murat chortled and toed Sam's ribs. "Go."

Sam wriggled upright, his hands still bound, and dashed for Jake, knocking into him and nearly sending him to the ground. Jake wrapped his arms around Sam. Murat held the gun loosely, pointing it in their direction.

"The money," Murat said, waving his pistol at Slatten.

Slatten slung his bag down and unzipped it, tipping it up so that in the glare of Niko's light the packets of bills spilled out like the stuffing in a carnival prize. Murat and Niko moved toward the money, kneeling down to examine it. Niko lay his light in the grass and sifted his hands through the stacks. Jake could smell ink and the filth of other people's greedy sweat.

"Good," Van Buren said, standing straight. "We both have what we want. There's just one more thing I need."

Murat and Niko both grinned up at the congressman.

"I need this to stay completely quiet," Van Buren said. "I need your word."

Niko blinked and nodded at Van Buren before returning his attention to the money. Murat grinned so hard that his teeth shone.

"Not really good enough though, is it?" Van Buren said, grinning back at them.

From the corner of his eye, Jake saw Slatten make a quick move with his hands followed by two flashes of orange flame and two snap ping metallic sounds.

Niko dropped in a heap.

Murat fell sideways, pawing at his throat, and struggling to get up. His long legs flexed stiffly as if they'd been yanked free from a spider. Slatten stepped closer, put his gun to Murat's eye, and fired a shot that burst through the back of the Albanian's skull, spraying dark matter across the grass.

Murat flopped back, dead.

84

Slatten whipped out a flashlight and he directed it over the bodies before he looked back at Jake and Sam.

Jake stepped protectively in front of his son, and Slatten turned his attention to Niko and Murat. Van Buren watched silently as Slatten worked over the bodies with his gloved hands.

Then Van Buren turned his attention to them. He frowned grimly and said, "Your life jacket and matches won't be enough."

"What?" Jake asked, wrinkling his face as though he'd tasted something sour.

"The *Titanic,*" Van Buren said, "sinking. Not as much room in the lifeboat as you thought."

The sound of the helicopter closed in on them.

Jake stiffened.

Slatten searched the grass. He grunted when he found the gleaming automatic Murat had carried and rose to his feet. He slipped his own gun back into his coat. Then he looked at Van Buren, pointed Murat's gun at Jake, and waited.

"She was no mother," Van Buren said, then he angled his chin at Sam, "and I couldn't have the bastard of that drugged-out hippie inheriting the bulk of the Van Buren fortune. The trust vested in his generation. He would have been the oldest."

"Everyone will know," Jake said.

Van Buren laughed.

"Really?" he said, nodding toward the gun in Slatten's hand. "You're killed with Murat's gun and the boy disappears, never to be seen again? It's very neat."

Van Buren looked to the sky. The helicopter was much closer now.

"They'll *know,*" Jake said.

Slatten leveled the gun at Jake.

"They'll know!" Jake screamed, the sound of the copter growing louder still.

When the white glare of the helicopter's spotlight flooded the tee, Slatten raised an arm up over his eyes and Van Buren staggered, crabbing sideways to get out of the beam.

"Shoot him!" Van Buren yelled.

Jake dug into his pocket and held up the

small round makeup case. He tossed it to Slatten. Slatten's free hand snapped it out of the air instinctively.

"Take some," Jake said. "You're on camera."

Jake glanced up at the helicopter, knowing Judy and her ex-husband had come through. "That's the Channel Nine news copter! Everything you do. Everyone will see it!"

The copter spiraled quickly down, hovering, and keeping the light trained on them, whipping them with the wind from its blades and deafening them so that it was hard to make out the sound of the coming sirens. Jake could see the camera strapped under the nose of the copter. From the cockpit, Judy's ex-husband gave Jake a thumbs-up. Van Buren took a few steps into the cone of light and stood with his hands raised as if he were a victim.

"I'm with you, Jake!" Van Buren shouted. The wind whipped thin strands of graying hair across the grinning skull of his face. "Slatten's been threatening me the whole time. I had no hand in any of this."

Slatten blinked as if he'd been struck by a board. His mouth sagged open, then it tightened into a frowning sneer.

He let the gun drop to his side, then turned it on the congressman. Van Buren's eyes grew. He thrust his hands out in front of him for protection.

"Slatten!" Van Buren screamed, turning to run.

"You," Slatten said, and fired into the back of the congressman's head.

Van Buren pitched forward.

Slatten tossed the gun to the grass, standing still for a moment in the glare of the light before he came back to life.

He let the disc of makeup drop, then scooped up the bag of money and ran for the trees, spilling ten-thousand-dollar packets like bread-crumbs as he disappeared into the night.

EPILOGUE

Jake held the door for Sam, then followed him down the Llewellyn House front steps. Drizzle drifted down, sheared by the skyscrapers from the bellies of low-hanging clouds. Jake unsnapped the umbrella's strap and popped it open, sheltering Sam and himself as they walked toward the park. The sidewalk glistened. Taxis hissed by in packs, gleeful and running free on the barren Sunday-morning streets. The fresh smell of rain blanketed the usual city offerings of dust, sewage, and trash.

Neither of them spoke until they reached the low stone wall of Central Park and its canopy of bright green leaves. They took a winding path, passing the hardcore runners who splashed along with faces like grim masks, wires dangling from their ears, headsets held in place by soaked terrycloth sweatbands, until they came to Bethesda Terrace. They descended the steps, feet echoing through the underpass until they stood at the foot of the Angel of the Waters fountain. The surface of the expansive blue stone pool stood still enough to catch the reflection of the bronze angel and her four cherubs below, hiding behind their curtain of droplets. At the balustrade by the pond, half a dozen Japanese tourists clustered like mushrooms beneath bright-colored umbrellas, peering at the far rugged shoreline and jabbering unintelligibly.

Jake removed the newspaper from under his arm and spread it out over a bench seat so they could sit without soaking their pants. Sam planted his elbows on his knees and hunched over, framing his face between both hands. Jake watched a pair of mallards glide lifelessly across the surface of the pond.

"It's nice that you're willing to do that," Jake said, patting Sam's knee. "Visit Martha, I mean."

Sam shrugged. "I like to come into the city to watch you do the show anyway."

Jake shook his head. "I always thought Sunday-morning TV was for old people."

Sam looked up at him. "You got some white hair going."

"That's what kids do to you."

"The stuff you do is good," Sam said. "It's real."

"Better than movie-star nannies?"

"Hey, it's network TV," Sam said. "House on the beach. Häagen-Dazs in the freezer, and all that. Even Ms. Dean watches. Every Monday morning it's 'Tell your father I liked his story, Sam.' "

Jake smiled and let that sink in.

"You think it really helps her?" Sam asked. "Me visiting?"

"The doctors say it does," Jake said. "You can tell she likes to see you."

"Sometimes it seems like she doesn't get that I'm not really her son," Sam said. "But she saw the report, right?"

"No, she knows," Jake said, putting an arm around Sam. "She just likes to forget a little, and it's nice that you let her."

"I'm glad you didn't let them use any more of that DVD you took of her. I should never have given it to them."

"You did what you thought was best. That's all you can ever do," Jake said. "You know, not letting *Outrage* run that stuff was what got me this Sunday gig."

"I thought it was because of the helicopter tape," Sam said.

Jake had given the tape shot from Judy's ex-husband's helicopter to Cambareri, even though *American Outrage* had offered him a hundred thousand for it, and his job. But the DA said the tape would be much more valuable for Slatten's trial if it hadn't been splattered across the potential jury pool's televisions.

"It was both," Jake said. "My agent said CBS kept talking about integrity and they mentioned Martha's tape, too."

The sky suddenly opened, pattering down on their umbrella. The tourists migrated toward the steps.

They watched the shattered surface of the pond. Rivulets began to run along the brick pavers at their feet. The sound of the rain and the fountain became one. In the middle of eight million people, they were completely alone.

"I talked with my producer the other day," Jake said, raising his voice just a bit to overcome the rain. "She said I could have some time to check out where Lukaj got his babies. It's a long shot, but I thought, you know, now that I'm settled into this show I could start poking around a little."

Sam's face revealed nothing.

"I was thinking of asking Don to let me look at some of the old FBI files on Lukaj," Jake said. "Maybe there's something there."

"I think," Sam said, freeing his face and

crossing his arms across his chest as if he were cold, "I think I'm good."

Jake allowed himself to smile.

Sam stood up. "Want to get a sandwich?"

Jake followed his lead and they began to walk toward the stairs.

"You sure about the FBI files?" Jake said. "I won't keep asking, but I want you to be sure. I don't mind."

Sam stopped and looked up at him. He patted Jake's shoulder and grinned so that his braces gleamed. "It's just you and me, Dad."

"Let's go."

ABOUT THE AUTHOR

Tim Green is the bestselling author of eleven previous thrillers and two works of nonfiction, including the *New York Times* bestseller *The Dark Side of the Game.* After playing eight years in the NFL and becoming a lawyer, he worked as a featured commentator on *A Current Affair, Good Morning America,* NPR, and FOX Sports. Tim lives with his family in upstate New York.